"What the hell kind of man do you think I am?"

Ross demanded harshly. "Do you really think I'd use you as a pawn in this game?"

"I wondered," Lilah murmured. "But you're not as ruthless as you make yourself out to be."

His eyes caught and held hers, and her heart skipped a beat at the intensity of his gaze. Suddenly she was locked against the lean strength of his hard body, feeling weak as the heat of him surrounded her. The room faded away, and Lilah caught her breath, her lips parting as she stared up at him.

She wanted Ross Bradford. God, how she wanted him. It was reckless and crazy, but in the heat of the moment, she didn't care. If he kissed her, she knew she would melt into his arms and forget about everything else in the world.

Even the reason she was here...

Dear Reader,

This is it, the final month of our wonderful three-month celebration of Intimate Moments' fifteenth anniversary. It's been quite a ride, but it's not over yet. For one thing, look who's leading off the month: Rachel Lee, with *Cowboy Comes Home*, the latest fabulous title in her irresistible CONARD COUNTY miniseries. This one has everything you could possibly want in a book, including all the deep emotion Rachel is known for. Don't miss it.

And the rest of the month lives up to that wonderful beginning, with books from both old favorites and new names sure to become favorites. Merline Lovelace's *Return to Sender* will have you longing to work at the post office (I'm not kidding!), while Marilyn Tracy returns to the wonderful (but fictional, darn it!) town of Almost, Texas, with *Almost Remembered*. Look for our TRY TO REMEMBER flash to guide you to Leann Harris's *Trusting a Texan*, a terrific amnesia book, and the EXPECTANTLY YOURS flash marking Raina Lynn's second book, *Partners in Parenthood*. And finally, don't miss *A Hard-Hearted Man*, by brand-new author Melanie Craft. *Your* heart will melt—guaranteed.

And that's not all. Because we're not stopping with the fifteen years behind us. There are that many—and more!—in our future, and I know you'll want to be here for every one. So come back next month, when the excitement and the passion continue, right here in Silhouette Intimate Moments.

Yours,

Leslie J. Wainger
Executive Senior Editor

Please address questions and book requests to:
Silhouette Reader Service
U.S.: 3010 Walden Ave., P.O. Box 1325, Buffalo, NY 14269
Canadian: P.O. Box 609, Fort Erie, Ont. L2A 5X3

A HARD-HEARTED MAN

MELANIE CRAFT

Silhouette®

INTIMATE™MOMENTS®

Published by Silhouette Books

America's Publisher of Contemporary Romance

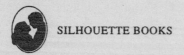

SILHOUETTE BOOKS

ISBN 0-373-07870-6

A HARD-HEARTED MAN

MELANIE CRAFT

is a freelance writer living in San Francisco. She read *Gone With the Wind* at age twelve, spent some time moping that she had missed the hoopskirt era, then discovered contemporary romance novels and never looked back again. She studied archaeology and English at Oberlin College, graduated in 1991 and set off to find some great stories to tell. In the past several years she has led safaris and taught Swahili in East Africa, excavated in Egypt's Valley of the Kings, traveled solo across the Sinai and devoured as many books as she could find. She has been a pastry chef, a bartender, a house cleaner and a copywriter. *A Hard-Hearted Man* is her first published novel.

Chapter 1

By ten o'clock, the African heat had settled in for the day. It hung in a shimmering haze, caught between the morning sun and the burning white concrete of Kenyatta International Airport.

If there was a breeze, Dr. Lilah Evans didn't feel it. The crowd pushed past, crushing her against the pay phone with the mass of several hundred yelling, shoving, sweating bodies all trying to clear paths in different directions. Taxi horns blared from the roundabout, and a muffled announcement crackled over the PA system. Lilah clamped one hand over her ear and hunched toward the phone, her fingers tight on the receiver as she strained to hear the voice on the other end of the line.

"I'm sorry," she said unsteadily. "What did you just say? Hugh Bradford *what?*"

"Passed away," the man said, raising his voice, and in spite of the heat around her, Lilah felt icy fingers grip her stomach. She hadn't misheard then. The stranger's voice seemed thin and unreal in the buzz of noise surrounding her, and she took a deep breath, trying to think clearly.

"He died, for God's sake," said the man irritably, mistaking her silence for incomprehension. "Heart attack. Last week. Are you a friend?"

"It…was a business relationship. We were going to meet for the first time today. I'm Dr. Evans."

"Sorry, I don't know the name. What business did you have with Hugh?"

This man worked in the Bradford office and he didn't know her name? Lilah frowned at the phone. "I'm the archaeologist from Wisconsin," she said. "The one in charge of the excavation at Hugh's ranch. And you are…?"

"This is Ross Bradford, Hugh's son."

"His *son?*" Lilah's voice rose in surprise. In the year she'd been discussing her excavation with Hugh, he'd never once mentioned a son. She'd been under the distinct impression that he was childless. "I don't remember hearing that he…"

She cut herself off, realizing that she was being rude. "Mr. Bradford, I'm so sorry about your father. I had no idea—"

"Obviously," Ross Bradford said dryly. "But thank you. Did you just arrive from the States?"

"Yes, I'm at the airport now. The excavation is scheduled to start in a few days, and I came early to do the preliminary setup with Hugh."

"I see. If I'd known about your plans, I'd have notified you about the changes before you left home. I've spent the past week trying to get my father's papers in order, but he had his own unique idea of a filing system, and I'm running behind."

"Oh, I understand," Lilah began. "I can—"

"Fine," Ross Bradford said briskly. "I'm sorry that your trip to Kenya had to turn out this way. You might want to ask a local travel agent about a safari while you're here. It's a good time of year to tour, and that would keep your visit from being a total loss."

Lilah was suddenly too alarmed to be offended that he'd cut her off. What did he mean, "a total loss?"

"Mr. Bradford," she said quickly. "It would be easy to fill you in on my arrangements with your father. My team is arriving tomorrow, and that way we can get started and not have to bother you again."

"You don't understand, Dr. Evans. It isn't possible to have any kind of excavation on the land now. I'm selling it to the Kenyan government to be added to the Nairobi Wildlife Reserve."

"You're *what?*" Lilah grabbed the edge of the phone.

"I'm selling it."

"When?"

"Now."

"But you can't do that!"

"No?" Ross Bradford's voice was cool. "I have to disagree, since I am doing it. The initial papers were signed last week."

"But your father and I have been discussing this excavation for months! This is a major project—"

"I'm sorry, but it's not going to happen. You'll have to find another project."

"Mr. Bradford, *you* don't understand. This is a critical site in African prehistory, not some dime-a-dozen thing! I have supplies and labor arriving to work there for a year!"

"Take them somewhere else. There's a lot of land in Africa. I'm sure you'll find another patch to dig up."

"But you—"

"Look, I'll be very clear. I couldn't change the situation if I wanted to. And I don't want to."

This can't be happening. The call had taken on a nightmarish feel, except that even Lilah's most anxious dreams about the project hadn't gone this far. Ross Bradford had barely waited days after Hugh's death to rid himself of the ranch.

"This project was important to your father," she appealed. "I have letters I could show you. I can't believe he never mentioned it."

"Given my relationship with my father," Ross Bradford said flatly, "I'm not at all surprised that we never discussed it. Now, if there isn't anything else, I have a lot of work to do."

"Wait, please, just let me explain how important—"

"I don't have time," he said. "Goodbye."

He hung up, leaving Lilah staring dumbly at the receiver in her hand, her pulse pounding so loudly that she could feel it thudding in her temples.

She took a shaky breath and closed her eyes, trying not to panic. What was happening here? Who was this man? Not once had Hugh said a word about having a son, yet suddenly one had appeared from nowhere and informed her that he was selling her site. In a few curt sentences he had snatched away the most important thing in her life, the work of three long years, with a glib "sorry"—and then hung up on her!

With awkward fingers, Lilah fumbled in her pocket for another Kenyan coin and pushed it into the telephone slot. She'd come this far, and she was damned if she was going to let this cold bastard turn her away now.

He picked up the phone on the first ring. "Yes?"

"This is Lilah Evans."

"I thought it might be. Look, Dr. Evans, we have nothing more to discuss. Believe that."

"I don't," Lilah said stubbornly. "Your father and I had a deal, and I think you owe me a chance to make my case."

"You're wasting your time. I'm selling the ranch, and that's the end of it."

"But your father told me that the land has been in your family for eighty years! He was so proud of that. You can't just sell it!"

"Lady, you know nothing about my family," he said, his words suddenly sharpened with the first hint of genuine emotion she'd heard from him. "And I'm not interested in discussing my father or my decisions with you. If you want to excavate the ranch, talk to the government and get a federal research permit."

"There's a four-year waiting list for federal permits!" Lilah was having trouble breathing, and she wondered if he could hear the horror in her voice. Four years was more than enough time for someone else, with the connections and experience she lacked, to work out a deal with the government and move in on her site. Hugh had promised it to her, but if the ranch became government property, the excavation would be up for grabs.

"Then I recommend getting your application in soon," he said, and the line clicked in Lilah's ear.

At least she hadn't cried in the middle of the airport, Lilah thought bleakly, as she sat on the edge of her double bed in Nairobi's New Stanley Hotel, a damp tissue wadded in her hand. She had saved it for the privacy of her own room. She could, at least, be proud of that.

The Bradford ranch excavation had always seemed a little too good to be true, from the day three years ago when it had literally been dropped onto her desk like a gift from fate. Two city detectives had knocked on the door of her university lab one quiet spring afternoon, carrying an assortment of stone tools just confiscated in the arrest of a major black-market antiquities dealer. The tools were piled in a shoe box like a child's rock collection, and before Lilah could protest, they were unceremoniously dumped into a dusty heap on top of her half-graded Anthropology 101 essays.

"Looks like a buncha rocks to me," one of the men remarked as she switched on her desk lamp. "Funny what some people pay big money for."

To the untrained eye, the pear-shaped stones were just oddly tapered rocks, flattish, gray and generally uninteresting, but as Lilah turned them over and over under the light, studying the pattern of stone flakes hewn from the edges and the odd mottling of the material, her initial curiosity gave way to astonishment and then to breathless excitement. Various tests over the next few days confirmed what she had barely dared to let herself hope: that the age and unique style of the tools strongly suggested that they had been looted from an unexcavated East African site.

It was hers for the taking—a junior professor's wildest dream.... All she had to do was find it. The chance of successfully tracing the tools back to their origin was slim enough to seem ridiculous, but the arrested dealer had plea-bargained by naming his sources, and from that first step, the trail back to Africa had slowly come together.

Two years later, Lilah had her site, a shallow canyon on the twenty-thousand-acre Bradford ranch, one hour's drive southwest of Nairobi.

Hugh Bradford, a crusty old rancher of British descent, whose family had been in Kenya since the early colonial days, had finally agreed to the excavation, but it took Lilah another exhausting year and a half of grant proposal writing, endowment hunting and shameless begging to pull together enough money to finance the excavation. By that point the dream had become a powerful thing. Somewhere along the line it had risen up and swallowed her, and she had eagerly dazzled herself with images of tenure and fame. Twenty-eight years old and head of a major excavation; cited in all the textbooks; in hot demand on the lecture circuit—it would be the ultimate "I told you so," spectacular enough to justify every hard choice she'd made along the way. *See what I've done?* she could say to her parents, who understood glossy photos in national magazines, but only nodded politely at her collection of dry academic papers. *See what I've done?* she could finally say to Jeff. *The stress, the work…the late hours in the lab…it was all worth it in the end! You gave up because you never really loved me.*

The dream, strong and swift as a river current, had carried her through the breakup, through all the ugly scenes of betrayal and blame. It had numbed her when Jeff announced that he was moving out; that he was in love with a twenty-year-old art major who loved to cook and was never too tired for sex. It had stiffened her spine, dried her eyes and sharpened her aim as she pulled the engagement ring from her finger and flung it at his head.

And the dream had been there to fill the void Jeff left behind. The Bradford ranch excavation had become everything to Lilah—her vision, her salvation, her reason for getting out of bed in the morning. It had promised her the world and never threatened to leave her.

Until now. Was this how it ended?

No! No, damn it. Never. Not while she could stand and fight. She swiped fiercely at her nose, and rose to pace the small rectangle of her room, kicking a discarded towel out of her way.

To save her excavation, she had to convince Ross Bradford to postpone closing the sale. But how? How could she make him hear what he was determined to ignore? He didn't care about her project, wasn't interested in her arguments. What would it take to capture his attention and buy herself enough time to sneak around the edges of his resistance and force him to understand the scientific gold mine buried on his ranch?

What kind of man was Ross Bradford? His voice echoed in her memory, the tone impatient as he fended off her horrified reaction to the news about Hugh and the ranch. Curt, no-nonsense. Not a man to try to sway with passionate declarations. His phone manner suggested a man who wanted facts, results. What if she dropped the emotional angle and presented him with cold, hard evidence? She could show him some of the actual tools from the site. If he could see and feel the evidence of what lay hidden on his property, he'd have to understand that it was worth exploring. And even Ross Bradford couldn't be completely immune to the almost mystical awe of holding stones worked by ancient human hands.

It was a long shot, but it was likely to be her only shot. And the first of many problems was that the original stone tools weren't with her. They were neatly labeled and stored in a lab drawer back in Wisconsin, and she had nothing in her luggage older than her favorite college sweatshirt.

She stopped in front of the window, tension tightening her shoulders as she stared out over the traffic-jammed streets of urban Nairobi. She needed stone tools, she needed them fast, and an hour's drive beyond the concrete and the skyscrapers would take her to the one place on earth where she could find them.

A plan began to take shape in her mind. It was crazy, dangerous and illegal, but what was the alternative? To sit here and watch her life crumble around her? She'd been gambling on this project for three years, and Ross Bradford had just turned it into an all-or-nothing game. This was no time to worry about propriety. After all, at this point, what did she have left to lose?

The main road of the Bradford ranch stretched for miles, rising and falling over the rolling savanna until it disappeared into darkness. Silver moonlight glazed the grassy African plains, and umbrella-shaped acacia trees stood in shadow, silhouetted against the sky. The air was spicy, slightly musky and the whisper of the grass mingled with faint animal sounds carried on the wind.

Lilah gripped the straps of her backpack, glancing around nervously as she walked. In the time she'd spent dreaming of her first visit to the ranch, never once had she imagined that she would come at midnight, creeping up the road like a criminal.

The wind gusted, making the long grass rustle as if an animal were slinking through it. The shadows beside the road were long and dark, and it was easy to imagine yellow eyes hidden there, peering out, watching her....

Lilah took a deep breath. This was a cattle ranch, and Hugh Bradford himself had assured her that there was nothing dangerous here. It would be bad for business to have anything eating the merchandise, so the entire twenty-thousand-acre ranch was circled by an eight-foot fence. This she could verify, since she had just climbed it.

She'd done a poor job of it, though. A sharp wire had

caught her on the chest as she swung herself over the top of the rusty steel-mesh fence, and now she had a tear in her shirt and a nasty gash that rubbed painfully against the strap of her backpack. She could mostly ignore the discomfort, but it had been a bad way to start off the night.

It figured, she thought grimly. What *hadn't* gone wrong since she arrived in Kenya?

The bilious anxiety she'd been battling all day threatened to rise up again, and she clenched her teeth, willing it away. She couldn't afford to dissolve into a mess of tears and worry, not now. It was still miles to the excavation site, and she had too much to accomplish before dawn.

Clouds were gathering in the distance, their dark shapes massing on the northern horizon, but the rest of the night sky was clear, with stars sprinkled like diamond dust around the full moon.

She'd spent the afternoon studying the maps Hugh had sent, planning her route through the ranch. But making the transition from printed paper to the vast darkness of this wide-open savanna was more than a little overwhelming.

The air was cooling rapidly around her, and Lilah shivered, trying not to think about how isolated she was out here. She fixed her mind on the road ahead, and reminded herself that every step took her closer to the site.

Her site. It was hers, Ross Bradford and his title deed be damned. What had he done to earn the land, inherit it? Ha. She'd spent three years planning this excavation, and all her life dreaming of it. Ross might own the land, but she had earned it.

She stopped suddenly. There was a new noise coming from somewhere nearby, blending with the raspy trill of the crickets. It had been hovering on the edges of her consciousness for several minutes, getting louder and louder until it had finally caught her attention. It was behind her, and it was...mechanical.

She turned quickly, looking back down the road, and saw with a sudden jolt of anxiety that car headlights had appeared down the road near the fence.

"Oh, great," she said, freezing in her tracks, staring toward the approaching headlights. The car was still half a mile away, at the bottom of the low hill, but this was the only road around, so it would have to pass her. Who would be up at this hour? What should she do?

The car was coming fast. She had to do something. She looked around quickly, then dashed up the road and dove off into the tall brushy grass behind a clump of scraggly bushes.

The thorny branches caught at her hair, and she jerked free, trying to crouch down as low as possible. She held her breath, peered through the grass and watched the car approach.

It was a brand-new, four-wheel-drive Land Rover, moving smoothly over the pitted road. Lilah huddled even lower as it neared, then stared, her stomach tightening in alarm. It seemed to be slowing down. She watched with an increasing sense of disbelief as it came closer and closer to where she lay hidden in the grass.

Was she hidden? Yes, she was sure of it. Could the driver of the car have seen her walking, silhouetted against the sky, just a few moments earlier? It seemed unlikely for a person without incredibly sharp eyes, but the moon was bright tonight, and it certainly looked as if the driver was searching for something. Or someone.

Me? Not me, oh, please, she prayed, afraid to move, afraid even to breathe. It was too late to try to slink away, now that the car was close enough for the driver to spot any motion in the thigh-high grass.

The Land Rover stopped, barely twenty feet from where she crouched, and the tall, broad-shouldered figure of a man swung out. She couldn't make out his features or expression with the inner light of the car at his back, but the harsh ring of authority in his voice was unmistakable, as was the long dark shape of the rifle he held.

"Out of the bushes *now,* or I'll shoot."

Lilah's heart was beating so loudly that she thought it would drown out the sounds of the night. Was he bluffing? Did he know where she was? He couldn't! No one could see that well in the dark.

She didn't move, didn't even breathe.

Go away, she commanded silently, trying to send him a telepathic message. *Go away.*

Before she even realized what was happening, the gun cracked and a shot whizzed over her head only a few feet to the left, buzzing like an angry bee.

Lilah gasped, and threw herself chest-down on the ground, trembling all over. He had a close enough idea of where she was, and he was going to kill her! What was she supposed to do? If she stood up now, would he shoot her? If she didn't, would he start shooting into the bushes? This wasn't fair! She might be trespassing, but killing her for it was overreacting, damn it!

"Out here, *right now!*"

He cocked the rifle again, and Lilah shrieked, jumping up. "Don't shoot! I'm coming out!" She sucked in a sharp, hot breath and stormed out onto the road.

"Are you crazy?" she yelled, seizing belligerence as the way to keep herself from dissolving into a quaking mass of fear and shock. "You could have killed me! You can't just *shoot* people!"

She faced the man, her hands clenched into fists to keep them from shaking, and stared at him as the white haze of panic began to clear from her eyes.

He was tall, standing inches over her, but in the sharp shadows of the moonlight he seemed even larger. There was a power about him above and beyond the gun he held, coming more from the intensity of him, the strength of his body poised there, his attention focused on her with a force that seemed physical. Lilah had never been easily intimidated, but facing off with this man made her fight for her bravado.

His eyes, shadowed by suspicion, bored into her as he lowered the rifle. "Who the hell are you?" he said coldly. "This is private property, so you'd better have a damn good explanation for why you're here."

Lilah stared at him, her heart pounding and her body icy-hot with adrenaline, trying to think fast and not succeeding. Who was he? If this wasn't the infamous Ross Bradford himself, she had a chance of bluffing her way out of this.

The voice on the phone hadn't been so refined, or so deep, had it? Could her ear have been tricked by the noise of the airport and the static on the line?

There was no way to be sure, so she took a deep breath and prayed for luck. "Of course it's private property," she said haughtily. "I happen to be a guest here. *Who are you?*"

"A guest?" he said incredulously. "*Whose* guest?"

He had a guarded face that disclosed nothing, but looked squarely and coldly down an aquiline nose at her as if she were a bug on a specimen tray. He reminded Lilah of a Roman emperor, powerful and remote on his arena balcony, and she had a sinking feeling that she was the one about to be thrown to the lions.

She braced herself. "Ross Bradford's guest," she said. "Really."

"Yes, really. And I don't think he'll appreciate hearing about this incident," she said sternly, encouraged by the fact that he was now watching her thoughtfully. "However, if you go away and let me get on with my walk, I promise I won't mention this to him."

"I'm Ross Bradford."

Lilah gulped. "You are?"

"That's right," he said coolly. "I own this property, and I don't recall inviting anyone for the weekend. You're going to have to come up with a better story than that."

Lilah managed a weak smile. "Okay, I—"

"You can think in the car. Get in."

"What? I don't want to—"

"I don't care what you want. You're in no position to argue." Ross Bradford stepped over to open the passenger-side door and waited, not taking his eyes off her. Lilah didn't budge, and he raised his eyebrows slowly, ominously.

"Get in."

Chapter 2

Ross Bradford didn't like being wrong, especially when it happened because he hadn't paid enough attention to his instincts.

His instincts had warned him earlier that day that this archaeologist might turn out to be a problem, but at the time he had dismissed the feeling, assuming that his message had been clear enough about where she and her excavation stood.

Or, rather, didn't stand. He had been direct to the point of being rude, but he simply didn't have time to let her down gently.

Thinking back, Ross realized that there had been clues in the grim determination, maybe even desperation, that he'd heard in her voice. And now here she was in the flesh, glaring at him like a cornered alley cat.

What the hell was he supposed to do now? It had been a long day, and it apparently wasn't over yet.

He waited, watching her as he stood with his hand on

the open passenger-side door, and something about her stance, suddenly light and edgy, warned him that she was thinking about making a run for it.

"Don't do it," he said, and saw her jump guiltily. She covered her surprise with a scowl, and folded her arms.

"I'm not going anywhere with you," she said. "Even if you do own this ranch, it doesn't give you the right to try to shoot anyone you see. And if you think I'm getting into your car, you're crazy."

"Actually," Ross said dryly, "I didn't try to shoot you."

"Oh, yes, you did. I was there, remember?"

"If I had tried to shoot you," he said, "you wouldn't be here talking to me. I never miss. Now, get in the car, or I'll radio the police and have them come out here and arrest you for trespassing."

"Arrest me!" she stared at him, horror on her face. "You can't! This is all a big mistake. M-my car broke down, and I thought I could find a house back here to call for help—"

"Your car broke down?"

"Yes," she said vigorously. "The fan belt broke."

"The fan belt," he said. "I see. What a shame. What were you doing here in the first place?"

She blinked, barely missing a beat. "Hiking."

"At midnight?"

"I got lost."

Ross gazed at her, not sure whether he was impressed or appalled by her brazen attempts to save herself. Whatever the case, he definitely wasn't flattered by her apparent belief that he was too stupid to connect her with the woman on the phone that afternoon. Did she think he had mysterious trespassers popping out of his bushes on a regular basis? It had taken him less than a minute to figure out who she was, even discounting the fact that the car headlights had briefly illuminated a Wisconsin decal on her bag. How dumb did this woman think he was?

She stared back, chin lifted slightly, the bravado of her expression not completely hiding the anxiety in her eyes. Looking at her, Ross had to admit that if he hadn't recognized that smooth, slightly low voice of hers, he actually might have written her off as some renegade student of Dr. Evans's.

Her hair was tied up in a messy ponytail, with escaped tendrils waving down to her chin. She wore blue jeans and a dark plaid button-down shirt that made her hair and skin look pale in the icy moonlight. With her scuffed sneakers and that backpack slung over her arm, she didn't look old enough to drink, much less to have a Ph.D.

"Have you ever seen the inside of a Kenyan jail?" he asked coolly. "It's not pleasant. And the American embassy isn't going to like having to deal with the police on your behalf. That kind of thing involves a lot of trouble and money, and it could be days before they get you out. Is that really what you want?"

"You wouldn't do that," she said, but her voice had lost much of its certainty, and she looked paler than ever. Her eyes flicked to the car and back to him again.

"Wouldn't I?" Ross said, and waited. She was probably right, but having her discover that wouldn't hurry this encounter along. His head ached from the hassles of the day, and he was damned if some stubborn archaeologist was going to cost him more sleep than he'd already lost.

"Are you sure you want to gamble on that? You don't know me at all. Get in the car."

The dangerous quiet in his voice was enough to convince her. She clenched her jaw and climbed silently into the passenger seat, where she sat, watching him warily as he shut her door and walked around the car to the driver's seat. As he started the car again and drove up the road, he glanced over to find her staring at him.

"You're not going back toward the gate," she said.

"That's right. I'm going home."

"But...what about me?"

He didn't answer. The truth was, he didn't know what to do with her, but it certainly wasn't going to involve leaving her alone out on the savanna. One of the herders had just killed a five-foot cobra by the side of the road that morning, and here was the professor, making swan dives into the shrubbery without thinking twice. She might be a nuisance, but she deserved to live through the night.

"I don't want to go home with you," she insisted. "Like I told you, this has all been a mistake. Let me go and I'll leave, I swear it."

"Sorry."

"Why not? Just stop the car and let me out! I'll walk right back to the gate and—"

Ross had had enough. "Walk back to the gate?" he repeated. She really was clueless, and lucky that she'd made it this far. "Do you know how dangerous it is out here? Are you aware that we've started taking down the divider fence between this ranch and the wildlife reserve? The whole northeast side of this property is open. We have lions hunting here at night, and you're walking around like it's upper Manhattan."

She sat quietly back against the seat, looking shaken, but Ross wasn't finished yet. "I find it interesting that you call *me* crazy," he said. "So tell me, Dr. Evans, what are you? Crazy, brave or just plain stupid?"

She didn't answer. Her hands were clasped in her lap, and she stared down at them, biting her lip.

Ross felt a flicker of guilt for being so harsh until he reminded himself that her presence here at midnight, carrying a backpack, said very bad things about her intentions. She didn't deserve sympathy.

"Well?" he said coldly, hardening his heart.

"All of the above," she said. "You do know who I am, then."

"You thought I'd believe the lost hiker story?"

She shrugged. "It was the best I could come up with at the moment. I don't have much to lose by now, in case you haven't noticed."

"And you're supposed to be a respectable professor?"

The mockery in his voice brought a flush to her cheeks, and she stiffened. "Yes, I am. I have a Ph.D. in African Archaeology, five papers published in highly respected scientific journals, *and* I happen to be the head researcher on the excavation here."

"I see. And since there isn't going to be any excavation here, I have to wonder what you're doing on my property at midnight, dressed like a teenager and carrying a backpack. It's not too hard to figure out, actually. You decided to trespass on the ranch and excavate without permission. I'll bet you thought you'd fill that bag of yours with artifacts and make a little money from them. That reads as theft in my book. Not very respectable, Professor."

Ross watched her with a sideways look, waiting for her reaction to confirm the truth of his words. It angered him to think that even someone who had claimed that her excavation was a "major site in African prehistory" would stoop to looting artifacts for cash. She didn't look like the type, which simply proved that appearances were deceiving.

Lilah was staring at him, openmouthed. "That is not true," she said vehemently.

"Oh, come on, Dr. Evans," Ross said. "Let's drop the pretenses and be honest at least once tonight. Why else would you be here, alone, with your bag? I think you finally accepted the fact that you can't work here, so you decided to make a profit to cut your losses."

"A looter?" she said incredulously. "You're accusing me of being a looter?"

"Perceptive, aren't you."

"How dare you! I'm a scientist!"

"Right," Ross said. This was just the kind of defensive reaction he had expected. How long would it take until she gave up and admitted the truth?

"Let's return to the question of why you're here. Are you a guest? No. Are you a hiker? No. If you have another half-baked story for me, let's get it out of the way, too."

"Fine," she said, her voice tight. "I'm here because you hung up on me, which was rude, by the way. I was going to try, tomorrow, to change your mind about the site, and since you were turning out to be...difficult, I thought it would help if I could actually show you some artifacts."

She sighed. "I thought that if you could touch the tools for yourself, you might realize how special they are, how interesting and it might help me plead my case. The bag is only to hold a map of the ranch, a flashlight and my notebooks."

"Why should I believe this story when you've lied to me since I picked you up?"

"Because it's the truth."

That was almost funny, coming from her. "The truth? That seems to be whatever suits your purposes, Dr. Evans. Right now, I'd say it suits you not to be caught stealing artifacts, so it's certainly a convenient story. I'll ask again, why should I believe you?"

"That does it," she burst out suddenly, and thumped a fist on the dashboard. "This is absolutely the last straw, damn it. Being hung up on, I can ignore. Being forced into a car, even being *shot* at, I can overlook. But if you dare insult my integrity as a scientist, you'd better believe one thing."

She pointed an accusing finger at him. "If you knew anything, you'd know that money is not the issue here. Having the chance to spend the months or years necessary to excavate a site as important as the one you unfortunately own—that, Ross Bradford, is what matters. Selling your family's ranch makes it clear that *your* only concern is your bank balance, but don't impose your values on me!"

It was only through the force of his willpower, well-trained by now, that Ross was able to clamp down on his own sharply rising temper as it flared with an intensity that surprised him.

He never allowed himself to get angry that way, not with the kind of fiery wrath that was blazing at him from Lilah Evans's eyes. He couldn't afford to. Anger like that revealed too much. It consumed you, then left you drained and vulnerable when it passed. He took a slow breath, then exhaled, drumming his fingers evenly on the gearstick, waiting for the heat inside him to cool.

From all appearances, Lilah's temper had already burnt itself out. She slumped back in her seat, folding her hands tightly in her lap and staring down at them as if she suddenly regretted her outburst.

Ross drove silently, the echo of her words still in his ears. *Interesting,* he thought. Tempers flaring out of control had a way of wrenching the naked truth out of people, and for that reason he was inclined to believe Lilah Evans when she said she was no looter. She really was still clinging to the hope of changing his mind.

What was it going to take to convince her that she was wasting her time? Too much was at stake to let anyone upset his plans, and it galled Ross that this woman could sit there self-righteously judging him, assuming that money was his reason for selling the ranch. Money! She had no idea.

"You don't know as much about this situation as you think you do," he said coolly, his anger settling like an icy weight inside him. He had turned the car away from the main road, onto the six-mile track that eventually became a driveway. Before long they were approaching the old ranch house. It sat, wood-sided and sprawling, on the top of a low rise in the land, its tall windows half-covered by a border of shoulder-high aloe plants.

He parked the car under a thatched overhang and got out, glancing back at Lilah, who was still sitting, frowning slightly, in her seat.

"Coming?" he said, turning toward the house.

He heard her door open as he walked away. "Wait a minute," she called urgently to his back. "What I said about borrowing artifacts to show you... I know it sounds weak, and I probably haven't given you any reason to believe me, but—"

He reached for his key and unlocked the wide wooden front door. "Actually, I do believe you."

"You do?" She sounded startled. "Really?"

"Does it matter?"

"Yes! I mean...wait, would you? I don't want to come..."

He stepped inside, missing the end of her protest, and

took off his dinner jacket, wincing slightly at the aching stiffness in his neck and shoulders.

It was the eighth long day he'd spent in the Nairobi office, and his father's affairs were still far from being in order. The office was overflowing with papers, some boxed and labeled, most still bursting haphazardly out of creaky filing cabinets and shelves. All of it had to go, either into storage or more likely into the trash. The business receipts for heads of cattle bought and sold, the contracts with meat and hide distributors and the rest of the ranching miscellany were bonfire fuel as far as Ross was concerned.

He dropped his jacket over the back of a chair, and looked around the living room. Ten days ago, he'd set foot in this house again for the first time in fifteen years, and he could still feel the strange mixture of comfort and anxiety that had assaulted him then.

But for a few minor changes that his father had made over the years, it was all eerily familiar, from the bright African weavings draped over the couches to the dusty leather-bound books lining the walls, to the faint smell of wood smoke and Hugh's tobacco lingering in the air.

Ross reached up to rub his forehead. Maybe he should have saved himself this unwelcome rush of emotion, not to mention an hour-long daily commute, by booking himself a room at the Hilton. He could have dealt with all of this from a comfortable distance, and then gotten the hell out of Kenya and back to his life, leaving old hurts and bad memories behind him for good.

He was pouring himself a glass of red wine when Lilah finally appeared in the doorway, her shoulders squared. The lamplight caught glints of dark gold in her hair, and her face was pallid except for the stain of color burning high on the edges of her cheekbones.

"Okay," she said grimly. "We need to talk."

Chapter 3

Lilah was still kicking herself for letting Ross Bradford goad her into blowing up at him. Trading insults was a luxury she couldn't afford if she wanted to save her excavation. She had followed him toward the house, preparing to plead her case and then stopped outside the door with a sudden case of nerves.

Being alone with Ross in the low light and soft shadows of his house seemed too far removed from the businesslike presentation she'd planned for the morning, and it made her feel awkward and off balance.

But she had steeled herself, pulling her arguments around her like chain mail and marched in to seize the only chance she was likely to get.

Ross had glanced up when she spoke, and his eyes moved over her thoughtfully. Lilah instinctively straightened under his gaze, and forced herself to return the look steadily, ignoring the sudden prickling warmth in her cheeks. She could read nothing on his face, and was startled when one corner of his mouth curved up.

"Talk?" he said dryly. "You look as if you're ready to slay a dragon, Professor. Should I be worried?"

"No. I'm not looking for dragons."

"You found one anyway. But my scales are thick, so you might as well come in. What do you drink?"

Lilah nodded toward the dull red glow of the wine in his glass. "The same, please."

She found herself watching his hands as he lifted the bottle. His fingers were strong and golden, and he moved smoothly, with the grace of a man at home in the lean strength of his body.

In the warm yellow light of the room, Lilah saw that he was wearing the remains of formal evening wear. The white shirt and black pants had wrinkled and wilted by this hour of the night, as if they had worn out in the fight to keep him confined.

She wasn't surprised. His clothes were clearly expensive, and cut to fit with a molded elegance, but there was a dark intensity about him that would frighten starched linen and pressed neckties into limp submission.

Ross silently handed her the stemmed glass.

"Thank you." She unexpectedly met his eyes. They were icy silver-gray, and light against his tanned face and dark hair. They appeared—and she suspected that they were—frozen.

She held the gaze and smiled charmingly.

"Forget it," Ross said.

"What?"

"Whatever you're planning. That smile doesn't go well with the steel in your eyes, Professor. If you're still hoping to change my mind about selling the ranch, save your-

self the trouble. It won't work. The answer is still no, and
that's the final word.''

''I don't believe in final words.''

''Believe in this one. As I said on the phone, the issue
is closed. The ranch is becoming part of the Nairobi Reserve, and it's not open to discussion.''

''Have you seen the site?''

''No, and I don't care—''

''You would if you saw it. Drive us down there, tonight. I'll show you why you should care!''

She stepped forward impulsively and put a hand on
Ross's arm. He tensed under her touch but didn't move,
and she was suddenly aware of the warm strength of him
under the thin linen shirt. The curve of his bicep was tight
against her fingers, and her skin prickled as she felt the
subtle heat of his body drifting out to surround her with
the scent of male skin and faint cologne. His eyes met
hers, looking faintly surprised, and Lilah felt a shiver rush
through her like liquid fire.

She jerked her hand back, trying to pull her thoughts
together before he noticed that she was shaken.

''Y-you have to see the site, at least. You can't make
this decision without considering all the facts.''

''I've considered the only important facts,'' Ross said.
His face was still unreadable, but his eyes were on her
with a disturbing intensity.

''Hear me out before you decide that,'' Lilah said, looking away to keep herself from getting flustered again.

She focused on the orange glow of the fire coals crack-
ling in the hearth, and took a deep breath. ''You can't—''

''I can,'' Ross said quietly. ''Give up, Professor.''

Lilah bit her lip. His voice was soft, but his tone was
cast-iron. She wasn't so blind that she couldn't recognize
utter defeat when it stomped on her. There really was

nothing she could do. It had been naive to think that arguments about science and knowledge could compete with the thrill of quick money. She had been a fool to come here at all.

"All right," she said stiffly, trying to pull the shreds of her dignity around her. "If that's the end of it, I won't bother you anymore. Will you take me back to the gate now, or do I have to walk?"

Ross smiled slightly. "Ready to take your chances with the lions to get away from me? I don't recommend walking. It's ten miles to the gate from here."

Lilah stared at him, her frustration growing. He was watching her thoughtfully, making no move toward the door or the car.

"I want to go," she said. "Now."

He shook his head. "Not yet. I want to talk to you."

"I really don't think we have anything more to say to each other," she said icily, still standing. "Please take me back to—"

"No." Ross's voice cut sharply through the quiet of the house, and Lilah looked nervously at him. What was going on? She hadn't exactly been pleasant company up to this point, so he should be anxious to get rid of her.

Except for the fact that he'd mentioned something about having her arrested for trespassing. But he hadn't meant it...had he?

Ross had paused, frowning as if he had intentionally stopped himself from speaking. He took a slow breath, tapping his fingertip against his wineglass.

"I gather," he said finally, "that I'm the bad guy in this drama. If I wasn't 'concerned only with my bank balance' as you put it, your project could have gone as planned, and everything would be wonderful, right?"

"Right."

"Wrong." He set his glass down on the table with a decisive thump. "And I'll show you why."

He crossed the room to where a set of glass doors opened onto what looked like an outdoor terrace.

"The other side of this story is out here, Professor. Take a look before you make judgments about what motivates me."

Lilah watched, surprised, as he stepped outside, then took another quick sip of her wine and followed him. The night wind met her in the doorway, lifting her hair gently back from her face.

Walking out onto the darkened terrace, away from the warmth and light of the house, was like casting herself out again into the wild African night. The terrace was bordered by a wooden railing, and beyond that lay a shadowed panorama of land and sky that stretched as far as she could see, from the dark curves of hills on one horizon, to the faint glow of Nairobi on another.

Ross was standing by the railing, looking out.

Puzzled, Lilah walked over to join him, shivering slightly in the cool air. The temperature was dropping quickly in the early morning hours, and the wind slipped in through her torn shirt to meet bare skin. She hugged herself, and leaned on the railing next to him.

He pointed out to the silent, distant lights of Nairobi. "I was born in this house," he said. "When I was ten, you could look in that direction and see nothing but darkness. Every year since then, the lights have gotten closer and brighter as the city swallows up the land. It's like a living thing, the way it grows."

He turned to Lilah, and his voice was fierce. "Things work very differently here than they do in America, Dr. Evans. The political climate can change without notice, and I consider myself lucky to be able to sell this land at a time when they'll preserve it as part of the park instead of turning it into an industrial complex. The development pressure is so strong that if I wait, I could lose the option of selling at all. The fact that my family has owned this land for four generations wouldn't be worth a shilling if the state suddenly decided to reclaim the land and put up a factory. It's that simple.

"My great-grandfather came here from England because he saw the chance to live in an open, untamed place that wasn't being divided up and paved over like his own homeland. Kenya is *my* homeland, and I'll do anything in my power to stop that from happening here."

Ross's hands tightened around the railing, and Lilah stared at him, astonished. His cool reserve had dissolved as he spoke, and now passion and determination crackled around him like a fire.

"Listen," he said. "What do you hear?"

Over the soft rustle of the grass she could hear the steady rush of the night wind as it swept over miles of green savanna. It sounded ancient and enduring, and it chilled her with an awareness of how tiny she was in the middle of this vast land.

"I hear wind," she said. "Coming from far away."

Ross nodded. "What else?"

"Crickets." They were trilling gently from the grass, their music light and throbbing in the darkness.

"What else?"

Lilah listened hard. There were animal sounds in the night, so faint and foreign that she had to strain to hear them clearly. Tiny high barks and snorts and odd ululating sounds like gurgles of water were barely audible on the wind.

"I...hear something else," she said hesitantly. "But I don't know what it is."

"Zebra," Ross said. "Down by the west watering hole. They came in from the park a few days ago. I've also seen giraffe and gazelle here since the fence came down. It's been seventy years since the native animals were last on this land."

His mouth curved dryly. "This week has been a long-overdue homecoming for everyone."

Lilah frowned, not understanding.

"When my great-grandfather took this land for ranching," Ross said, "he did what every other rancher was doing at the time and cleared it out to make room for his cattle."

"He chased out the gazelle and giraffe?"

"No, he had the ranch workers shoot them. In masses. They wiped out huge herds and left the bodies out for the vultures."

"Why?" Lilah said indignantly. "That's a terrible thing to do."

Ross shrugged. "That was the colonial mentality. Imposing proper British law and order on wild Africa. No matter that they were also destroying it."

Lilah blinked at him. "This isn't quite what I would have expected to hear from the heir to a colonial cattle fortune."

"You're not alone," Ross said dryly.

"The product of four generations of ranchers…"

"Three. I'm the fourth."

"Okay," Lilah said. "Three is enough. How did you manage to stray so far from the…er…herd?"

Surprisingly, his mouth curved. "Pun intended?"

Lilah grinned encouragingly. "Of course."

He shrugged, staring down at his hands on the rail as his face darkened again. "I'd been in American boarding schools since I was ten, which didn't do much to foster family unity. By the time my father figured that out, it was too late.''

''For what?''

''Everything,'' he said flatly, and turned around to lean against the rail, his back to the savanna night. ''So, Professor, is this clearing up the reason behind my decision to sell the ranch? Or am I still on trial for being a greedy sonafabitch who doesn't care about anything but my own fat pocket?''

The sudden coolness in his eyes told Lilah that he regretted letting the conversation take a personal turn. She was beginning to see that Ross Bradford was not a man who shared himself easily or lightly.

But he was also a man capable of great emotion, at least when it came to his land. Had that same fierce passion ever been directed at another person? How would it feel to be the one who kindled that slow-burning fire in his eyes?

She took a deep breath. *Stop that*, she ordered herself. She was here to save her excavation, and she needed a clear head now more than ever. If love for his land was what motivated Ross Bradford, then maybe she could use that angle to reach him.

''I can see that you care about protecting Kenya,'' she began.

''I do. And I can see that you're leading up to something,'' he said.

She flushed, but hurried on. ''If this land really does matter to you, how can you justify letting an important part of this country's past go unexplored? Wait a few months to sell the ranch. There's no hurry—''

''But there is,'' Ross said. ''You don't know the whole story. There's no time to waste, and I'm far more concerned with saving something that's dying than I am with preserving something that's already dead.''

"Archaeology isn't *dead*," Lilah said indignantly. "It's as alive and significant as your land, just in a different way."

Ross raised his eyebrows. "I have a hard time seeing how you can equate old pottery pieces with the survival of an endangered species."

"It's not that simple. You can't just divide everything into 'now' or 'then' as if the past doesn't count."

"The past counted when it was happening. Now it doesn't. It's finished, so it's not important."

"But it is!" Lilah exclaimed. "Ignoring the past is like trying to study a flower but ignoring its roots. Just because you can't see them, does that mean they aren't important? They're part of the whole thing. Cut the flower and it dies."

"That's a nice metaphor, but your point isn't valid."

"No? Why not?"

"Because," Ross said, "flowers eventually die anyway, and the one in question might be glad to be free while it can. Roots have serious drawbacks."

Lilah blinked, aware that the discussion had somehow moved beyond the merits of archaeology. From the bitterness in Ross's voice when he'd spoken of spending his childhood in boarding school, it wasn't hard to guess that he'd had a less than perfect family life. Was dismissing the past his way of avoiding painful memories?

"I think roots have advantages," she said carefully. "For flowers or people. They mean connection and security. Why would anyone choose to be cut off?"

"Sometimes the choice is made for us." Ross said. "As I see it, the past is good for only one thing. Reminding us not to make old mistakes again."

"But there's so much more to it," Lilah protested. "Look out there, at the plains. Everything you see is just the latest step in the whole line of history. The past, the future...it's right in front of us!"

She flung out her arm dramatically, then winced as the motion split open the fence-wire cut on her chest.

"What happened?" he asked.

"Nothing. It's nothing. I was just saying that—"

"It looks like something to me."

He took her by the shoulders and turned her toward the pool of light spilling out from the living room. His fingers were gentle but firm as he pulled aside the torn edge of her shirt to expose the wound.

"Really, it's no big deal," she said weakly. There was a strange heat burning through the shoulder where he held her, and the feel of his rough fingertips exploring her bare skin made her tremble.

"I wouldn't say so. That's a nasty cut. Doesn't it hurt?"

Lilah looked up and met his gaze, feeling a shiver of awareness move through her at the contact. "Not...at the moment."

"No?" His eyes were the color of glacial ice, but now, perhaps, not so cold. Lilah suddenly saw a flicker of amusement there, and it was enough to snap her back to herself.

"I'll take care of it tomorrow," she said, pulling back, but Ross held onto her shoulder and steered her firmly toward the house.

"Sit down." he said. "I'll get what you need."

"Really, I don't—"

But he had gone. Lilah sighed and folded her arms. She didn't have to wait long. Ross was back in a minute, carrying a wet cloth, gauze and an iodine bottle.

"You're not sitting," he said mildly.

"Right," Lilah said. "You see, this isn't necessary. It's only a scratch, and it'll be fine. I appreciate your good intentions, but—"

"Are you this argumentative with everyone?"

"No."

"Then pretend I'm someone else, and sit down," Ross said. "I don't like to have injured women bleeding in my living room."

He stepped toward her, and Lilah found her knees buckling. Quickly she sat on the edge of the couch. "Fine," she muttered. "Maybe I will sit."

"Looks like you could use some fence-climbing practice," Ross remarked, then added dryly, "Don't look so surprised. All the rust on you makes it rather obvious that you didn't come in through the gate. Have you had a tetanus shot?"

"Probably. Before I left, the university clinic gave me more shots than I could count, so I..."

Lilah's voice caught in her throat. Ross had moved to stand before her, so close that the heat of his body touched her like a caress. The male scent of him surrounded her, druglike and dizzying, and while she was still reeling, he leaned over, holding her good shoulder, and deftly unfastened the top three buttons of her shirt.

Ross's chest was in front of her at eye level, wide and firm under the white linen, and Lilah had the sudden aching desire to run her palms over it, feeling the warmth and strength of him under her fingers.

What was happening here? She swallowed hard, wondering if she should sit on her hands, just to be safe.

"Um...Ross?"

Her shirt fell open to the shadowed cleft between her

breasts, and she glanced down at it and back up at him as he slid it gently away from her injured shoulder.

She cleared her throat. "Ross."

"Yes?"

He gazed down at her, waiting, and Lilah could suddenly feel her heart thudding in her chest. She had no idea of what to say next. A spell was slowly and alarmingly tightening around her, and she only knew that she had to break it.

She took a deep breath. "You said you were fighting some development pressure?"

Ross's mouth curved up slightly. "You have a one-track mind, Professor," he said.

Little did he know. "I'm curious," she said.

Her shirt slipped down her arm to bare the lacy edge of her bra, exposing the full length of the scratch. It was an angry red against the pale skin of her chest, and had started to bleed again, but Lilah barely felt it. She was aware only of the confident motion of Ross's hand as he slid his fingers under her bra strap, easing it away from the cut and off her shoulder.

"Pressure is a gentle word for what's turning into a small war," he said. "But that's not a story I want to go into tonight. Lean forward."

Lilah closed her eyes as he reached toward her with the wet cloth and began to sponge out her cut. A trickle of warm water ran down between her breasts, and she shivered, feeling flushed and dizzier than three sips of wine could explain.

She took a breath and opened her eyes to find Ross watching her with a very slight, almost thoughtful frown. His gray gaze caught and held hers for a moment, then broke away to focus down on her wound.

"Next step," he said briskly, uncapping the iodine bottle. "This might hurt a little."

He wasn't kidding. The cut was deeper than she had realized, and the iodine began to sting fiercely.

"Ow!" she said, instinctively trying to pull back.

Ross had her firmly by the shoulder. "Hold still. I'm almost done.... There."

He pressed on a strip of gauze, secured it with tape and stepped back to survey her. "You don't look very happy, Professor. Aren't you glad to be saved from all those tropical germs?"

Lilah stood up, clumsily pulling her ripped shirt back over her newly bandaged shoulder. "Well," she said, "you were definitely very thorough. No germ could possibly survive that tidal wave of iodine. Thanks, I think."

Ross smiled sardonically. "Better to be safe. In the future, be more careful when you climb other people's fences."

"Corporal punishment with iodine. Is this some kind of vigilante justice?"

He shrugged. "It'll have to do. I've had a long day, and I don't feel up to pressing charges."

"Then you're not going to make me rot in prison."

"Not this time," he said. "You're off the hook."

"Thank you. Will you take me back to the gate now?"

"No."

"No?"

"No," he repeated, looking pointedly at her. "I wonder if you won't go searching for the site once you think you've gotten rid of me."

"Why would I do that? You've flat-out refused to let me excavate. I just want to go back to my hotel!"

He shook his head. "Sorry. You're staying here tonight."

"What?" Lilah exclaimed. "That's ridiculous! You don't have to baby-sit me until morning just to make sure I don't go to the canyon."

He walked over to the hearth and picked up the iron poker, using it to spread the embers of the dying fire. "Maybe not, but even the suspicion that you might be turning yourself into lion bait again is enough to ruin my sleep. I'd rather not worry about it. You can sleep in the guest room and leave in the morning."

She stared at his back, her face getting hot as she imagined how this twist might appear to her colleagues. If they heard that she spent the night here, after Ross Bradford had denied her access to the site...well, it certainly would look as if she had used more than an appeal to his kindness to try to change his mind.

"I can't stay here," she said.

"Oh? Why not?"

"Because it's not proper," she said stiffly.

Ross looked amused by her prudish choice of words. "Fence-climbing, trespassing and unauthorized midnight excavation work *are* proper?"

Her blush deepened. "You know what I mean."

"Yes," he said. "I do. But you don't have a choice about this. What time do you need to be awake?"

Lilah gritted her teeth. "Six. I have to go to the airport to meet my group. They left the States before I could reach them."

"What are you going to tell them?"

"I don't know," she said, trying to ignore the knots of anxiety forming in her stomach. It wasn't pleasant to think about what the next day held in store. "I'll try to explain what happened to our project."

"And then?"

She lifted her chin and looked fully at him. "Then I'll

go to the Park Bureau and do everything I can to talk them into giving me a federal research permit.''

"Do you ever give up?"

"No, I don't. Even if I end up on a plane headed back over the Atlantic, I'm going to figure out a way to make this damned excavation work."

"Why, Lilah?"

It was the first time he had used her name, and the sound of his deep voice shaping the word sent a sudden quiver up her back.

"Because I want to," she said fiercely. "That site is important, Ross, and it's mine. I want it just like you want your wildlife reserve, and I'll do whatever I have to do to get it."

There was an odd look in Ross's gray eyes as he watched her, but he didn't press any further, and Lilah was glad. As determined as she tried to sound, a large part of her felt exhausted and defeated, and she had to draw on her deepest core of strength to even think about the upcoming day.

"Your room is the second door down the hall," he said finally. "Let me know if you need anything. And don't wander away from the house. There are *askaris,* armed guards, who patrol here. I wouldn't want one of them to mistake you for a trespasser."

"Me?" Lilah said with a straight face. "How ridiculous."

"Right," Ross said dryly. "Good night."

He left the room, and Lilah heard the low creak of his footsteps moving down the wood-floored hallway. She exhaled hard, and reached up to rub her eyes. The room suddenly seemed hot and stuffy, and on an impulse, she walked over and opened one of the terrace doors.

The air outside was cool, and the clouds she had seen

in the distance were closer now, sharp and dark against the full moon, drifting silently with a beauty that made her ache.

She clenched the railing as her throat tightened. Kenya was ancient, beautiful and lost to her. How could everything have gone wrong so quickly, and so irrevocably? She should have protected herself, should have planned for a disaster like this. And now it was too late.

A rustling sound startled her out of her thoughts, and she glanced around anxiously. Everything was gray and fuzzy in the moonlight, but she was suddenly sure that she had seen the shape of a man only yards away, moving stealthily through the patch of seven-foot aloe plants that bordered the house.

She stared out into the darkness. There he was again, and then he was gone. Was it the guard, coming up to order her back inside? Lilah moved cautiously away from the railing. It should make her feel safe, knowing that he was out there to protect the house, but there was something creepy about the way he moved, slinking through the shadows like that.

She stepped back toward the doors and the security of the house, then heard the rustle again, now closer. Did this *askari* guard know that she was a guest? The way the man was lurking in the bushes unnerved her.

"Hello!" she said with forced cheer in her voice.

There was absolute silence from the dark thicket of plants.

Imagining a rifle being trained on her for the second time that night, she said loudly, "I was getting some air, but I'm going to bed now. Good night!"

A chill, black silence. Nothing stirred.

To Lilah, it seemed menacing. Her heart suddenly thud-

ding, she scurried back through the door, shoved it closed
behind her, and locked it.

The warm lights of the living room bathed her in a
reassuring glow, and the curtains on the doors fell back
into place, covering the glass panes and blocking out the
darkness.

She took a deep breath and stepped back, feeling the
flood of panic recede, leaving only embarrassment. What
on earth had gotten into her? The guard must have thought
she was crazy. Her imagination was suffering from jet lag,
and it was definitely time for bed. The early hours of the
morning were ticking by, and if the day ahead turned out
as expected, she was going to need the help of a good
night's sleep to face it.

Chapter 4

The next morning, Ross was sorting through a stack of papers when he heard the sound of a car chugging toward the house. Surprised, he checked his watch. He'd sent a car and driver to the airport at eight, but hadn't expected them back yet. The hassle of getting foreign visitors through customs usually took at least an hour, and a group loaded down with archaeological excavation equipment should have been tied up until noon.

But one glance out the window assured him that it was the ranch Land Rover approaching, packed with people and luggage. The archaeologists were here, and Lilah Evans, as far as he knew, was still asleep.

Ross himself had been up by six, and the red-eyed reflection greeting him in his shaving mirror had been almost enough to send him back to bed. He had lain awake for a long time last night, frowning at the ceiling, thinking over his encounter with the prickly but interesting Dr. Evans.

What was it about her that caught his attention? She was attractive enough, in a clean and distracted way, but that wasn't it. He had known many beautiful women, and a merely well-proportioned face didn't do much for him. No, it was the vitality in Lilah's face that made it fascinating. She lived and breathed as though she meant every bit of it, and that raw energy intrigued him.

By the time he said good-night to her, a plan had begun to shape itself in his mind, but it wasn't until the clock hands crept to three that he had finally come to a decision. It would be possible, under one condition, to delay the sale of the ranch. But meeting that condition was going to require Lilah's help, and Ross had his doubts about whether she would agree to cooperate once she heard the entire story.

The guest room door was still closed, and Ross couldn't hear a sound inside, which didn't surprise him. He had seen exhaustion falling over Lilah like a fog last night, and he had intended to let her sleep until at least eleven. But now that wasn't possible. Mama Ruth, the housekeeper, could stall the new arrivals with a pot of Kenyan coffee, but hopefully Lilah wasn't the kind of woman who needed an hour to pull herself together.

He raised his hand and knocked sharply. Inside, there was a soft sound of blankets moving, then nothing. He knocked again.

"Come in?"

Lilah's voice was hazy with sleep, and Ross paused, suddenly wondering if he should have asked Mama Ruth to awaken her.

Too late now. He squared his shoulders and opened the door. "Morning, Dr. Evans," he said briskly. "Rise and shine."

Sunlight filtered through the gauzy curtains, washing the room in clean brightness. He glanced around, uncomfortably aware of the clothes draped over the armchair, and of Lilah, sitting up in the middle of the rumpled bed, clutching the sheets to her bare shoulders and blinking at him as fuzzily as a newborn kitten.

"Ross," she said unsteadily, and cleared her throat. "What time is it?"

Her honey-colored hair caught the light as it tumbled down to her shoulders in sleepy disarray, and her skin was pale and smooth against the white sheets. There were dark smudges under her eyes, and Ross felt himself tensing as he looked at her.

He didn't want this image of Lilah in his mind, rumpled and vulnerable, looking every bit the way she would if she had just awakened beside him after a passionate night of—

Damn it! Enough. He fixed his gaze on a framed print of wildflowers hanging on the far wall. "It's ten," he said.

"Ten?" Her voice lost all traces of sleepiness. "Oh my God, I was supposed to be at the airport two hours ago to meet the flight!"

She swung her legs over the edge of the bed, holding the covers against her in a death grip. "Ross, excuse me, I have to get dressed, and then I need to..." She paused as he held up one hand. "What? Are they late?"

"They're here."

Lilah goggled at him. "Where?"

"Pulling into the driveway as we speak."

A flash of horror crossed her face, and she reached up to touch her hair, winced and dropped her hand. "*Now?* What are they doing here?" She stared at him. "You sent a car to pick them up?"

He nodded. "I thought you could use the sleep."

"Oh." She looked as stunned as if he'd suddenly done a back flip, and then her face softened into a hesitant smile. "That was nice. Thank you."

The subtle scent of feminine skin was in the air, mingling with the sunshine, drifting over him like a drug. It stirred up an ache that he didn't want to acknowledge, and he steeled himself against it.

"Don't thank me. It was the least I could do." The cool edge to his voice brought a wariness back into Lilah's eyes, just as he had intended.

He took a deep breath. "I'll meet you in the living room," he said, and walked out, his hands jammed into his pockets to hide the fact that they were clenched into fists.

What in God's name was happening to him? Had he been alone so long that the sight of one woman tangled in her bedsheets could affect him like this? That kind of emotional vertigo was exactly what he didn't want or need, and he was damn well going to make sure that it went no further. If he decided that he wanted Lilah Evans in his bed, he'd seduce her and be done with it. Period.

"Ross."

A deep voice cut into his thoughts, and he looked up to see Otieno Kasu, the ranch manager, beckoning to him from the open kitchen door.

The kitchen was warm and bright, with the smoky smell of coffee lingering in the air. There was a board of half-chopped carrots on the wooden table, but no sign of Mama Ruth.

Otieno motioned Ross into the room and closed the door behind him. "The archaeologists are here?"

"The car just pulled up," Ross said, and tapped the side of the enameled coffeepot on the stove. It was lukewarm, but he poured himself a cup anyway. "They'll be knocking on the door in a minute. Is this all the coffee? If I have to act like a Bradford, I'll need more."

His friend's expression was disapproving. "You need a night of good sleep. Sleep is better than coffee."

"But coffee is more available than sleep," Ross said. It was sad but true. The events of the past ten days hadn't done much for his rest or his peace of mind.

He leaned against the edge of the counter, listening for the sound of the group at the door, and heard nothing.

"I'm going to go see what happened to the archaeologists," he said. "Just to make sure they aren't out there excavating my yard."

The front door was standing open, letting in a pool of tropical sunshine. Through it Ross could see the group outside, huddled into a conference.

"But you talked to him about it?" one of the two men was saying urgently, and as Ross paused in the doorway, he saw with surprise that the man was speaking to Lilah.

Less than five minutes from bed to work? Definitely a new record for a female of his acquaintance. She must have bolted into her clothes the moment he left her room.

The man interrogating her was about thirty, red-haired, with a stubborn chin and a soft body that looked as if it spent too much time behind a desk. "Wouldn't he discuss it with you?"

"Yes, we discussed it," Lilah said. She sounded stoic, as if she expected the worst and was grimly prepared to take it.

"And? You do know that this sale means that we'll need a federal permit to work on the land."

"I know that, Ted. And we'll get one, but it'll take time. I'm going to meet with the director of the Park Bureau, and it's possible that I can convince him to—"

"Convince him? Not likely," Ted said. "You can't just

walk right in and talk someone into bypassing all the rules. Let's just face the fact that we've lost this site."

Ross grinned, watching Lilah's shoulders stiffen. He didn't have to see her face to know that she suddenly had fire in her eyes. Ted, whoever he was, had just said the wrong thing.

"I am not going to face any such fact," Lilah began.

Ted snorted, ready to argue, and Ross decided it was time to step in.

"Good morning," he said briskly, and the conversation halted. Lilah turned quickly to face him. Her hair was damp, as if she'd splashed her face in a rush, and the curling tendrils he'd seen earlier were now tucked firmly behind her ears. Her cheeks were freshly scrubbed, but there was a tense, tired look about her that made Ross wonder if she'd slept any more than he had.

His eyes moved over her, and he realized that she was wearing one of his shirts. Mama Ruth must have given it to her to replace the one she had torn on the fence. It was a white oxford button-down, and it hung loosely on her slender body, obviously too big. Seeing her wrapped in it sent an unexpected jolt through Ross.

Lilah must have noticed something in his expression, because there was a sudden rush of color to her cheeks, and she raised her hands, awkwardly smoothing the cloth against her.

"Mr. Bradford," said the second man, stepping forward and extending his hand. He was in his fifties, the oldest of the group, and he looked like a rounded, slightly crazed Albert Einstein. Horn-rimmed glasses sat crookedly on his nose, and a shock of gray hair rose from his head at an alarming angle. "I'm Elliot Morris," he said, shaking Ross's hand.

Ross blinked at him, noticing that he was wearing the

unlikely combination of brown plaid pants and a blue striped shirt. Both were baggy and comfortably rumpled.

"And this is Dr. Ted Garvey," the man continued.

Ross nodded briefly to Ted, and turned back to Elliot. "I was under the impression that there were more of you."

"There are," Elliot said. "We have three graduate students and our illustrator along, but they stayed behind at the airport to get our equipment through customs." He raised shaggy eyebrows at Ross. "Though from what I'm hearing, we may not need it after all."

In the sudden, expectant silence, Ross glanced at Lilah, who was the only one not watching him. Her gaze was on the ground, and she looked faintly gray.

"No," Ross said. "You'll need it."

Lilah's head snapped up, and if Ross had intended to try for dramatic effect, he would have been pleased by the astonishment on her face.

"What?" she said, staring at him. "What are you saying? Are you postponing the sale?"

A flash of raw, wild hope lit her face, and the nakedness of her expression embarrassed Ross.

"That's right," he said briskly.

Lilah composed herself with visible effort. "I see," she said. "Well. How interesting. When exactly did you decide this?"

"Today. I just phoned the Park Bureau. They're willing to wait six weeks to finalize the sale, so I can give you that long to excavate. After that, the ranch becomes government property."

"Six weeks?" Ted Garvey echoed. "You obviously don't understand what kind of time and work is involved with an excavation like this. Six weeks is barely long enough to get started."

"Sorry, but that's my offer. Take it or leave it."

Ted shook his head. "We can't possibly—"

"Take it!" Lilah exclaimed. "Of course we'll take it! Ted, don't be stupid. Anything could happen in six weeks' time. If this site turns out to be important, we can use the early success to convince the government to let us stay."

Ted scowled. "And if it doesn't?"

"It will," she said, pinning him with a fierce look. "I came here to start an excavation, and that's what I'm going to do. You make your own decision about whether to stay."

"Lilah's right," Elliot said. "Take a chance, Ted. You're not old enough to be stodgy yet."

Ted muttered something under his breath.

"Was that 'yes, I'll stay and be a team player?'" Elliot asked.

"I suppose so," Ted said grudgingly. "Since I already went to the trouble of flying here."

"Ted doesn't respond well to plane trips," Elliot explained. "Little peanuts make him cranky."

"It's not the peanuts, it's the recycled air," Ted objected. "It gives me a sinus headache."

Ross felt a sudden insistent tug on his arm, and looked down to see Lilah beside him. "Okay," she whispered. "What's going on? Why are you doing this?"

He bent his head toward hers. "Are you complaining?"

"No! But I'm confused. Why this sudden gift of six weeks?"

"It's not a gift."

She recoiled, looking wary. "What do you mean?"

"Not now. We can discuss it later, if you really do want the six weeks."

"You know I do," Lilah said slowly. "But I don't see why—"

"Later," he said firmly, and straightened up to address the rest of the group. "So, it's official. Dr. Evans and I will take care of the paperwork."

"Thank you," Elliot said. "Very much."

Ross glanced at Lilah, and succumbed to a wicked urge. "You should thank Dr. Evans," he said. "She had an...unusual approach to the matter."

Lilah's eyes widened with alarm. And gave a barely perceptible shake of her head, which Ross pretended not to see. Elliot looked enthusiastic. "Lilah? Yes, she can be persuasive, all right. This project has been hers from the start. She's very dedicated."

"Yes," Ross said. "Very. I would say that she had to climb some fences to get where she is today. Figuratively speaking, of course."

"Well," Lilah said loudly, shooting Ross a glare that could have frozen molten lava, "Just look at the time. We know how busy you are, Mr. Bradford, so we won't keep you any longer. We really do need to start setting up camp, so..."

Ross grinned. "I don't mind a break. Are you sure you wouldn't rather come inside for a cup of coffee?"

Elliot's eyes widened. "Oh, that sounds—"

"Nice," Lilah interrupted, "but we can't. With only six weeks to work, we'd better get started right away."

"You're sure? Mama Ruth just made some great short-bread cookies."

"Cookies?" Elliot said wistfully. "Really?"

"Later," Lilah said.

Ross met her gaze and her lips tightened at the amusement she saw in his eyes.

"Next time then," Ross agreed. "I know you're in a rush. Dr. Evans and I can talk business tonight. We have a few important things to discuss."

"Oh yes," Lilah said, fixing him with a look that promised that his joke would come back to haunt him. "Yes, we definitely do."

"Ross, I must speak with you," Otieno said, as the carful of archaeologists pulled away from the house. Ross turned to see his friend standing in the doorway, a frown creasing his normally impassive face.

Ross smiled briefly. "You overheard. And you're about to tell me that I'm making a big mistake, right?"

"No. It is your decision to make."

"True," Ross said. "But you'd still be justified in asking me what the hell I'm doing. I know this caught you by surprise."

Otieno shrugged. "I think you must have a good reason to delay the sale."

"What qualifies as a good reason? Natural disaster? War? My father's ghost coming back to haunt me for selling his land?" He sighed. "No. I don't have a good reason."

"This woman, the archaeologist," Otieno said, then paused.

"What about her?"

"She is quite pretty."

"I hadn't noticed," Ross said shortly. "So, what was it you wanted to talk about? I haven't turned up a copy of the grain invoice yet, so if the supplier is still hounding you, tell them to sit tight."

Otieno shook his head. "This is not ranch business. Someone was outside the house last night."

"What do you mean? A prowler?"

"The *askari* found a man's footprints by the windows of your bedroom. He saw no one, only the prints, and broken branches on the bushes by the house. Nothing was disturbed.''

Ross drummed his fingers on the coffee mug, holding back a surge of anger. "Wyatt," he said. "Damn the bastard. He's behind this."

Even the man's name left a bad taste in Ross's mouth. Jake Wyatt was the force behind a group of developers pushing the government to use nearby land, including the western side of the Bradford property, as the site for a major meat-and-hide processing plant. Wyatt was greedy, conscienceless and very well-connected. Ross had learned that hard truth years ago, when he was seventeen and still living at home. He'd stumbled across proof that the rancher was using a cheap, illegal pesticide to dip his cattle, a poison known to cause long-term health problems in the workers exposed to it.

Angered, Ross had gone straight to the authorities, only to find that Wyatt had the Bureau of Agriculture in his pocket.

"We're looking into it," he was assured, over and over, as nothing happened. It was like slamming up against a wall, and the only thing he'd eventually accomplished was to make his hatred of Jake Wyatt reciprocal.

The man hadn't mellowed since. In the past ten days, Ross had seen enough shady maneuvering and foul play to think he'd seen it all.

"Interesting that we suddenly have a prowler," he said grimly. "I'd call it coincidental, but I don't believe in coincidence. Wyatt wants his factory badly, and he's made it clear that he'll do whatever it takes to win."

Ross's words hung in the air as the two men gazed at each other. What was Jake Wyatt capable of? It would be foolish to assume any limits, and they both knew it.

"This time," Otieno said, "we will teach him to lose."

There was steel in the older man's voice, and Ross nodded, recognizing the same grim determination he felt.

"I'm glad you're on my side," Ross said dryly.

"Never doubt that."

"Never," Ross said, his throat suddenly tightening. It was true. Otieno Kasu was Ross's older brother in every respect but blood, and more of a family than Ross's blood kin had ever been.

Fifteen years ago, it had been Otieno, not Hugh, who had understood and accepted Ross's decision to take a wildlife conservation position with the World Bank instead of coming back to Kenya and the ranch. It had been Otieno who answered Ross's letters when Hugh wouldn't even acknowledge them, and Otieno who encouraged Ross to start ECO, his own environmental consulting firm.

Now, as the two men stood silently under the morning sun, Ross was surprised by how right it felt to be home. He had expected to return to Kenya awkwardly, even guiltily—an intruder in his father's house. How else could it be? He was here to act on the beliefs that had alienated him in the first place. Hugh would be furious to see what he was doing.

Or would he? Ross had been stunned to learn that his father had left him the ranch. Hugh was neither a fool nor an idealist, and would have known exactly what Ross would do once he owned the property. Was it simply that the old man had had no one else?

Ross had voiced these questions to Otieno soon after he returned, and the other man had introduced an odd idea.

"I think your father began to realize," his friend said, "that it is a great wrong to cast away your family. I think he began to see that at the end of a life, it is not land or business that matters, but *umoja.*"

Unity. Connectedness. The Swahili word came easily off Otieno's tongue, but Ross found it difficult to apply such a concept to his father's life.

"That sounds too deep for the Hugh Bradford I knew."

"A man can take on different ways as he grows older. He looks at the world around him and at the path he has cut behind him. In some, age does bring wisdom."

"If he was changing, why didn't he contact me? He knew I was writing to you. I would have come back. I would have come...to see him."

There was quiet empathy in Otieno's dark gaze. "Perhaps he thought he had more time."

Ross cleared his throat and stared down into his coffee mug. Maybe leaving him the ranch was Hugh's gesture of acceptance of Ross and his choices. It was hard to imagine, but there was a certain peace in thinking that it might be so.

At any rate, he had more immediate problems to deal with. This news about the prowler warned him that he might have underestimated Jake Wyatt, which meant that the six-week delay would be more of a risk than he'd expected.

But he had given Lilah Evans his promise, and he intended to honor it. The plan he had in mind should keep the odds in his favor, but just the same, he was going to have to be careful. Very careful.

"They're here," Elliot said.

Lilah looked up from the tent stake she was hammering into the rocky ground and squinted up the road. "Already?"

Sure enough, through the thorny screen of acacia branches, she could make out the dust cloud raised by the rented Land Rover as it chugged down the hill toward them.

"And to think that you doubted them," Elliot said airily. "You should know that a professor of my caliber does not train just any average bumbling graduate student. It takes more than a few puny customs officials to hold back my trainees."

"Nothing personal, Elliot, but I'll bet you money that Denise is responsible for this. See? She's even driving."

Denise Johnson, the scientific illustrator, waved at them as she pulled the loaded-down car into camp.

"I deserve an honorary degree from you people," she said, jumping down from the front seat. "Do you know how long it took me to talk those bureaucrats into letting your gear through? And do you think I got any help from this group? No.

"This one," she pointed to Peter Lee, who began to look sheepish, "thought it would be a good time to practice the Swahili he learned in his quickie course, so as the customs guy is eying your boxes, Pete says—"

"I meant to say that we were a group of many people," Peter interrupted, his ears turning red. "I told you, I thought it would help explain why we had so much stuff."

"Right, but he got his nouns mixed up and ended up saying something which translated into 'we have many guns.' You can imagine how well that went over."

"Oh, dear," Elliot said sadly.

"Yeah, no kidding. Fortunately, as soon as we switched back to English, they realized that we were only lousy Swahili speakers, and not terrorists, and let us through. But not until they combed through every inch of your stuff."

"I'm glad you made it," Lilah said, hugging her friend, whose crisp new safari hat topped off a sparkling clean ensemble of khaki shorts and matching shirt. A neatly pressed red bandanna was tied jauntily at her neck. "You look different," she said, stepping back to take a look at her friend. "But strangely familiar. Wait, I know, you're Indiana Jones!"

"No, he's my cousin. I'm Indiana Johnson." Denise grinned. "I figured it would help your luck if I looked the part. To tell you the truth, though, I'm not sure I want you to have any luck. If you find nothing at all, then I can just laze around and work on my tan."

Lilah had known from the first stages of planning the excavation that she wanted to bring Denise along to work with them. Photography did a poor job of capturing the subtle flaking patterns on stone tools, but a specially trained artist could record that information in a pen-and-ink drawing.

Peter emerged from the back of the Land Rover, his long arms wrapped around boxes of data sheets. "Where should I put these?"

"We'll use the big tent as our lab," Lilah said, pointing. "You can just pile those on the floor until we set up the tables."

She and Elliot exchanged glances, and he stepped closer to her.

"Do you think," he said in a low voice, "that we should bother to unpack everything? It might be wiser just to leave some of those boxes alone. Save ourselves the trouble of repacking if we have to go."

Lilah sighed. "That would be practical. But you know what, Elliot? I don't want to be practical. I want to unpack every box here and make myself believe that we're going to stay."

"That may be out of our hands."

''Not if I can help it. I'm going to start working on the permit right away.''

''And you might just get it. But if you don't, Lilah, don't take it personally. There are a lot of factors involved here, and a major one is whether we find anything significant down at the site in the next month. It's going to be a gamble, so do what you can and hope for luck.''

''Luck.'' Lilah shook her head. ''Yuck.''

Elliot chuckled. ''Well put.''

''I mean it, Elliot. I hate depending on luck. This time there's too much at stake. Hoping that we pick the right spots to excavate, hoping that we have enough time to find what's out there and use it to convince the government to let us stay...it's too iffy for me.''

''That's the archaeologist's cross to bear, my dear.''

''Maybe so, but in the meantime, I'm going to get everything set up to make use of this luck if—no, *when* it happens.''

The afternoon sun was dissolving into rosy evening light by the time camp was set up. The four canvas sleeping tents and large laboratory tent were nestled in a rough circle under the overhanging shade trees, and a stone fire circle marked the center of the group. Elliot and Denise, self-proclaimed gourmet cooks, were busily putting together a dinner that involved opening a lot of cans.

Lilah was hungry, but not so hungry that dinner felt more important than a canyon visit. After their late-morning start, there hadn't been a spare minute to sneak away all day, and now she intended to grab her chance before it was too dark to see.

Only a few hundred yards from camp, the thigh-high savanna grass gave way to the edge of the canyon. From there, the land sloped gently down, becoming a stretch of dry, crumbling earth dotted with tough-rooted plants.

Moving sideways for better balance, she picked her way slowly down the slope to where the gorge leveled off onto a sandy, rocky soil floor. She wandered slowly, keeping her eyes fixed on the ground.

The warm glow of the late-day sun brought out the rich earth tones of the pebbles scattered around her feet, and she squinted slightly as different colors and shapes caught her eye. Her trained gaze picked out an unusual stone in the mixture around her, and she squatted down to get it.

Aha. It was a flake of chert, a smooth and very hard type of stone that came in an amazing variety of colors, from white to black to red. This piece was the same mottled gray as the tools they had already recovered from this site.

"What did you find?" asked a voice behind her.

Lilah jumped, startled, and lost her balance. Dirt grated into her palms as she sat back hard on the rocky ground, and she turned to see Ross Bradford walking toward her, looking amused.

Chapter 5

"What's the idea of sneaking up on me like that?" Lilah stood, ignoring the hand he offered, and dusted herself off.

Ross raised his eyebrows. "Actually, I called to you twice, but you didn't answer. Did you find something interesting?"

"A flake," she said grudgingly, and offered it to him. "Here."

He took it, his fingers brushing lightly against hers, and Lilah bit her lip as she watched him examine the scrap of stone. The sun's golden light picked out strands of mahogany twined into his hair, and his silvery eyes seemed to glow against his face.

The wind gusted, hugging Ross's shirt against his broad chest, and Lilah averted her eyes with considerable effort. There was no good reason why she should be reacting like this to a man she barely knew, and it needed to stop.

Now. Ross Bradford had already brought more than enough chaos into her life.

"I am here to work," she said under her breath. "Work. Work."

"What did you say?"

"Nothing. Look, Ross, I...wanted to thank you for your trouble in getting us these six weeks to work here."

"Really."

She frowned. "Yes."

"You're not convincing, Professor."

Lilah exhaled sharply, annoyed that he could read her so well. "I'm trying to be polite."

"Be honest instead. You're wondering why, if I can give you six weeks, can't I give you six months? Or even three months? You're glad for a chance to start your project, but you resent the hell out of me for dropping crumbs in your lap to make up for the loaf I stole. Am I right?"

He was, but Lilah wasn't prepared to admit it. "Look," she said. "This is your ranch, to do with as you please, so obviously I have to be grateful for any crumbs you want to give me. Our priorities may be different, but—"

"And what are my priorities?"

Lilah's face heated up. "I'd rather not discuss this."

"You still think that the reason I'm so anxious to sell the ranch is that I want to make a quick profit."

"I didn't say that."

"Not since last night, you mean?"

"Ross—"

He held up one hand. "I could make a lot more money by selling this ranch to the industrial developers instead of to the government. But I want this land put out of the reach of those developers. Forever." His gaze held hers as he spoke. "Money is not the issue here. Do you believe me?"

"Does it matter whether I believe you?"

"Yes, because I need your help. I'm taking a risk by delaying the deal, and I want to ensure that the delay doesn't work against me."

"I don't understand."

Ross half turned, shading his eyes against the setting sun. "Ten miles to the west," he said, "my property borders a working cattle ranch owned by a man named Jake Wyatt. He and his powerful friends have been working behind the scenes to convince the government to industrialize my land."

"That's why you're in such a hurry to sell?"

He nodded. "I want this settled. Like I said last night, if I wait too long, I could lose the option of selling at all. The government has been known to seize land when it suits them."

He gave her a significant look, and continued. "Wyatt is going to see this delay as a gift from heaven. What I need is someone who can get close to him, listen to what he says about his plans and then report back to me, so I can keep one step ahead of him."

"Hold it right there," Lilah said. "I get the feeling you're talking about me, and if you are, you'd better think again. I'm an archaeologist, not an industrial spy. I came to Kenya to excavate, and that's exactly what I'm going to do. Sorry, but no way."

"You should let me finish before you put your foot down," Ross suggested.

"It isn't necessary. I can't do it. I know you're doing us a favor, and I'd be glad to repay you in some other way, but espionage is where I draw the line."

"That's your final word, then?"

"Absolutely."

"That's too bad. I was looking forward to seeing what your group found at the site."

Lilah stared at him as his meaning became clear. "You can't," she said, appalled. "You *wouldn't* refuse to let us excavate just because I won't do this for you."

Ross raised his eyebrows. "Actually, I can and I would. The risk of being taken by surprise and losing my deal is too great without your help. It's not worth it."

"That's not fair! I know I said that I'd do anything to keep my site, but I didn't expect you to take me up on it!"

"Surprise."

"Oh, very funny. Look, Ross, I'm not cut out to be a spy. I get nervous, and I trip over things, and—"

"You're overdramatizing this," he said. "All I want is for you to attend a few reasonably boring receptions with me and talk to Wyatt. That's it."

"Go to parties with you? What else? What makes you think that this Jake Wyatt person would give me the time of day, much less tell me his intimate business secrets over champagne and crackers?"

"Because Wyatt is his own biggest fan, and he loves to hear himself talk. If you steered him in the right direction, and there was enough of that champagne flowing, my guess is that he'd take it from there."

Lilah was silent for a moment, frowning at the ground. It was clear from the cool determination in Ross's voice that he had no intention of backing down.

"Fine," she said grudgingly. "I'll do it."

"I thought you would."

She rolled her eyes. "You don't leave much to chance, do you?"

"No. I take care of my own business and let other people leave theirs to chance."

"I try that, too, but things don't always work out so neatly," she said. "Trust me, I know."

Ross laughed suddenly, really laughed, with an open, genuine sound that enchanted her. She looked up at him, and was amazed to see that lines had crinkled up around the corners of his eyes, and his mouth had released its usual cynical curve.

"Having your own problems with luck lately, Professor?" he asked.

"You know it," Lilah said. When he looked at her like that, she suddenly felt as if she were basking in a light warmer than the sun. "But at least I have six weeks to improve it."

"Then the price is worth it?"

"I won't answer that, because I don't want to ease your conscience."

Amusement flickered in his eyes. "I should have known by now that you don't take defeat graciously."

"Everybody tells me that," Lilah admitted, a reluctant smile tugging at her mouth.

The sun had dropped behind clouds massed low on the western horizon, outlining them with gold fire, and the coolness of the evening began to settle in as the shadows lengthened and melted together.

"We should head back," Ross said. "It'll be dark soon."

Lilah nodded, and stepped forward to walk with him, matching his easy stride.

Ross's plan meant that she would be spending time with him, which was an unnerving thought. Something about him awakened all of her senses, made her feel more alive, as if the air around him crackled with an inexplicable electricity. It was a strange sensation, and not a completely comfortable one, but it attracted Lilah as much as it unsettled her.

The next few days rushed by in a flurry of activity at the site. The archaeologists had been able to hire some of the ranch workers to help speed up the early excavation, but in spite of the increased pace, nothing dramatic had turned up. This was completely normal, but still a disappointment to Lilah, who had half expected wonderful things to come leaping out of the ground to greet her.

On Friday afternoon, she was on her way back to camp for a water break in the shade of the trees when she crossed paths with Denise.

"I was just coming to find you," her friend exclaimed. "Some guy just came by with a message for you. He said to tell you that Mr. Bradford will pick you up tonight at eight, and that you should dress as formally as possible. Does this mean what I think it means?"

Lilah took off her wide-brimmed straw hat and fanned herself with it.

"I hope he knows that 'as formally as possible' means a sundress to me," she said. "I came here to work, after all. Nobody warned me that I'd need my tiara."

"Lilah!" Denise grabbed her arm urgently. "I'm dying of curiosity. Are you going out with Ross Bradford?"

"We're going out, but—" Lilah began, and Denise whooped, cutting her off.

"You have a date!"

"No!" Lilah said quickly, feeling her face get hot in spite of the shade. "It's not a date. I'm just going out to some embassy party in Nairobi with him, that's all. Why are you looking at me like that?"

"Come on, Lilah. You're going to a party with him? Where I come from, that's what we call a date. Now I realize that you've been working pretty hard lately, and maybe you've forgotten about stuff like that, but—''

Lilah groaned. "I know what a date is, Denise, and believe me, this isn't one. Among other things, the word 'date' means something you choose to do, and I definitely didn't have a choice here."

Denise looked mystified, so Lilah explained the condition Ross had imposed on letting them stay at the site.

"That's amazing," Denise exclaimed as Lilah finished. "Why don't things like this ever happen to me? What I would do for a date with that man."

"I don't have a date! This is business, nothing more. Underhanded business. Blackmail, you could call it. Anything but a date, okay?"

Denise appraised her with a look. "Lilah, you're weird. Maybe it is supposed to be just business, but this is a golden opportunity, can't you see it? Don't tell me you haven't noticed that Ross Bradford is one very sexy man."

"I've noticed," Lilah said.

"So…" Denise looked expectantly at her, waiting for Lilah to provide some reason why Ross Bradford was not date material.

Lilah shook her head. "No. No way. You don't understand."

A new clarity began to dawn on her friend's face.

"Aha," Denise said. "I do understand, Lilah Evans. In fact, it's becoming crystal clear that you are protesting too much. You already like him a little, don't you?"

"What? Have you been listening to me?"

"I sure have. And I know you. You're trying to convince yourself that you're not interested in Ross Bradford because you're afraid that you might be falling for him."

"That's not true. I'm here to work. That's all."

"This is classic avoidance behavior," Denise said.

"I knew you should never have taken that psychology class."

"Lilah, you know I'm right. You haven't had a date in six months. I know, because I set up the last one for you. That was Philip, and you said you didn't like him because his teeth were too white."

"Well, they were."

"Too *white?*" Denise demanded. "What kind of person rejects a man because his teeth are too white?"

"Me. It didn't look normal. Every time he smiled, there was this blinding flash of—"

"This absolutely proves my point. You're doing everything you can to avoid ever falling in love again. Why?"

Lilah frowned at her toes. "I've been busy for the past six months."

"Busy? Or just afraid? You know, you can't allow Jeff the Jerk to scar you for life."

"I'm not scarred," Lilah said. "I'm just a lot better at being careful. I'm never, ever getting dumped again. The next time I let myself fall in love, it's going to be with someone so safe and devoted that he'll be completely under my thumb and I'll never have to worry about him walking out on me. I want a nice, boring, risk-free relationship."

"Loving someone is always a risk," Denise said. "And I don't think you can necessarily choose who you love."

"I can," Lilah said grimly. "And I will."

"Hmm," Denise said. "We'll see. And in the meantime, there's no way I'm going to let you go to an embassy party in a sundress. Not with that man. It just so happens that I brought along my favorite little black dress, and you can borrow it."

"You brought dress-up clothes with you?" Lilah was

impressed. Denise, with her usual aplomb, was prepared for anything. "You didn't happen to bring a parachute, in case we have to dive out of a burning plane one of these days?"

"Do not joke," said her friend solemnly. "And never, ever, underestimate the universal need for a little black dress. Lilah, you may be a Ph.D., but there are a lot of things I could teach you."

"Don't you think I should wear my business suit?" Lilah said doubtfully. The idea of wearing a sexy dress did make it seem like a date. The suit would definitely be safer.

"Absolutely no suit. Think about it, a boring business suit at a glitzy evening party? All wrong. You'd look out of place. In my dress, you'll still stand out, but in the right way. This Jake Wyatt guy will be eating out of your hand."

True to her word, Denise personally took over the preparation of Lilah for the evening. The promised "little black dress" turned out to be a slim and silky sheath held up by tiny straps. It managed to combine sophistication with just the right degree of sexiness, and after seeing it, Lilah was a slave to the temptation to wear it.

"It isn't too short, is it?" she asked, tilting Elliot's shaving mirror up and down to try to get an idea of how she looked.

"Are you kidding?" Denise said, and sighed. "That darn dress doesn't look the same on me. If I weren't so selfish, I might give it to you. You should wear clothes like this more often."

Lilah grinned. "Right, to department meetings, and all those other glamorous things I do. What time is it?"

"Almost eight."

"Do I have time to go for a walk?"

"Right now? No."

"Not even a quick one?" Lilah smoothed the dress anxiously.

"Nervous?"

"A little." Lilah laughed, but the sound was stiff. "Isn't that dumb? It's this spy thing, of course. That's the only thing I could possibly have to be nervous about."

"Of course," Denise said diplomatically. "Makes perfect sense to me. But you definitely don't have time for a walk, because I hear a car coming. Your date...ahem, I mean your business meeting, is here."

Chapter 6

The British Embassy was located in the lushest, most upper-class suburb of Nairobi, an area which Ross had always thought seemed more like a winding tropical road in Beverly Hills than a section of official buildings. Most of the embassies were here, housed in huge, beautiful villas which had originally been built by wealthy British colonists back in the early part of the century.

The embassy was brightly lit and crowded that night, and guests milled around on the terrace and lawn, enjoying the cool evening air. It looked like an elegant house party, if one ignored the high-security fence and the armed soldiers who carefully checked everyone coming through the gate.

With a hand on her shoulder, Ross guided Lilah in through the front door. Her skin was smooth and warm under his fingers, and the silky material of her dress shimmered around her, somehow emphasizing exactly what it concealed.

Ross was having a hard time keeping his eyes off her. It had been days since he'd seen her, which was intentional on his part. He had stayed away from the archaeologists' camp, partly to avoid giving Lilah any chance to back out of his plan, but mostly to try to clear his mind of her.

It hadn't worked. He'd been having trouble concentrating as he sat at his father's desk in the Nairobi office, and when his thoughts drifted away from the paperwork in front of him, they came to rest on the image of Lilah that first morning in the guest room. He remembered her sleepy, unguarded eyes, her hair tumbling down over her shoulders, and how her mouth looked as soft and swollen as if someone had been kissing it.

Earlier that evening, when he'd finally seen her again, he had been rocked by a wave of desire intense enough to demand attention.

Soon, he thought. He had to be patient, although it was difficult to maintain the faint touch on her shoulder when what he really wanted was to slide his polite, neutrally placed hand down along the curve of her side, tracing the shape of her under his fingers. He could sense that Lilah wasn't as immune to him as she wanted him to think, and he was disciplined enough to wait until her own desire had reached the critical point.

Heads immediately began to turn as they entered the room. Ross knew that his own sudden return to Kenya had been of great interest to local society, and the small war developing over the fate of his property was probably keeping the gossips buzzing. The appearance of a lovely but unknown woman on his arm would only spice up the situation.

Under the pretext of nodding hello to a few acquaintances, Ross scanned the room. Where was Wyatt? His

body felt jumpy, alert, as if even the man's presence behind him could somehow make him prickle like a wary
lion. But the large room was crowded, and there was no
sign of Wyatt. Yet.

"Ross Bradford?" A man with a nose which could
only belong to the British upper class was approaching
them eagerly.

"Yes," Ross said. "Have we met?"

"Sorry, no," said the man, in a crisp accent that reminded Ross of his first few years at the embassy school
in Nairobi before his parents had packed him off to America. "But I know your work, and I'm delighted to meet
the man behind ECO. I'm Simon Caldwell, assistant to
His Excellency, the Ambassador."

He shook Ross's hand enthusiastically, then hesitated.
"I'm terribly sorry about your father."

"Thank you," Ross said. "You knew him?"

"Somewhat," Simon Caldwell said. "Not as well as I
would have liked. He rather kept to himself."

Ross nodded, not surprised to hear that. He saw Simon
look inquiringly at Lilah.

"Dr. Lilah Evans," Ross said.

"Hello." With classic American forthrightness, Lilah
stuck out her hand and smiled at Simon. "Nice to meet
you."

"Delighted," he said, shaking her hand. "You're with
ECO also, Dr. Evans?"

"Er...with who?" she said, looking startled. "Eco?"

"My company," Ross murmured to her.

"Oh! No, I'm with the University of Wisconsin. We're
doing archaeological work on the Bradford property."

"You don't say." Simon raised his eyebrows. "I'd
love to hear about it, after I've done my duty and greeted

everyone. Archaeology has always fascinated me. We Brits have it in our blood, you know.''

"I'd be glad to tell you about the site,'' Lilah said, then stepped forward and touched the consul's arm. ''By the way, would you happen to know anything about government research permits? I've applied for one, but I'm a little worried about whether it'll be approved.''

Simon Caldwell's brow wrinkled. ''Research permits? Well, we don't really deal with that. But I've heard they're hard to come by.''

"I know," Lilah said, and sighed delicately. "I just wondered if you might have some advice for me.''

Ross suppressed a groan. He liked to think that any sane man would see through this act in a second, but Simon Caldwell was disappointing him. The consul was gazing down into Lilah's suddenly wistful hazel eyes with the expression of a man about to volunteer to slay dragons. It was hard to watch.

"Come to think of it,'' Simon said, ''I do have a few friends at the Park Bureau. I'd be glad to put in a good word for you.''

"Would you?" Lilah's smile grew as bright as the sun, and the consul blinked, dazzled. ''Thank you.''

Ross was beginning to think that he had enlisted the right person to deal with Jake Wyatt. Ms. Evans was good, all right. He was going to have to be careful to keep himself from getting lost in those lovely eyes. It would serve him to remember that Lilah had an agenda of her own.

She looked up at him as Simon moved away, and grinned. ''How about that?'' she said. ''Not bad, huh? I surprise myself sometimes.''

"Well done,'' Ross said.

She chuckled. ''Some might call me shameless.''

"'Savvy' would be a better word. The consul could be a useful connection."

"Hopefully so," Lilah said. "I need all the help I can get."

"Ross Bradford!"

A short, square man in his mid-sixties was headed straight for them, wife in tow. They had familiar faces, and he recognized them as friends of his father's, but he had to struggle for a few uncomfortable seconds to remember their names.

It was strange, how he slipped into feeling as if he'd never left Kenya, until minor things hit him suddenly with the weight of fifteen years.

"Well, son," said the man, Desmond Peters, who Ross recalled was an executive of some sort with a coffee export company. "I hear that you're trying to unload your family property on the government. They say you're a big conservation man now. Read all about you in that *Newsweek* article."

"Really," Ross said, gazing evenly at Peters. There was something in the man's voice that he didn't like.

"I never thought I'd see a Bradford sell the family land, especially to make another national park. Seems to me that we have plenty of parks around here, son. What we need are businesses like ranches to create jobs, and bring in money. Your father knew that."

"Actually," Ross said coolly, "you might be surprised about what brings money and jobs into a country. A bigger park needs more rangers, more administrators, more tour group leaders, more safari drivers, more road maintenance workers…stop me any time."

Des Peters's smile had slipped. "Well, I don't know about that—"

"Not to mention that the trickle-down effect of an increased rate of tourism will impact local travel agencies, restaurants, hotels—''

Peters was flushed with ire and alcohol, and he waved his hand at Ross. ''Sure, right, I've heard all this before. But do you want to know what I think?''

Ross raised his eyebrows at the man, suspecting that he was about to hear it regardless of whether he wanted to.

Peters did not disappoint him. He pointed a beefy finger at Ross and snapped, ''I think it's bull, and I'm not the only one. You'd probably like to take out more than your father's land, wouldn't you? I bet you're trying to figure out a way to really screw up this country by getting rid of all the ranches. Hell, you'd probably like to tell me to get rid of all the coffee fields, too, since they aren't *natural*. Let the damn animals have the land back, right? Let's just make one big national park. Who the hell cares about our jobs?''

Ross listened to Peters's outburst with contempt. Why didn't people realize that letting their emotions run away with them only made them look weak and stupid?

''I don't have any immediate plans to destroy Kenya's coffee industry,'' he said dryly. ''In fact, I had a good cup of the local brew this morning. Maybe you should return the favor and drop by to visit the new reserve.''

''Not likely,'' Peters said, glaring at him. ''And I wouldn't be so sure about that new park, or you'll be in for a surprise.''

He turned and stomped off into the crowd. His wife, who had hovered there looking upset, hurried to follow him.

''What a rude person,'' Lilah exclaimed. ''Where does he get off descending on you and shoving his half-baked opinion in your face?''

''Never a dull moment.''

"You're not kidding. Has this been happening a lot?"

Ross shrugged. "Enough to show me that I don't have a high approval rating in the ranching community."

"They'd rather see a huge industrial complex on your property?"

"Of course. It's good for business. Wyatt certainly thinks so."

"Is he here?"

That was a good question. It was at just that moment, as if Lilah's question had made him materialize, that an ebb in the stream of people moving past them revealed Wyatt leaning on the bar across the room, deep in conversation.

Lilah sensed Ross's sudden tension and clutched his arm. "Do you see him? Where is he?"

"Over there, by the bar," Ross said, taking her by the shoulder just as she turned to look, and trying to walk her in the opposite direction.

Typically, she balked. "That's all the way across the room. He can't possibly tell that I'm looking at him. I just want to see—"

"Not now. There are too many people watching. If you start staring at him, they'll notice. Just follow me for a minute."

"Okay," she grumbled.

He guided her over to the far wall, against the heavy wine-colored window drapes.

"Is this where I get my strategic intelligence briefing?" Lilah asked.

"Your what?"

"You know, when the secret agent gets the rundown on her mission. You're supposed to give me stuff now, like a very tiny microphone disguised as an earring, and a stiletto knife I can tuck into my garter."

"Are you wearing a garter?" Her long bare legs gave no indication of it.

"No. That's a problem. If you were better at picking your spies, you wouldn't have chosen a discount archaeologist, and you could have gotten someone who owns garters. Your loss."

"For someone who had to be dragged here kicking and screaming, you're adapting well."

Lilah looked evenly at him. "We made a deal. I agreed to do this, and I will."

Ross didn't buy her matter-of-fact tone. The edge to her voice revealed that she was more nervous than she was letting on. Her tough-kid facade was oddly endearing, making him wonder if he'd done the right thing by forcing her into this.

"Wyatt is on the right end of the bar, wearing a gray jacket," he said. "He's Australian, so you should be able to pick out an accent. If you walk over there, ask for a drink and look slightly lost. He's likely to start a conversation with you."

"Piece of cake. I'm on my way."

He caught her by the arm. "Wait a minute."

Having her poised to go in search of Wyatt made Ross suddenly, unexpectedly, anxious. In the car, he had told her more about the rancher, but did she truly understand what kind of man he was? Was it wrong or even foolish to involve her in this?

Lilah was gazing up at him, her hazel eyes seeming oddly vulnerable. Ross knew that she was tougher than she appeared, but still…

"Be careful," he said finally. "I don't want you to be nervous, but this is serious. He's smart. Don't underestimate him."

"Don't worry about me. I'll see you around."

She flashed Ross a smile and mingled into the flow of the crowd, but he frowned as he watched her disappear. Lilah was smart enough to sense for herself that Wyatt was a dangerous man and to act accordingly, but just the same, Ross knew that he would be keeping a discreet eye on what was happening.

This wouldn't be so tough, Lilah reassured herself as she approached the bar. All she had to do was strike up a conversation with this Jake Wyatt person. If nothing came of it, Ross would just have to find himself a more experienced spy.

"What can I get you?" the bartender asked as she squeezed in at the end of the bar.

"White wine, please—" Lilah began, furtively glancing sideways, only to discover with a flash of alarm that Wyatt and his friend were picking up their drinks, preparing to go.

Lilah turned to watch as they moved away from the bar. Great, what now? She hadn't even had a chance to take a good look at Jake, and now he and his companion were merging into the crowd, about to vanish.

"If you want wine," the bartender said, "the waiters have a good chardonnay."

One such waiter, balancing a tray of glasses, was moving through the crowd not far from where Jake had just been, and Lilah suddenly had an idea. It even seemed like a good one, but she was short on time to consider it.

"Perfect," she said to the bartender, and dove back into the crowd.

She wormed her way along the path Jake had taken. He and his friend were walking slowly, talking as they moved through the throngs of people, and Lilah was able to get near them in a matter of minutes. She was pleased to see that the wine-carrying waiter was also circulating close by. It looked as if his path would take him into the perfect position in just moments...and there he was! It was now or never.

Lilah squeezed out in front of her protective screen of bodies and descended on the waiter, declaring loudly, "Chardonnay? How wonderful!"

It worked like a brilliantly choreographed dance. In one swooping move, Lilah plucked a long-stemmed glass from the tray, thanked the waiter brightly, turned as if to leave, and collided head-on with the arm of Jake Wyatt.

Score, an inner voice crowed triumphantly as she found herself holding an empty glass and staring at Wyatt's now-soaked coat sleeve.

Lilah was so amazed that it had actually worked that she had no trouble assuming a shocked expression.

"Oh my goodness," she gasped, clutching his arm and gazing contritely into a pair of piercing blue eyes. "I'm so terribly sorry. I didn't even realize you were there!"

"Don't apologize," Wyatt said, as the waiter came to the rescue with a handful of paper napkins.

Lilah was relieved to hear an unmistakable Australian accent, indicating that she had indeed drenched the right man. He appeared to be in his late fifties, a powerfully built man shorter than Ross, but as thickly muscled as a boxer. His face was darkly tanned, and deeply lined. He could be considered handsome, in a battered sort of way, but a certain pale-lashed hardness about his azure eyes gave them a sharp, snakelike look.

"In fact," Wyatt continued, "It was my fault. I stepped right in your way, Miss...?"

"Evans. Lilah Evans," she said, and bit back a laugh. It had sounded too much like "Bond. James Bond."

"Well, Miss Evans, there's no damage done." Jake removed his jacket and tossed it to the waiter. "Here, have this cleaned up."

"You see?" he said, showing Lilah his shirtsleeve, which was only spotted with wine. "Nothing to worry about."

"Yes, but—"

"If you insist on feeling guilty, come outside and keep me company while my shirt dries. I'm Jake Wyatt, and I know we haven't met."

"That sounds lovely, Mr. Wyatt," Lilah said. "I could use a little fresh air."

A quartet was playing outside on the lit terrace, and a few couples were dancing. The canopy of stars had been entirely covered over in the past hour by low-hanging, ominous clouds that had quietly rolled in overhead. The breeze brought a faint scent of ozone to her nose, and thunder murmured in the distance.

"I'd have thought the rainy season would be over by now," Jake said, and shrugged. "Keeps the watering holes high, at least."

"You're a rancher?"

"Biggest ranch in the area. About an hour's drive southwest of the city."

He slid a patio chair out from a small candlelit table. "Have a seat."

"Southwest?" Lilah said innocently. "Why, you must be near where I'm staying. Do you know the Bradford ranch?"

His hard eyes narrowed and locked onto her face. "I certainly do. What are you doing there?"

"Working. I'm running an archaeological dig."

Wyatt was still staring at her. "You're one of the archaeologists."

"You've already heard about us?" Lilah forced a

laugh. "I can't believe it. We haven't been here very long."

"I make it my business to hear about things. Are you a friend of Ross Bradford?"

"Not at all," Lilah said, hoping that she sounded convincing. "I was a friend of his father's. I didn't hear a thing about Ross's plans to sell the land until I arrived last week. He finally agreed to a delay, but—"

"Six weeks," Jake said thoughtfully. "So, you were responsible for that. Interesting."

"The original plan was to work there for over a year. Ross was completely unreasonable about it, so you can imagine how I feel about his park project."

Lilah was surprised at how difficult it was to inject hostility into her voice. A week ago, she would have said those words to Jake Wyatt and meant them, but now it was hard to gather up her original animosity.

"I've had my own…conflicts…with Ross," Jake said. "But I thought he was gone for good. He left Kenya fifteen years ago, you know, and hasn't been back until now."

This was startling news to Lilah. "What happened?"

"A falling-out with his father. Everyone thought he'd been disowned." Jake's mouth tightened. "It would have made my life easier if he had been."

This sounded promising. "What do you mean?"

But Jake shook his head and stood up, suggesting that they dance.

"I'm afraid I'm not very good at this," Lilah warned him.

"They don't send girls to dancing school anymore?"

"Not in my family."

Jake's arm hooked around her waist like an iron belt, and she looked up to meet the flat glitter of his blue eyes.

"Just follow my lead," he said. "And relax."

But Lilah couldn't relax. Her heart was thudding, and she moved stiffly, stumbling as he guided her through the steps.

Jake's hand slid upward, along her back, the heat of his thick fingers burning through the fabric of her dress. She tried not to shudder as she felt his hand moving subtly down again in a slight caress.

"I have an idea that may interest you," he said smoothly, dropping his voice so that only she could hear. "I'm in a position to help you with your problem."

"Oh?"

"Ross thinks he's going to have a park, but he's wrong. The government plans to put an industrial complex on that land once they have it. I'll be working with the developers who are going to build the factory."

His breath was hot on her cheek. "I could arrange to leave the canyon area untouched for as long as you want to excavate there."

Lilah pulled back to stare at him, genuinely stunned. Her entire excavation, handed back to her on a silver platter? Jake's offer rang with the confidence of a man who knew what was going on behind the scenes. Could he be right? Could Ross be fighting a losing battle?

And what would it mean to her if he was? If Jake had already won, then her excavation was doomed unless she quickly reassessed her priorities. It would be foolish to cast her lot with Ross if an alliance with Jake Wyatt would save her site. After all, it was her career on the line.

But there was something else. Only a week ago, she wouldn't have cared a whit about Ross and his plans, and the idea of aligning herself with his opponents wouldn't have fazed her at all. But now, strangely, she did care.

She didn't want to see a factory complex spread over

the wild and beautiful savanna, and she didn't want to be Jake Wyatt's friend at the price of being Ross's enemy.

Why did she care about what happened to Ross Bradford and his wildlife reserve, damn it?

Jake was silent as they danced, probably pleased that his suggestion had had such an impact.

"You're right, Mr. Wyatt." Lilah said finally. "That is a very interesting idea. I'd like to discuss it with you later."

"Of course. Enough business talk. Why don't we—"

"May I cut in?"

The voice behind her was chilly but familiar, and Lilah's heart jumped as she turned to see Ross standing there, facing Jake with steel in his eyes.

Chapter 7

"Well, hello there, Ross," Jake Wyatt said, stepping back to look him over. His voice was mild, but his smile did not reach his eyes. "I was wondering when we'd see you. You've been neglecting your lovely escort. Not a smart move, son, though I do enjoy picking up what you let slip through your fingers."

Ross's jaw tightened, and Lilah nearly stepped out of the way. It didn't take a genius to read the double meaning in that remark.

"Miss Evans," Jake said, turning to Lilah, "I'll plan to see you again."

He raised her hand to his lips and kissed it, then turned his back on Ross and disappeared into the crowd.

The hot imprint of Jake's lips burned on Lilah's hand as she stepped awkwardly into Ross's arms, her breath catching as they began to move and she felt the contours of his lean body against her.

"Wyatt liked you," Ross said, an edge to his voice.

"That was the idea, wasn't it?"

It was hard to think with him so close. His cologne was warm and spicy, and Lilah had the sudden desire to press herself against him, to reach up and brush her lips against the hollow at the base of his throat.

She took an uneven breath. "Do you want to hear what happened?"

"We'll talk about it later."

"Okay," Lilah said. "You know, he's not what I expected, from your description. I thought he'd be a little blustering guy with a Napoleon complex. But he seems...predatory. I can see why you're wary of him."

"Lilah," Ross said tightly, "right now, I don't want to hear about damned Jake Wyatt."

She was confused by the sudden tension in him. He'd brought her here to deal with Jake, but now he seemed angry. There was no way he could have overheard the other man's murmured offer, so what was bothering him?

"What made you cut in so abruptly?" she asked.

"I thought it was time."

"Did you happen to notice that Jake was running his hands all over my back?"

"I noticed."

"Hmm. I'm surprised you didn't see that as a useful step toward my squeezing information out of him."

Ross stopped. "For God's sake, do you think I want you to take it that far? I never asked you to *seduce* him. What the hell kind of person do you think I am?"

"Ruthless?"

"But not unprincipled," he said roughly. "I didn't like seeing Wyatt with his hands all over you, and I assumed that you weren't enjoying it either."

"This is a relief," Lilah murmured.

He frowned. "What is?"

"That I'm not just some pawn you're using to win a high-stakes game. I can handle Jake Wyatt, but it's good to know that you care about...limits."

"You even questioned that?"

"I wondered. But you're not as ruthless as you make yourself out to be, Ross. Thank you for coming over to save me."

"You're welcome."

His eyes caught and held hers, and her heart skipped a beat at the intensity of his gaze. Did she lean forward, or did his arm tighten around her? Lilah was suddenly locked firmly against the lean strength of Ross's body, feeling weak as the heat of him surrounded her. The noise and activity of the room faded away, and Lilah caught her breath, her lips parting as she stared up at him.

She wanted Ross Bradford. God, how she wanted him. It was reckless and crazy, but in the heat of the moment, she didn't care. If he had kissed her then, she would have melted into his arms and forgotten about everything else.

Something in her eyes must have given her away. There was a sudden awareness in Ross's own gaze, along with a spark of some indefinable emotion. He took a deep breath, and abruptly let her go.

"Let's take a break."

Lilah nodded, dazed. "Okay."

At that moment, the previously grumbling thunder gave a wholehearted crash, and a spattering of fat raindrops began to dot the terrace stones.

Ross took Lilah's arm and led her back into the brightly lit embassy just as the skies opened up and let loose great watery sheets of rain. Stragglers from the lawn rushed inside, and waiters hurriedly began to close the tall windows.

"This looks nasty," Ross said. "We should head back."

"Can't we wait it out?" Lilah asked. The prospect of returning to her dark, lonely tent wasn't appealing.

"We could, but if a lot of rain comes down, the roads inside the ranch are going to get bad, fast. I've spent too many nights digging cars out of the mud to want to risk getting stuck again."

"Okay," Lilah said halfheartedly as another clap of thunder shook the building. Other guests were retrieving their coats, and it looked as if the party was breaking up. "Let's go."

By the fourth time Lilah felt the Land Rover slide in the new mud covering the ranch road, she realized that Ross had been right. Even with his expert handling of the car, they had come close to getting bogged down several times since they turned off the paved highway from Nairobi.

"How can so much mud appear so fast?" she asked, as the car skimmed sideways. It was as slick as ice under the tires.

"Amazing, isn't it? This savanna soil doesn't drain well. It's especially bad now, at the end of the rainy season. The ground is already saturated, so water piles up on top and makes a swamp."

The back of the car fishtailed as Ross rounded a bend in the road. He steered the front into control, and Lilah saw through the curtain of rain on the windshield that they were approaching the turnoff to the half-mile track leading down to the field camp. The back wheels of the car began to bog down, churning slightly, and the car slowed.

"Hold on," Ross said, and veered off the road to take

the car onto the grass, where the rough plants provided enough traction for the tires to grip.

"I hate having to do that," he said. "It tears up the land, but this track is getting bad. I'm not going to be able to get you down there tonight."

"What do you mean?"

"Your friends are camped on one of the lowest areas of the ranch, and are probably ankle deep in mud and water right now. Even if I could get the car down there without getting stuck, there's no way I'd get it up the hill again. There's a reason why the ranch house is built on high ground."

"So we're going to the house?" Lilah kept her voice carefully neutral, but she felt a warm, secret pleasure that she wouldn't have to leave Ross's company yet. How on earth had she gone from wanting to avoid him to this new longing to be near him?

"We're going to the house," Ross confirmed. "Unless you'd rather we both spent the night down in your camp getting slowly submerged in cold muddy water and praying that your tent doesn't leak."

By the time they reached the ranch house, the rain was coming down so hard that it looked like a solid curtain of water between the front door and the overhang where Ross parked the Land Rover. A simultaneous burst of thunder and lightning shook the sky as Lilah stepped out of the car. The storm was right overhead.

"Wait here," Ross said. "I'll get an umbrella from the house and come back for you—"

"That's okay," Lilah said. "Let's just run for it. I won't melt."

She bent down to slip off her pumps, and tossed them back into the car, reminding herself to pick them up in the morning. Getting muddy feet was better than ruining her only pair of good shoes.

"Are you sure?" Ross asked.

Lilah nodded, and gave him the thumbs-up sign. "Let's go."

He grabbed her hand, and pulled her out into what felt like one of the smaller Niagara falls. She sputtered, half running, half stumbling after him, unable to see anything at all, and clinging to his hand like a drowning person.

All at once they were in the living room, dripping into a rapidly spreading puddle on the floor, with the door slammed firmly behind them and the noise of the rain reduced to a muffled drumming on the roof.

"Good grief," Lilah gasped, leaning against the door, feeling water streaming down from her wet hair. "They don't make storms like that where I come from."

"Welcome to the tropics."

"Thanks a lot." She looked up at Ross and started to laugh. "Boy, are you wet. You look like you went swimming in your suit."

He grinned. "I think I did. And you're not much better, Professor. Is that a puddle I see under you?"

"Yes. Oh, dear. I'm ruining your carpet."

"Don't worry, it'll dry. I'll get you a towel and some clean clothes, and you can have a hot bath."

"Sounds great," Lilah said, starting to shiver.

She followed him to the large master bathroom, where he turned on the taps over the old-fashioned clawfoot tub. Lilah sat on the porcelain edge, holding one chilly hand under the stream of water, and hugging herself with the other arm. Ross left and returned a moment later, carrying two large towels and a pile of clothing.

"Here," he said, setting them on a chair. "You look

nice in my shirts, but I thought my pants might be a little large, so I brought you a *kikoy*."

Lilah recognized the brightly woven cloth wrap. It was fringed on the edges, and worn like a sarong by the Swahili tribesmen who lived near the coast. Folded on top of it was another of Ross's soft linen shirts.

"Thanks. I still have to return that first shirt you lent me. If it keeps up like this, it won't be long before I have all of your clothes."

"Then I'll have to come naked down to your camp to get them back."

"Denise would love that." Lilah said. She knew better than to let herself imagine Ross naked, but the image was persistent, and she could feel a blush beginning. She stopped it by fiercely fixing her attention on the bar of soap next to the tub. It was white. And square. The tub was getting full, so she reached over to turn off the taps.

"Denise?"

"My friend. The artist. She thinks you're…ah…very attractive."

Ross just smiled enigmatically, but his eyes were on her with an unnerving intensity.

"This is her dress," Lilah added, flustered.

"I like it on you," Ross said, his gaze sweeping over her body, making her breath catch in her throat.

Her blush rose up again. "Thank you."

There was a brief silence. "Your water is getting cold," he said, making no move to go.

Lilah swallowed hard, and nodded.

"Better get in," he said softly.

Their gazes met, and Ross raised his eyebrows at her as he turned to go. "I'll make you some tea," he said over his shoulder. "Come find me in the kitchen when you're ready."

The door clicked shut behind him.

Lilah exhaled hard. For a minute, she had almost thought that he wasn't going to leave, that he would— never mind. This growing ache she felt to be touched by him was making her imagination run wild, and she was going to make a real fool out of herself if she wasn't careful.

She peeled off Denise's dress, draped it carefully over the back of the chair, and slipped into the warm water.

She stayed in until the water cooled and her fingers wrinkled, and when she finally padded barefoot into the kitchen, Ross was at the stove, warming his hands over the teakettle steam.

He had showered and changed, and was wearing a pair of faded chinos and a dark green T-shirt that fit tightly over his broad shoulders. His dark hair was damp and tousled on the back of his neck, and Lilah wanted to reach out and twine her fingers into it. Instead, she leaned against the door frame and watched him.

It was only a moment before he noticed her. "Feeling better, Professor?"

"Much."

"Good." He poured a mug of tea and handed it to her. "If you're hungry, there's leftover *ugali* in the fridge."

"Leftover what?"

"*Ugali*. It's a staple around here—cornmeal paste, cooked thick. Mama Ruth has been stuffing me with it for as long as I can remember, and nothing's changed since I came back. I don't want to hurt her feelings, so I spice it up with hot sauce and eat enough to make her happy."

"That's nice."

"Not really. I just know better than to get into a battle of wills with Mama Ruth over dinner. She's tough."

"Sounds like she mothered you well."

"Lucky for me. Between her family and Otieno's, I always had someone looking after me."

"Not your father?"

"No. The ranch was his first priority."

Ross's face suddenly seemed cooler in the dim kitchen light, and the shadows playing there gave him a withdrawn, closed look. He obviously didn't want to talk about his family, but Lilah was curious to hear what he would tell her.

"What about your mother?"

"Claire wasn't cut out for motherhood," Ross said. "My father was the one who wanted an heir."

"As opposed to a son?"

He acknowledged her comment with a short nod. "That's about right."

"Did they divorce?"

"No. Claire was killed in a car wreck when I was young, so it's just as well she never spent much time being a parent. You can't lose something you never had in the first place."

His voice was expressionless, as if he were describing someone else's life.

"When did that happen?" Lilah asked quietly.

"A long time ago. I was fourteen."

He saw the look on her face, and his mouth took on a cynical twist. "That day she was on her way to meet whoever she was sleeping with at the time."

Lilah would have been shocked at how callous he sounded, except for the sudden tension in his shoulders and the fact that his voice seemed intentionally flat.

"Fourteen is still just a kid," she said. "You must have missed her terribly."

"I'd been in boarding school for years."

"Wouldn't that make it harder?"

"No, easier. I was building my own life by then."

"That's a lot to ask of a fourteen-year-old."

His mouth curved again, bitterly. "It wasn't asked of me. It was required."

"Were you really such a tough kid?"

He was silent for a long moment, then said finally, "Yes."

Lilah was beginning to get a clearer picture of the reasons for the invisible wall Ross seemed to carry around himself. A past like that would convince anyone to keep the world at a distance. Feeling at all vulnerable would be unbearable to this man.

"I'm sorry, Ross," she said softly.

"Don't be. My family life wasn't ideal, but I did all right. I don't use it as a ploy for sympathy."

"I guessed that, since you don't seem to enjoy talking about it. I think you deserve more respect than sympathy, for overcoming it all."

"Thanks," he said. "Now drink your tea."

Lilah sipped dutifully, but she was mulling over what she had just heard. There was much, much more to Ross Bradford under the strong and polished outer layer that he presented to the world. She was glad to know it. It made him real.

"Your father never remarried?" she asked casually.

"You were right," Ross said. "I don't enjoy talking about this."

"Do you ever talk about it?"

"No. It has nothing to do with who I am now. And I've learned that giving out personal information can be dangerous. People have their own reasons for wanting to find your vulnerable spots."

Lilah frowned. "That's an awfully cynical way to look at the world."

"Cynical? I'd say practical. I'm not naive or romantic when it comes to human relationships."

"Practical for business, maybe," Lilah said. "If you're in the kind of high-powered corporate environment where you always have to watch your back. But you can't apply ruthless business principles to every part of your life."

"No?" Ross said. "I wonder."

Lilah stared at him, trying to read his face, but it was completely neutral, and she had the sudden sensation that he was gazing at her from behind a wall of one-way glass.

"You don't need to apply them right now," she said firmly, meeting his eyes. "With me."

"Really? How do I know that? It's interesting that you're suddenly asking me personal questions, considering what you have to gain."

"Gain?" Lilah felt a chill in her stomach. "I don't like the sound of that. Do you think I have a hidden agenda?"

"I don't rule it out. I do own something that you desperately want, after all."

And there it was. Ross was watching her, waiting to see her reaction to his words, and Lilah was almost too stunned to speak.

"I see," she said finally. "Now, let me get this straight. You think I'm looking for a way to manipulate you into not selling the ranch so I can have my excavation back? You think that's why I'm asking about your family? To…gain your trust, or find your vulnerable spots, or something?"

Ross shrugged. "I don't know, but I believe in being careful."

"Did it even occur to you that I might be asking because I want to know you?" Lilah said indignantly, then cut herself off.

It was such a small thing to say, but it felt like the first step into unmarked and dangerous territory. Ross's gaze fixed on her with an attentiveness that demanded she proceed.

"It's true," she said. "I want to know you, all right? I find you interesting."

"Interesting," he repeated thoughtfully.

"Right, interesting." She took a deep breath. "And if you really want to know, I...like you. Satisfied?"

"Not really," Ross said. "The last time I checked, you resented me for selling the ranch and forcing you into this plan with Wyatt. What changed so suddenly?"

"I got over it."

"Just like that."

"No, not just like that. You helped me understand why you want to sell the ranch, and I respect that. I also happen to enjoy your company."

"When you're forced to."

"God, you're cynical," she said, frustrated. This was far beyond the point where she would have given up on anyone else. But she wanted Ross to believe her. Her archaeologist's instinct told her that there was something precious buried inside this man.

"No," he said. "I'm honest. Every time you've been in my company, up until this moment, has been because you had no choice in the matter. You wouldn't be here now if there were no storm tonight."

He watched her with a strange gleam in his gray eyes.

"Isn't that right?" he asked. "I want to know. If there were no storm, and I had asked you to come back with me, would you have done it? To ask me questions? Because you like me?"

There was mockery in his voice, but she could hear a challenge there, too. He was daring her to answer honestly, to speak the words that hovered in her throat.

He stepped forward, looking down at her with a gaze that made her knees weak.

"Tell me this," Ross said, reaching out to touch her face with fingers that trailed fire behind them. "If you could go back to your camp right now, what would you do? Do you know?"

"I know," Lilah said, her heart beating fast. "I'd stay."

Ross didn't speak for a moment, but he was so close that Lilah could feel the heat of him warming her like sunlight. He tensed as she reached out to touch him, and she felt his breath catch as she slid her palm up the warm length of his chest and looked up to meet his eyes.

"God...Lilah..." he said, almost in a groan, and pulled her to him.

His kiss was as cracklingly alive and demanding as the rest of him, and Lilah, crushed up against the lean hardness of his body, couldn't press herself close enough as she returned the embrace with equal urgency. She reached up to twine one of her hands into his hair, clinging to Ross as he kissed her until her mouth felt hot and bruised.

Her other hand found its way up under the loose edge of his shirt, to stroke up the smooth naked skin of his back, her fingers spreading to feel the firm curves of the muscles there. They were hard and tight as he held her, and Lilah could suddenly feel the hard, steady pounding of his heart against her chest.

His mouth left hers to sear a path down her throat to the hollow at its base, and she gasped softly as his hand at her waist touched bare skin. Lilah felt as if waves of heat were sweeping through her, and she held Ross as if she wanted to sink into him.

His hand slid up from her waist, rumpling her shirt as it rose, his strong fingers stroking over the naked skin of her midriff. She could feel cool air against her skin as the shirt was pushed up, and the slight roughness of his fingertips as he touched her.

Lilah murmured his name and arched herself toward him, slipping her own hands between them, under his shirt and up over his wide chest. Ross groaned, and she could feel the muscles in his thighs tense as his arm tightened at her waist.

She opened her eyes to see him watching her, his gaze locking onto hers as his hands traced the curves of her body. Lilah's breath caught in her throat. It was almost too intense, too personal, to have his eyes on hers as his hands moved over her skin, as if he were touching not just her body but her soul.

A shudder, dark and aching, passed through her, and Ross bent his head to capture her lips again. Lilah wrapped her arms around him, and caught his lower lip in her teeth in a gentle play-bite.

Suddenly, he froze. Lilah thought at first that she had hurt him, and then realized that he was listening intently to something.

Now she could hear it, too, as she struggled to quiet her breathing. It was faint, but definitely audible over the growl of the thunder.

"Someone's shouting," she said, feeling disoriented.

Her words seemed to confirm what Ross was thinking.

"Damn it," he said, pulling away from her. "That's Mtuko."

The urgency on his face was enough to alarm her, though she had no idea who Mtuko was, or why he would be shouting in the middle of the night.

"Lilah," Ross said, looking down at her, "stay here. Don't leave the house. I'll be back."

There wasn't even time to answer before he was gone.

Chapter 8

It was the prowler again. Ross had known it the moment he heard the *askari's* voice, shouting over the sound of the receding storm.

The intruder had been right next to the house when Mtuko spotted him, but he had bolted away into the darkness before anyone could get more than a quick look at him. The *askaris* had chased him, and Mtuko had gone out in the truck to search the roads, but Ross doubted that it would do any good. On a night like tonight, with mist and shadows everywhere, it was easy to hide on the open plains.

He came back to the house, chilled and frustrated. It was no surprise that in the noise of the storm, the prowler had been able to get to the house unnoticed, but it angered him that the man had escaped again. What the hell was he doing here in the first place?

And his timing… Ross reached up to rub his forehead.

Damn, it was hard to know whether he should resent or welcome the interruption.

The scene in the kitchen had been totally unexpected, and it had surged forward with the momentum of a freight train. His own desire for Lilah had spiraled out of control, moving him like a puppet in the grip of something larger than himself. The thought appalled him. It was too soon, too intense. If there was going to be an affair, it needed to be clearly defined for what it was...and wasn't.

Lilah was sitting on a kitchen chair, nervously twisting a cloth napkin. She jumped up when she saw him. "What happened?"

"Our night visitor came back," he said, frustration leaking into his voice. "And we missed him again."

"What night visitor?"

"There was a prowler outside the house the first night you were here. You didn't happen to see anything strange, did you?"

Her face went white with a suddenness that startled Ross. He stepped forward instinctively, but stopped when she raised her hands.

"I'm okay," she said.

"You saw someone."

"No, that's the stupid part. I was outside, on the terrace, and I heard someone slinking around in the bushes." She laughed shakily. "Can you believe, I thought it was the *askari?* I couldn't figure out why I had the creeps. Guess I should start listening to my instincts."

"Did you get a look at him?"

"Not really. Just a shadowy figure, slim and medium-height. Then I got spooked and ran inside." She took a deep breath. "A prowler. Why do you have a prowler? This isn't related to the land conflict, is it?"

"It could be."

"Boy, you people sure take your business deals seriously. Or is there something else going on that I don't know about?"

"You know everything I know," Ross said.

It seemed strange to be talking to her like this, as if nothing had happened between them, when he could still vividly feel the warmth and softness of her body against his.

"Maybe Jake could tell me something. I'll try to—"

"No," Ross said, surprising himself. "You won't. You're out of this."

"What?"

"Our deal is off, Lilah. This is starting to feel dangerous to me. I don't want you involved after all."

It was the right decision. There were too many unknowns, and the alarming feelings he was developing for Lilah only complicated the issue. It would be much better to disentangle her from his business and his life before anything else happened.

He had expected her to take the news happily, but now she was shaking her head.

"No way, Ross," she said. "I'm still doing it."

He stared at her for a moment, confused until he realized what was at the root of her apparent change of heart.

"Don't worry," he said. "The six weeks at the site that I promised are still yours. I gave you my word, and I'm not reneging on it."

"That's not what I'm worried about," she said impatiently. "You know you need my help, or you wouldn't have gone to all the trouble of getting it in the first place. I'm not reneging on the deal, either."

"That's not an issue on your end. I'm simply telling you that you aren't involved anymore. Period."

"Well, save your breath. I want to see you get your

reserve, and I'm not quitting now. You need me, I'm help-ing you, and you can't just dump me when the going gets tough.''

He frowned. "We'll discuss this later."

"No, we won't. There's nothing to discuss, because I'm still in. Deal with it."

Ross folded his arms against his chest, drumming his fingers impatiently against his biceps. He had been sure that she'd take the first chance to get out of her obligation to him, but now she was fighting to keep it. And she *knew* that the six weeks weren't at risk, so what was going on?

"Ross, do you need me?" Lilah said.

Need? Damn. Ross winced. He had never been a fan of that word. Needing someone—for whatever reason— was the same as admitting that you couldn't make it on your own. And that, he knew, was putting yourself into a very bad position. It was simply common sense. Other people had their own interests at heart; they might appear to be on your side, but that only lasted as long as your plans didn't conflict with theirs. Only a fool would trust anyone else with his professional or emotional survival. As far as Ross was concerned, feeling as though you needed someone was the clearest warning you should run like hell in the other direction.

"Do you?" Her voice was gentle, but firm.

He shook his head. "It makes no difference."

"Well, that's a sudden change," she remarked. "Not very long ago, you told me that the delay was too risky without my help. You said that you needed someone to get close to Jake Wyatt. You said—"

"I know what I said!" She was right, damn it. How had this happened? Stupid, stupid, he berated himself, aware that he was in an impossible position. He couldn't back out of the promise he'd given the archaeologists. It was a matter of personal pride. How was he supposed to deal with this?

"You said that you couldn't do this without me," Lilah persisted. "Remember?"

Ross clenched his teeth. Of course he remembered. But when he'd said that, he'd been supremely confident that he held all the cards. Now, aces were suddenly popping up all over the place, and he was scrambling to pull his hand back together.

"Admit it, Ross. You'd be much better off with my help. It's true, and you know it."

"Maybe," he said gruffly.

"That sounds like a reluctant 'yes' to me."

"I can do this without you if I have to."

"Well," she said. "Fortunately, you don't have to."

Ross regarded her warily. Her determination to stay involved was the only clear fact in an otherwise very muddy situation. But why was she suddenly so committed? It didn't make sense.

All of this—the delay, bringing in Lilah—had been a major misjudgment on his part, but now he had to deal with the consequences. He wasn't so weak that he couldn't handle temporarily needing Lilah's help. He'd stay with their original plan because he had no choice, but he would keep a cautious eye on her until he saw her real motivation.

"Fine," he said at last. "You're right. I will be better off with your help. But you need to understand that this could be dangerous. The developers are playing for high stakes, and I don't want you taking any risks."

She smiled like the Mona Lisa. "Whatever you say."

Ross exhaled. This was already going badly. "Promise me that you'll be careful."

"Of course."

"And from now on, I want you to tell me immediately if anything unusual happens."

Lilah's face was unreadable, with only that small, thoughtful smile curving her lips. He had the sudden, frustrating feeling that for all his effort to take control of this situation, somehow it was still trickling through his fingers like a fistful of dry sand.

"And you will absolutely check with me before you do *anything* involving Jake Wyatt."

"Quit treating me like a Girl Scout," Lilah said.

Her clear hazel eyes met his, and he felt something catch inside him. She was beautiful; there was no denying it. Her features had somehow imprinted themselves in his mind so that she seemed almost familiar as he gazed at her, his eyes gliding over her dark, straight brows, down the gentle arcs of her cheeks to linger on her mouth.

"Believe it or not," she added, "I'm as tough as you are, Ross."

"I hope not," he said quietly. She was standing right in front of him, so close that her scent drifted delicately around him. He could still feel the sensation of her soft curves under his hands, and without thinking, he reached out to stroke her cheek. Her skin was velvety under his fingers, and she trembled at his touch.

A rush of desire shuddered through him, and he had the sudden feeling that even if he took her in his arms right now, crushing her up against him, he still wouldn't be able to hold her close enough to satisfy the ache inside him. His hand slipped around to caress the nape of her neck, lifting her silky hair, and she made a soft sound, her eyes meeting his with sudden entreaty.

It was more than Ross could stand. He stepped forward, pulling her to him, and kissed her again with a fierce hunger that overwhelmed him. She clung to him, melting against him, until they were both breathing in short, ragged gasps.

He bent his head to trace the line of her collarbone with his lips and tongue, tasting the sweetness of her skin. He felt her quiver, then tense against him.

"Ross..." Lilah's voice caught in her throat. "Wait."

Her hands slipped up his arms, her body stiffening.

There was an edge of anxiety to her plea, and one look at her face was enough to alarm him. She was flushed, her eyes wide and worried.

"What's wrong, Lilah?"

"I'm sorry," she said unsteadily, avoiding his gaze. She stepped back, wrapping her arms around herself like a child.

Ross could feel cool air move in against him where Lilah had just been. Having her pull away was almost a physical pain, but he was careful not to betray that in his expression as he stood quietly, watching her.

She took a deep breath, still refusing to look at him.

"I didn't mean for this to happen again," she said to the ground. "While you were gone, I was thinking..."

A chill formed in Ross's stomach, and began to curl slowly upward. *He* was supposed to be the one bringing up the second thoughts. Hadn't he just decided to slow this down until it could be brought under control? Yet here he was, caught in the grip of his desire for her, losing his damned head again only moments after he thought he'd settled everything. What was happening to him?

"This...just can't work," Lilah said.

Ross felt as if he were falling, somehow struggling for footing as he stood there, listening to her halting explanation. Without even seeming to realize it, Lilah had taken control of the situation, and left him fumbling. It was completely unacceptable.

"Actually," he said slowly, making his voice intentionally seductive, "it seems to me that it was working."

She bit her lip. "It's not that simple."

"No? I think it is."

He stepped forward again, reaching out to curve his fingers possessively around her cheek and jaw, brushing briefly against her lips, fighting the tremor of desire that weakened his hand.

"I won't believe you if you tell me that you don't want me," he said. "Not after what's already happened. Is this too fast for you? Do you want to slow down?"

Lilah closed her eyes, and Ross felt a flash of triumph as she leaned slightly into his touch. But it was only for the briefest second, and then she seemed to realize what she was doing, because she stiffened again, and pulled away.

"I think I should go to bed," she said. Her gaze flicked up to meet his, and he was startled by the mixture of anxiety and unhappiness in her expression.

What was upsetting her so much?

"I think you should stay here and talk to me," he said. "Just talk. Nothing more."

"I can't. I have to go."

"Not yet. I want to know what's happening here. Are you involved with someone else?"

Surprise lit her face. "No!"

"Then what's wrong? We don't have to go on with this. But if we don't, I want to know why."

"It's a bad time for me," she said weakly. "The excavation...I'm busy—"

"You're saying that you don't want to be in a relationship right now. That you're too busy."

"Right," she said quickly. "That's exactly it."

"That's fine," Ross said. "I'm not looking for a relationship, either. But there are other, less complicated ways of being involved. We're obviously attracted to each other, so why not just enjoy that? There's no need for either of us to worry about anything more in the short time we'll be here together.''

Lilah recoiled as if he had slapped her, and Ross frowned. After what she'd just said, he had expected her to agree without hesitation, but the expression on her face told him that he had said something very wrong.

''What do you want, Lilah?'' he asked, trying to keep his frustration out of his voice. Once again, things had slipped away just as they seemed to be falling into place.

She looked up, and her eyes were unnaturally bright. ''I don't know,'' she said.

''When you do,'' Ross said, ''tell me.''

She nodded, and hurried out of the kitchen, leaving him wondering if he had seen the faint sparkle of tears in her eyes as she turned away.

The ranch house was stuffy with the windows closed and locked against the evening breeze, but Ross was willing to bear a little discomfort for the sake of security.

He walked down the hall, listening, in spite of himself, for any sounds coming from Lilah's room. He heard nothing, and passed quickly by, resisting the urge to knock on her door. He had waited in the kitchen, watching the minutes tick by on the wall clock, until he was sure that she'd gone to bed.

Halfway down the hall, a draft tickled his face, and he stopped, frowning. The door to the library was ajar, and he looked in to find one of the two windows standing open, letting in the rain-scented wind. The curtains tossed damply against the frame, and the papers on his desk ruffled in the cold air.

''What the hell?'' he said, staring at the scene.

He had closed that window before he'd left that evening. Had Mama Ruth opened it to air out the room, then forgotten to shut it before she'd gone home?

He ran his fingers over the desktop. The desk and phone were dry, except for a fine mist brought in by the post-storm wind. If Mama Ruth had left the window open earlier that evening, everything would have been soaked from the torrential rain.

No, this window had been opened more recently, within the past few hours, when there was supposedly no one else in the house.

Instinctively, he froze where he stood, checking over the room to see if anything else had been disturbed. His briefcase and papers were on a chair, untouched, but now he could see faint traces of mud on the wooden floor around the desk. Someone had been here, all right.

He crouched down to examine the marks. They were dry by now, and indistinct, as if the person had taken care to minimize the traces he left.

Ross leaned out the open window, and sure enough, even in the dim square of light spilling out of the house, he could see the new footprints in the wet ground. The marks nearest the house were deep and blurred, as if the man had jumped quickly through the window and taken off into the night.

Ross closed the window, and locked it. The mud specks inside went no farther than the desk, only a few feet from the window, so the prowler hadn't come far into the house.

Nothing on the desk seemed to have been touched, so it looked as if the man had aborted his plan, whatever it was, and backed out in a hurry, at which point Mtuko had spotted him and started yelling.

What had the intruder wanted? Information? Ross's personal business papers were piled on the desk, but everything important pertaining to the ranch was locked up in the Nairobi office. Money? No. His watch and a few Kenyan pound notes were still scattered around. Wilder possibilities crossed his mind. Could it have been a failed kidnapping attempt? A bomb? A quick inspection of the room ruled out the last possibility.

What then? And what would have happened if the man hadn't bolted away? The thought left Ross cold and angry. There was no excuse for letting this happen. It wasn't the *askaris'* fault. Two men could do a good job but still miss a wily prowler in the darkness and noise of the storm.

No, the responsibility was his for not locking the damned window. He never made mistakes like that, and this one was inexcusable. It also felt like a small but pointed reminder that he was slipping. Everything these days, from the ranch sale to Lilah Evans, seemed to be shifting shape when he tried to get a grip on it.

Frowning, he closed the library door and walked down the hallway to his room. He stretched out on the big bed and stared at the ceiling, his mind churning over everything that had happened that evening. This trip back to Kenya was turning out differently than he had planned, and he didn't like it. It was time to straighten out all of these uncooperative events, and force things to work out his way.

Whatever that meant, in Lilah's case.

When he finally drifted off, his sleep was light and troubled, and suffused with the low growl of thunder from the receding tropical storm.

Chapter 9

Cold mud squished up between Lilah's bare toes as she walked quickly over the lawn in front of the Bradford house. It was six in the morning, much earlier than she had expected to awaken, and her head felt groggy after the short and restless night.

Ross was still asleep, or at least, his door was still closed, which was a relief. She couldn't forget how she had felt in the kitchen last night, torn between the desire to lose herself in his arms and the fear of what might happen if she did.

Falling in love with Ross Bradford would be about as safe as throwing herself into the path of a bulldozer. He had proved it when he said, very clearly, that he wasn't interested in a real relationship. Ross might not have any trouble with the idea of a quick affair, but she knew that her own heart wasn't so well protected. In a few weeks where would she be? Slinking back home to the States with no excavation, no tenure and a broken heart? No thanks. Better to pretend that last night had never happened.

But that was easier said than done. She opened the door of the Land Rover to retrieve her pumps, and stopped as she caught the faint scent of Ross's cologne, lingering against the leather seats. Even that ghostlike hint of him brought back the memory of his hands on her body, the heat in his eyes as he pulled her toward him, his rough passion as he kissed her....

Emotion flooded her without warning, leaving her shaken by a wave of longing so intense that she wanted to scream and pound her fists against the car.

I don't want this! I don't need this! Not now, not him! She was here to work, to focus entirely on the excavation, to lose herself in it as deeply and surely as she could ever lose herself in a lover. Concentrating her hopes and desires on the excavation was better, saner and a whole lot smarter than letting herself love a man who had no intention of loving her back.

It was early enough to be misty from last night's rain, and water sparkled on the tall aloes bordering the house. The air was damp and clean, and the rising tropical sun painted the lawn with pale pink and yellow light.

"Good morning!"

Lilah froze, even as she realized that it wasn't Ross's voice behind her. Taking a breath, she turned to see Otieno Kasu, the ranch manager, walking toward her. She'd met him briefly on the morning that her team had arrived, and had liked him instinctively then, partly for the quiet strength of his face, and partly for the way Ross seemed to relax around him.

Otieno wore work clothes and muddy boots, and gave the general impression that he'd been up for hours.

"You are looking for Ross?" he asked. "It may be too early. I don't think he is awake yet."

He took a closer look at her rumpled shirt and sleepy eyes, and seemed to reconsider, though he gave no indication of surprise. The corners of his mouth turned up almost imperceptibly. "*Is* Ross awake?"

"No," Lilah said. "Not yet, and I don't want to wake him, but I need to get back to the canyon to work. Please, is there anyone who could give me a ride?"

Even she could hear the urgency in her voice. She told herself that it was because she was anxious to get back to the site. She was *not* trying to run away before Ross woke up.

Otieno was kind enough not to ask questions.

"I will," he said, turning toward the car. "It would take you too long to walk."

He was quiet as they drove away from the house, and Lilah wondered what he was thinking.

"Do you have a family here?" she asked, his silence making her feel as if she should speak.

He nodded. "I have a wife, two sons and two daughters, older than you. My sons are grown, also, but the youngest is still at university."

"Do you see them often?"

"Not as much as we will when we move to the city. Mary has a new baby now, and my wife wants to be near her. We'll find a flat there."

"Do you have to find a new job when the ranch is sold?"

He smiled. "I have a new job. I'm going with Ross to work on the rain forest project, and then to Tanzania with his company. He has been trying to hire me for years, but I was busy with the ranch, and my children were too young. Now, I will go."

Lilah glanced at him. "He must be happy about that. He told me that he was practically raised by you and your family."

Otieno nodded, turning the car onto the track leading down to camp. The road was still slick with mud, but it had dried enough to be navigable.

Everyone in camp was just waking up, with the exception of Elliot and Denise, who were wearing their mud boots and toasting bread over the fire. They looked over at the car and Elliot waved.

Lilah sighed, and was about to thank Otieno, but he spoke first. "So, why don't you ask me what you really want to ask me?"

"What do you mean?"

He humored her with a patient smile. "About Ross."

Lilah blinked at him. Either her feelings were more obvious than she realized, or Otieno was remarkably perceptive. He was right; there were a thousand things she wanted to ask him, but given the opportunity, she couldn't voice a single one of them.

How could she say, "Who is Ross, really?" or "What does he want?" or especially "Do you think Ross might ever fall in love with me?" As much as she wanted the answers, those weren't the kind of questions she could ask.

Otieno saved her the awkwardness of groping for something to say. "I will tell you this," he said. "Ross keeps himself alone. Once, I think it helped him. His family was very rich, but not very happy. He learned to protect his heart when he was just a child, but now I think this is not good for him."

"Does he talk to you about this?"

"Not much," said Otieno. "I talk to him. I tell him

what I think, and he hears me, but my words only go as far as his ears.''

"But you're his closest friend."

"Yes," Otieno said with a glimmer of quiet humor, "but I am not a young woman. Perhaps you can do what I cannot."

"You have a lot of faith in me," Lilah said. "But you don't know anything about me. What if he doesn't—"

"I know that you and I share something," Otieno said firmly. "We both care about Ross."

Lilah glanced at him with ever-growing respect. This man definitely didn't miss much.

"You're right," she said, and it was a relief to admit it. "We do."

"Well, then, perhaps it will do some good," he said.

Elliot glanced up over the rim of his coffee mug as Lilah walked into camp. "Morning," he said with studied casualness. "Have a good time? How's Ross?"

Denise choked on her toast, and shot him a reproachful glance. "Great, Elliot. Really subtle. Now I'm in trouble.

"Lilah, I swear," she appealed. "I had to tell him when you didn't show up for breakfast, or he would have been running around looking for the lion that ate you."

"It's okay," Lilah said, picking her way carefully across the campsite toward her tent, trying to avoid both the largest mud puddles and the scattered acacia tree thorns.

Denise jumped up to follow her. "Well, good. I'm glad you're not mad at me. Now that that's taken care of, you better start talking. Where have you been? What have you been doing? What changed 'Denise this is *not* a date' into staying out all night? Am I being nosy? I don't care."

Lilah unzipped her tent and ducked in, tracking mud onto the vinyl floor as she dug her work clothes out of her duffel bag and found her boots. Denise hovered expectantly in the doorway.

"It was too muddy last night to get down the road to camp, so I spent the night at the ranch house," she said, pulling on her jeans. "The party was fun, and I met Jake Wyatt, who gives me the creeps."

"Lilah," Denise said sternly. "You're giving me the runaround. Tell me what happened with Ross. Are you two on better terms after last night?"

Lilah managed a weak smile. "You could say that."

"So do you like him any better now that you're getting to know him?"

Lilah bit her lip, wondering how she was supposed to answer that. "I like him," she said finally. "A lot."

Denise looked sharply at her. "How much is a lot?"

That did it. Lilah sat down on her cot and groaned. "It's a lot more than I should. I'm falling in love with him. Or maybe I've already fallen. I don't know. What am I going to do?"

"Okay," her friend said slowly. "Let me see if I follow you. You're falling in love with Ross, but yesterday you didn't like him at all—"

"I lied," Lilah mumbled through her fingers. "I didn't want to admit it."

"You dope. It figures. I knew you were trying too hard to convince me that he isn't your type."

"I even convinced myself," Lilah said. "Mostly."

"Um…so, last night. Did you…?"

"I kissed him. Actually, he kissed me."

"Yippee!"

"No! Denise, it's complicated."

"You like him, he likes you, he kisses you, it feels

good... What's so complicated about that?'' Denise paused, looking worried. "Unless it didn't feel good. You're not about to tell me that that beautiful man is a bad kisser.''

"Ross is a very good kisser,'' Lilah said, color rising to her cheeks at the memory of just how good he was.

"Apparently so,'' Denise said. "What's the problem then?''

"This whole thing is a problem. I've known him for a week. A week! It took me more time than that to decide what color to paint my kitchen, and this is a little more serious, not to mention dangerous.''

"I keep trying to tell you that love isn't safe.''

"Well, it should be! I have a job, and a life, and I don't have time to have my heart broken. I need something with a warranty.''

"I can't figure out why you're so convinced that your heart is going to be broken.''

"Because he's only interested in a quick affair, no strings attached.''

"Did he specifically tell you that?''

"Yes,'' Lilah said unhappily. "Very clearly.''

"Oh, dear. Are you sure?''

"I'm sure. Physical intimacy and emotional intimacy are very different things in his book, and he makes it sound so simple. We like each other, we're attracted to each other, so why not jump into bed and have a fling?''

Denise rolled her eyes. "Oh, God, that is such a guy thing. What did you say when he brought up this fabulous idea of his?''

"Nothing,'' Lilah confessed. "I left and went to bed. I didn't know what to say, Denise. Things were getting pretty intense just before we kissed, and I felt like we were making a...connection. Like he was telling me things that he doesn't tell other people. Things he needs to talk about. For me, the kissing and the…'' She paused. ''And the other physical stuff—''

''Don't spare the details for my sake,'' Denise urged. ''I'm living vicariously.''

Lilah ignored her. ''For me, it's all connected. It has to be. I don't know how to have a heartless fling.''

Denise nodded. ''You're very loyal. You'd have to be, to stay with Jeff for so long.''

''It's true! I get attached. I'm devoted and monogamous by nature. I know it's old-fashioned and unhip, but I can't help it. So what am I supposed to do?''

''A lot can happen in a few weeks,'' Denise ventured.

''I want to believe that. Something in me thinks I should just try this, on whatever terms, and hope that it all works out. But I'm scared. I thought I was going to die when Jeff left me. I can't handle loving another man who decides to dump me and move on. I can't. If I'm setting myself up to have my heart ripped out…''

''Look,'' Denise said. ''Here's what I think, and I'm sorry if it sounds unsympathetic, but life isn't about hiding in a cocoon and protecting yourself. It's about going after what you want and facing whatever happens with guts and pride that you did your best. You know that.''

''Are you an artist or a therapist?''

''I am all things to all people,'' Denise said. ''You're stronger than you think, Lilah. If you're falling in love with Ross Bradford, go for it. See what happens.'' She wagged an emphatic finger, adding, ''Because if you don't, then you'll always wonder what could have happened if you'd been just a little braver. Personally, that's not the way I'd want to look back over my life.''

Lilah sighed. ''You're right.''

"Eventually," Denise said, "you'll figure out that I'm always right. But you can start by listening to me now."

The water from the night's rain had collected into one continuous puddle at the base of the canyon, and the slopes were dark and muddy. Rain runoff had swept mud over some of the excavated areas, and Lilah resigned herself to spending the morning cleaning off her previous day's work.

She had just settled down when her eye caught something new.

Three feet up the slope from where she sat, she could see a dull gray stone tool sitting half-out of the mud, only visible now that the rain had washed away the soil covering it.

As she reached for it, Lilah realized with a shock of excitement that it was not the only tool there.

"Elliot!" she yelled, scrambling up the slope on her hands and knees. There had to be a hundred of the hand-hewn blades scattered on the slope above her. "Ted! Come look at this."

Everyone within hearing distance caught the urgency in her voice. Elliot and Ted were both there in a moment.

"Look at what the rain uncovered," she said excitedly, gesturing over the stones. "Cross your fingers. I think we may have something here."

By the time the late afternoon shadows began to lengthen, Lilah had blisters on her hands and a sunburn on the back of her neck. They had moved an enormous amount of earth out of the side of the canyon in order to expose more of the promising soil level as it stretched back into the hillside. What they found as the day wore on was more than enough to keep them working.

Stone tools, bones and more of the scattered flakes appeared in the giant screens they used to sieve the soil removed from the test trench.

Lilah was elated. It was just what she'd been praying to find, and now she might just have a chance at getting that federal excavation permit.

The mood at camp that evening over dinner was jubilant, and Elliot ceremoniously popped the cork on a bottle of champagne he had secretly brought along for just such an occasion.

After dinner, they all crowded into the lab tent, where Lilah found herself giving an impromptu lecture on fossil bone analysis to a small but very eager audience.

"And here," she said, turning the end of one bone under the bright light of the battery-powered halogen lamp, "you can see a few very light cut marks right along the edge. See? This is what you get when you use a sharp stone tool to slice the meat away from the bone."

She picked up several fragments of an antelope femur and laid them out in their original positions. "And look at this. See these broken edges? This bone was probably intentionally split...."

There was a soft rustle of canvas in front of her, and Lilah's heart skipped a beat as she looked up to see an acutely familiar figure step into the tent and stand, with his arms folded against his chest, behind the group of students.

Ross's eyes met hers, and he gave her a cool half smile.

Lilah gulped, sheer force of will keeping her from blushing a horrible shade of rose as she fingered the bones. Everyone else in the tent, noticing her sudden awkwardness, turned to see who was there.

"Hi, Ross," Elliot said easily. "Welcome. Lilah was just giving us a brushup on Bones 101."

"Sounds interesting. Don't let me interrupt," he said, and Lilah knew that he was absolutely aware that his sudden appearance had rattled her.

She swallowed again and continued automatically. "I was saying that this bone was probably broken to get the marrow. It takes work to hunt down a big animal, so you have to be efficient about using everything you can."

After she finished, Lilah intentionally took her time getting the graduate students started on labeling and bagging the newly recovered artifacts, all the while acutely aware that Ross waited outside the tent. Denise's pep talk had made it sound so noble and right to live dangerously and follow her heart, but suddenly the idea of launching herself into an affair with Ross felt something like getting behind the wheel of a Ferrari with no brakes.

Ross and Elliot were standing outside the tent, deep in conversation, and Lilah attempted to casually sidle past them and out the door into the late evening light. She didn't get far.

Ross's hand whipped out and caught her firmly by the upper arm as she passed by.

"Going somewhere?" he asked pleasantly.

"I...need some water," she said, trying unsuccessfully to twist out of his grip without calling attention to the fact that she was doing it.

"Water," Ross said skeptically.

He still had her by the arm, and Elliot, sensing tension, excused himself to go check on the students.

"Right, water," she said. "Too much talking. Makes my throat dry." She manufactured a cough. "See?"

"I see. I think I'll come get some water, too. I want to talk to you."

If Lilah had had any conscious control over her heartbeat, she would have told it to slow down and shut up, because it was pounding too loudly as she and Ross walked over to the row of water storage jugs near the campfire circle.

She wasn't actually thirsty, but she filled her mug anyway, took a sip and looked at him. He was wearing casual clothes and work boots, and the faded blue of his shirt picked up glints of the same color hiding in his eyes.

Lilah took a deep breath. "So," she said. "Did you hear that we had good luck today? We dug up a hunting site about halfway down the ravine slope, and I'm guessing that it's more than four hundred thousand years old. On Monday morning I'm going into Nairobi to send samples back to the States. We should have a date for it in a few days."

Ross was gazing at her with an inscrutable face. "Sounds like just what you wanted," he said.

"It is. It seems to be mostly undisturbed, which is really rare," she said a little too fast. "We found a lot of stone flakes, some tools—what?"

Ross's mouth had quirked into a smile, and he was looking at something over her shoulder.

She turned around, and looked across camp to the open flap of the lab tent to see Elliot and Denise peeking out at them. They looked surprised and embarrassed when they realized that they had been spotted, and their heads disappeared quickly back into the tent.

Lilah sighed and looked up at the sun, which was getting low on the savanna horizon. "Why don't I just show you the site," she said. "Come on."

Chapter 10

The canyon seemed to glow with an inner fire as the rocks and sand reflected the deep, molten-gold light of the sinking sun. Ross followed Lilah down the slope, checking back over his shoulder to see if any of her unusually curious friends had decided to follow them.

It looked as if they had been warned off by the glare she had given them, so he was alone with her. Again. Wasn't this how they had gotten into trouble before?

Ross had worked all day, trying to forget about Lilah, but thoughts of her kept creeping into the corners of his mind. Eventually he had gotten tired of the struggle for concentration, and decided to come confront her.

But here she was, acting as if he were some tourist arriving to see the sights. Was she so deeply regretting what had happened between them that she could hardly face him? Well, too bad. She was going to have to.

He stopped walking, and she turned, looking uncertainly up at him.

"The area we excavated is just down there," she said, pointing.

"Lilah," he said, folding his arms, "you and I both know that I didn't come down for an archaeology lesson."

It didn't help to notice how lovely she was. Her dark blond hair caught the light of the setting sun and turned into warm honey tumbling down to her shoulders in a way that reminded him of how she had looked last night, hot and disheveled with passion. But the worried look in her eyes and the smudge of dirt on her cheek made her seem oddly vulnerable.

"Oh," she said.

Ross had a fleeting urge to shake her. "You took off in a rush this morning," he said coolly.

"I had to get back to work, so I—"

"Otieno told me that you were outside, looking for a ride at the crack of dawn. Sounds like you were anxious to escape."

"No," she protested. "I woke up early, so I thought I should leave."

"I think you did more than leave. I think you ran away, just like you did last night. What are you so afraid of?"

Lilah bit her lip, looking trapped, and her silence was enough to convince him that he was right.

"Tell me," he said.

She hesitated a moment longer, then took a deep breath. "Okay," she said. "Last night you asked me what I want, and I didn't know. I had to figure it out. That's why I ran away."

"And did you figure it out?"

She looked up to meet his eyes, and there was a sudden resoluteness on her face, like a person about to take that first dive from the high board.

"Yes."

"What do you want, Lilah?"

She shook her head. "First you tell me what you want."

He frowned. Was she playing with him? If so, her game made no sense. He had no hesitation about repeating what he'd told her last night.

"I don't believe in wasting time," he said. "We have five more weeks together, and I think we should enjoy them. I want you to come back to the house tonight, and I want to wake up tomorrow morning with you next to me."

"I see," Lilah said, giving him a small, resigned smile that left him highly dissatisfied. What was the matter with her? He couldn't remember the last time he had said something like that to a woman, and he would have appreciated a slightly warmer reception.

"I just wanted to clarify that," she added.

"And you want...?"

"I want the same thing."

Her green-flecked eyes met his squarely, but something in their expression hinted that she had more on her mind than she was telling.

But Ross didn't bother to probe any further.

"No more running away, then?" he asked, reaching out to take her hand, then raising it to his lips. He turned it over, and pressed a kiss into her palm.

"No more running away," she agreed in a low voice, as he slid his lips down to the delicate skin of her inner wrist. Her fingers curved around his jaw for just a moment, then stopped, tensing, as if she had intentionally cut off her reaction to him.

Ross knew a challenge when he saw one. He had no intention of letting the momentary awkwardness of defining their relationship interfere with the reason it existed in the first place. Lilah might not be moving, but he could feel the throb of her pulse under her skin, against his lips. He slipped the tip of her forefinger into his mouth, catching it gently between his teeth.

Her eyes flicked up to meet his, startled, and just as quickly looked away again. Ross took her motionless hand and slid it down, holding it in place against his chest, feeling the heat of her skin burning into him. He felt a tremor pass through her, and immediately returned her hand to his lips.

"I think I was right," he observed in a murmur against her palm, trying to provoke her. "I think this does scare you. You want me as much as I want you, but you're afraid to admit it."

"That's not true," she said unsteadily. "I'm not afraid of you."

"No? Prove it."

Lilah looked at him for a long moment, not speaking, and then to Ross's surprise, she smiled. It wasn't a casual smile. Her lips curved upward into an expression that seemed almost feline, and Ross felt a sudden and unexpected flicker of alarm.

She moved toward him, stopping when they were chest-to-chest. He could feel her breasts brushing against him as she breathed, and only intense self-control and curiosity about what she was doing kept him from reaching out for her. He could feel himself getting aroused, and if she moved any closer, she would feel it, too.

She did. Moving so that her hips were pressed teasingly up against him, she slid her hands up his chest to his shoulders, then began to deliberately glide her fingers over the sensitive skin at the nape of his neck.

Ross clenched his teeth, refusing to move in spite of the fact that her hands and body were sending small elec-

PLAY "LUCKY 7" AND GET
THREE FREE GIFTS!

HOW TO PLAY:

1. With a coin, carefully scratch off the silver box at the right. Then check the claim chart to see what we have for you — **FREE BOOKS** and a gift — **ALL YOURS! ALL FREE!**

2. Send back this card and you'll receive brand-new Silhouette Intimate Moments® novels. These books have a cover price of $4.25 each, but they are yours to keep absolutely free.

3. There's no catch. You're under no obligation to buy anything. We charge nothing — ZERO — for your first shipment. And you don't have to make any minimum number of purchases — not even one!

4. The fact is thousands of readers enjoy receiving books by mail from the Silhouette Reader Service™ months before they're available in stores. They like the convenience of home delivery and they love our discount prices!

5. We hope that after receiving your free books you'll want to remain a subscriber. But the choice is yours — to continue or cancel, any time at all! So why not take us up on our invitation, with no risk of any kind. You'll be glad you did!

YOURS FREE!

PLAY LUCKY 7 FOR THIS EXCITING FREE GIFT!

THIS SURPRISE MYSTERY GIFT COULD BE YOURS FREE WHEN YOU PLAY

LUCKY 7!

NO COST! NO OBLIGATION TO BUY!
NO PURCHASE NECESSARY!

PLAY THE

Just scratch off the silver box with a coin. Then check below to see the gifts you get!

YES!

I have scratched off the silver box. Please send me all the gifts for which I qualify. I understand I am under no obligation to purchase any books, as explained on the back and on the opposite page.

245 SDL CH5M
(U-SIL-IM-07/98)

Name _____
PLEASE PRINT CLEARLY

Address _____ Apt.#

City _____ State _____ Zip

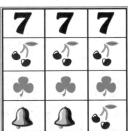

WORTH TWO FREE BOOKS PLUS A BONUS MYSTERY GIFT!

WORTH TWO FREE BOOKS!

WORTH ONE FREE BOOK!

TRY AGAIN!

The Silhouette Reader Service™ — Here's how it works

Accepting free books places you under no obligation to buy anything. You may keep the books and gift and return the shipping statement marked "cancel." If you do not cancel, about a month later we'll send you 6 additional novels, and bill you just $3.57 each, plus 25¢ delivery per book and applicable sales tax, if any.*
That's the complete price — and compared to cover prices of $4.25 each — quite a bargain! You may cancel at any time, but if you choose to continue, every month we'll send you 6 more books, which you may either purchase at the discount price...or return to us and cancel your subscription.

*Terms and prices subject to change without notice. Sales tax applicable in N.Y.

If offer card is missing write to: Silhouette Reader Service, 3010 Walden Ave., P.O. Box 1867, Buffalo, NY 14240-1867

BUSINESS REPLY MAIL
FIRST-CLASS MAIL   PERMIT NO. 717   BUFFALO, NY

POSTAGE WILL BE PAID BY ADDRESSEE

SILHOUETTE READER SERVICE
3010 WALDEN AVE
PO BOX 1867
BUFFALO NY 14240-9952

NO POSTAGE
NECESSARY
IF MAILED
IN THE
UNITED STATES

tric shocks up and down his spine. God, that she could do this to him with just her presence, with just the tiniest touch. It was everything he could do not to grab her and tear off her shirt, push down her pants and take her right there on the rocky ground.

Lilah's hands moved down to undo the first two buttons of his shirt. She raised herself up on her toes, and Ross felt his hands clench into two iron fists at his sides as she began to kiss him on the flesh she had just exposed, her soft mouth and warm breath searing his skin.

She opened another button and paused, looking up into his face. "You know what I think?" she murmured, and he just waited, unable to speak.

"I think you're the one who's afraid," she said.

"What?" he said with some effort, his voice hoarse. "That's crazy. Why would I be afraid of this?"

"Not of this," she said softly, as her fingers continued their work. "Of everything else."

Ross could barely think right now, much less consider what she could possibly mean by her cryptic remark. All he was aware of were her hands and mouth, and the fingers which, on opening the last button, had managed to slip even lower, brushing against him for the briefest second, making him inhale sharply.

She pushed the shirt off his shoulders. He felt the cool air of the evening against his back, and the heat of Lilah against his front. Her hands were playing with his skin, stroking silkily up his back and around his sides, sensitizing his entire body.

It was with this new, buzzing skin that he could feel her breasts through her thin shirt, their nipples hard against his chest, and he knew, in some dim, far-off way, that he was about to lose this showdown.

It was too much. His resolve was crumbling fast, and

he was so far gone that he hardly cared. His hands reached for her as if they had a life of their own, and he moved quickly, linking one leg behind hers to knock her off balance. Before she knew what he was doing, he had her on the ground.

"Enough," he growled, pinning her arms at her sides.

Lilah's mouth was curved into a satisfied grin, and he kissed it off her, roughly, thoroughly, with an urgent hunger for the taste of her.

Her arms linked around him as she responded, her silky mouth and warm body welcoming him. Her own ardor, the feel of her undisguised hunger for him, was amazingly erotic, as if her own passion fueled his desire for her to an almost insatiable level.

It took every bit of willpower in his body to lift his head from hers. "We're not in the best place to continue this."

Lilah smiled up at him. "You don't want to walk back into camp with twigs in your hair and dirt all over you? I guess that would be a little obvious."

"Come back to the house with me," he said. He wanted her badly, but on his own terms. She had caught him off-guard too many times, and he planned to start all over, his way.

"To continue this in a more suitable place?"

"Yes. Do you want to?"

Her hazel eyes were wide and vulnerable in the fading evening light, and they shimmered with a longing that astonished him.

"Yes," she whispered. "I do."

It was dark by the time they arrived at the house, and the one lamp burning in the living room cast a pale glow out over the savanna. Everything was dim and indistinct in the low light, and as Lilah waited for Ross to unlock the front door, she felt as if she were in a dream, drifting on a warm current of desire through a place where anything was possible.

He held the door open for her, and she stepped into the house, a shiver of nervous anticipation coursing through her.

What now? Were they supposed to talk, to relax and work their way up to whatever happened? Lilah hesitated in the middle of the room as Ross closed the door behind her.

It had never seemed so awkward before. Her heart was beating so hard that she could feel it pounding against her chest, and she bit her lips, trying to find something to say.

But Ross made it all unnecessary. Before she knew what he was doing, he stepped behind her, linking his arms around her waist, and Lilah automatically leaned back, feeling the rise and fall of his breath against her back.

"Lilah," he said, taking her shoulders in his strong hands and turning her slowly around to face him. "Look at me."

She could feel a stain of color in her cheeks as she met his eyes. His gaze traveled over her face, searching it, then slid boldly down to move over her body.

A shock of excitement rippled through her as Ross's eyes consumed her. He seemed to be barely restraining himself from doing anything more than holding her silently by the shoulders, and there was a feeling of energy held in check, of action frozen for a moment like a camera still.

"I've told you what I want," he said, his voice low and intense. "Now, before this goes any further, you tell me. Exactly."

Lilah leaned forward to brush her lips against his chest and felt him shiver. He groaned, then pushed her away, holding her away from him.

"No. Say it. I need to hear you say it."

"I want you," she said, urgency tearing the words out of her. "I want you to make love to me, Ross, please..."

It was as if her words had released him. His arms curved around her, pulling her against him, and his mouth met hers hungrily, kissing her until she was gasping for breath.

He lifted his head, and she sagged slightly against him.

"Oh, no, don't..."

"Don't what?"

"Don't stop," Lilah said. "Please..."

Ross laughed softly, low in his throat, with a husky sound almost like a growl. "We've had too many interruptions already, haven't we."

He guided her back toward one of the living room couches, where he gathered her into his lap and began to touch the skin of her neck with slow, shivery kisses. "Now it's time," he murmured, his lips against her collarbone, "to take care of unfinished business."

He slid one hand possessively around the curve of her hip, and his fingers began to trace long, smooth trails up and down her legs.

Lilah's breath caught in her throat as his rough fingertips curved in toward her inner thighs, stroking the delicate skin there with teasing, circling motions, slipping under the hem of her shorts to move higher, and higher...

A soft whimper escaped her, and as she struggled to sit up, Ross shifted, turning her so that she was suddenly below him, with the weight of his body crushing her into the soft couch.

"Hey," she said weakly, but the exclamation was smothered on her lips as Ross's mouth claimed hers again.

Lilah kissed him back with reckless abandon, her hands pushing up under his shirt to explore the hollows of his back.

She felt him inhale against her lips as her fingers stroked over his naked skin, and he broke off the kiss to raise himself on one elbow, reaching between them to undo the buttons of his shirt. It fell open around him, exposing his tanned, muscled chest.

He smiled. "Your turn."

Lilah leaned her head back against the cushions as Ross caught the edge of her T-shirt, pulling it up and off. She closed her eyes, suddenly shy as she felt the touch of his lean fingers at the clasp of her bra.

"My God, Lilah," he murmured, his voice low and rough with passion. "You're beautiful."

Her bra fell away, and his hands moved up to stroke the curves of her breasts, tracing small arcs there, each feeling like a tiny trail of fire that lingered hot on her skin.

The light, exploratory touch was maddening, and Lilah pushed up slightly, into his hand, and moaned as his fingers opened to cup the weight of one swollen breast.

She opened her eyes to see his tousled dark hair as he bent his head over her to caress her with his lips, bringing her nipples to taut, aching points as he kissed them. Her body arched toward him, and he began to brush her skin with fiery-hot kisses in a trail that moved lower and lower until his hands and mouth were stroking over the exquisitely sensitive skin of her abdomen and upper thighs.

She cried out, she couldn't help it. His touch made her nerve endings jump and crackle, and she writhed beneath him against the cushions.

It was almost more than she could bear when he pushed down her shorts and panties and slid one hand around to the inside of her thigh to stroke, gently but relentlessly, between her legs where she was damp and aching. His lean fingers kept moving silkily back and forth as she struggled for breath and clenched her thighs together around his hand.

"Oh, God, Ross...please," she gasped, feeling as if she was going to explode.

Ross moved back up to cover her with his body, twining his strong legs with hers, and Lilah felt him reach down to undo the buttons of his pants. Her hands slipped over his back and traveled downward, helping him to push away the rough khaki cotton, wanting no more barriers between them.

"Ross, please, now. Don't wait. I can't..."

She heard him laugh softly, huskily, his breath hot against her skin. "I won't," he said. "I want you too much to wait any longer."

Moonlight glinted palely on his shoulders as he leaned over her, caging her between the two strong pillars of his arms.

"Look at me," he whispered, and when Lilah met his eyes, the heat she saw there sent a sizzling mixture of fear and excitement through her.

She made a soft, imploring sound, and Ross bent to kiss her with an urgent passion, smothering her gasp as their bodies merged.

Lilah could feel the tension swelling inside her, rising fast and hot like a cresting wave, and just when she was sure that it was too much to bear, it exploded in a glorious blaze of sensation, leaving her limp and wracked with shudders of pleasure.

She clung blindly to Ross, loving the strong, smooth

motion of his body against her as, with a ragged groan, he allowed himself his own release.

He collapsed on top of her, his face buried in her hair, and Lilah reached up to stroke his back as they rested, tangled together, their breathing slowing to normal.

Her eyes began to feel heavy as her body relaxed, and she closed them, letting herself sink down into a warm languor, feeling Ross's even breathing matching her own.

She woke as she felt Ross move, and opened her eyes to see that he had rolled away to lean on his elbow, and was gazing down at her, his eyes smoky in the darkness. Cool air drifted between their bodies, chilling Lilah's sweat-damp skin, and she sighed, without intending to.

There was a sudden wariness on his face. "Regrets already?"

"No," she said, snuggling closer to him and pressing her exposed skin against his warm chest. "I'm cold. Don't move."

He laughed softly, and she felt him relax. "I didn't want to crush you."

"I don't mind." Sleepiness dulled the edges of her mind, and she was glad. She didn't want to think right now, not when everything felt so right. She needed the strength of him against her, and she wished that she could melt into the heat of his body.

He bent his head to kiss the slope of her shoulder, tracing lines on her skin with his lips and tongue until the tickling, feathery feeling was too much for her still-sensitized skin. She began to squirm, and felt his arm tighten around her waist, holding her firmly against him.

Her skin quivered as he teased it, and she moved her head to catch his mouth with her own. His lips were cool and firm but his tongue was hot, and they kissed slowly, lingeringly, exploring the feel and taste of each other. Lilah felt her tired body awakening to a warm flow of desire moving like honey through her veins.

Before she realized what he was doing, Ross reached down to hook one arm under her knees, and curved his other around her back, scooping her toward him as he stood up.

Lilah gasped, and instinctively linked her arms around his neck. "What are you doing?"

Amusement flickered in his eyes. "Taking you to bed."

"To sleep?"

"Not necessarily."

She smiled up at him. "This is much nicer than the first night I spent here. I never thought this would happen."

"I did."

"You did? When?"

"The next morning, when I came into the guest room and saw you tangled up in the sheets. You were all flushed and sleepy, and that's when I knew I wanted you in my own bed, sooner or later."

"I see," she said slowly. "And here I am. Do you always get what you want so quickly?"

He nodded. "I told you that I don't like wasting time."

His gaze was warm and intimate, but his words troubled her. Wasting time was only a concern when it was something limited, needing to be rationed, and that was exactly how Ross saw their time together.

Shadows pooled in the contours of his face, and the beauty of him made her heart ache.

"What are you thinking?" he asked.

She took a deep breath. "I'm thinking about how much I wanted this, too," she said. "I'm glad I'm here with you."

It was the truth. Whatever the circumstances, whatever the terms, the only place she wanted to be was here with Ross, in his arms. That was all that mattered right now.

Chapter 11

Lilah was rummaging around her tent early on the morning of her Nairobi trip when Ted poked his head in through the canvas flap. "Looking for these?"

"Hey, my letters. Thanks."

"I found them in the storage tent. In the dry food box." Ted frowned at her. "You're not usually so absentminded, Lilah."

"No, I guess not," she said, and shrugged. "Oh, well."

"I think you have something on your mind."

"I have lots of things on my mind. The excavation, the research permit—"

"Ross Bradford?"

Lilah put down her bag. "Ted, that's personal, and I'd rather not discuss it. Do you want anything from town? Stamps? Chocolate? Don't tell me you don't want chocolate. I have an order from everyone else."

"Not for me. Look, Lilah, I have something here you should see." He held out a magazine, folded open. It was an old *Newsweek,* the one with the article about Ross and his company, ECO.

"Read this," Ted said. "You might be surprised."

Lilah looked suspiciously at him. "Why?"

"Well, you're dating Ross Bradford, aren't you? Has he told you what he *really* does for a living?"

"Of course he has," she said. "He's the head of ECO, a big international company that does conservation work."

Ted snorted. "The man is a radical. Did he tell you about his latest project? He's setting up a new national park in the Central African rain forest, and he's turned the area into a war zone. Read it! It's all right here." He shook the magazine at her. "The research group he sent out there is trying to keep poachers from slaughtering the forest elephants for ivory."

"What's wrong with that?"

"Lilah, I'm trying to look out for your best interests, that's all. Illegal ivory is a big business, and everybody out there has automatic weapons. It's like the old Wild West. The poachers are shooting at Ross's group, and his group is shooting back. Is this the kind of man you want to be involved with? Some kind of conservation commando?"

"I don't want to continue this discussion," Lilah said coldly, and stepped past him, out of the tent.

She could hear Ross's Land Rover coming down the camp road, and she quickened her pace, aware that Ted was following her.

"What if he gets killed out there?" Ted called out. "What if he kills someone else? He may be legally right, but morally?"

Lilah ignored him, not wanting to hear any more. She was surprised and shocked by what Ted had just told her.

Was Ross's work really so dangerous? He did seem to play for high stakes, if the issue of the ranch was any measure. She would have to ask him herself. It couldn't really be that bad.

"Morning," Ross said to the group, as he stepped out of the car. He was dressed for business, but at the moment his tie was loosened and his shirtsleeves were rolled up to expose his tanned forearms.

"Hi," Lilah said, her heart leaping at the sight of him. In spite of his professional clothes, it wasn't hard to picture him out in the jungle, his rifle in his hand. What was it he'd said to her that first night when he caught her trespassing? *I never miss.* How much experience did he have with guns anyway?

She took a deep breath. "You're here early. Want some coffee?"

"Thanks, no. I just had my morning cup. We can go when you're ready."

Lilah felt someone poke her in the back as she stepped forward, and she turned to see Ted standing behind her, giving her a disapproving look.

"I hope he has his *gun,*" Ted said in a sarcastic stage whisper. "He might want to *shoot* somebody!"

Ross couldn't help overhearing, and raised his eyebrows, but Ted suddenly appeared to be very interested in the bread he was toasting over the fire.

"What was that all about?" Ross asked, as he helped her into the car.

"Ted's been trying to tell me that your work involves running around in the jungle shooting people," Lilah said. "Of course he must be exaggerating."

She paused, waiting for Ross to agree, but he didn't say anything.

She looked sharply at him. "Isn't he?"

"Not entirely. It's been bad over there for the past few months."

"Wait a minute, are you telling me this is true? That you are shooting at people? I thought you were setting up a national park."

"I am. And it's mainly the other way around. Certain people out there are shooting at us."

"Why?" Lilah asked incredulously.

"Because we're trying to stop the illegal ivory trade before it wipes out all the area's elephants."

"I can't believe this. How bad is it?"

"It's been getting progressively worse. Ken Harding, one of my biologists, ran into a group of poachers last month when he was doing a game count. They fired at his car and it was either luck or damn good driving that got him out of there with only a bullet in his shoulder."

"That's crazy."

"I couldn't agree more. But this is big money. Black-market ivory is a multimillion dollar business."

"I can't believe this," she said again. "Here I was, thinking that you were just a nice, peaceful CEO with a desk job."

Ross grinned. "You should know by now that I'm not nice or peaceful."

"Then this situation with Jake Wyatt and the ranch isn't unusual for you at all."

"No, it's not," Ross admitted. "And it's small-scale compared to most of the deals my company handles. It may look like conservation, but it's really about money. It didn't take me long to stop being surprised at what some people will do for money. You look troubled," he said, glancing at her. "Why?"

"Why? Isn't that obvious? People are shooting at you

on a regular basis and you want to know why I'm troubled?''

"Don't tell me you're actually worried about me."

"Don't tell me you'd care if I was," Lilah said, imitating his mocking tone. She sighed. "Is it worth it, Ross? I know elephants are an endangered species, but putting yourself on a firing range to set up a park to protect them?"

"Yes," he said immediately. "Absolutely worth it. If I stayed out of this because of the danger, instead of working for what I believe in, I wouldn't be able to live with myself. Safe and guilty is not how I want to spend my life. I'll be damned if I'll sit back and watch a few criminals get rich and powerful by selling illegal tusks on the black market. Does that make sense?" he added. "Or do you think I'm crazy? A lot of people do, so you'd have company."

"No," she said reluctantly. "I understand. It's an important thing to do, and you're probably very good at it. Just...be careful, okay?"

It was a useless thing to say, really, but Ross didn't seem to mind. He smiled slightly. "I'm always careful."

"I hope so."

They were silent for a moment, and Lilah frowned down at her hands. Why couldn't she have fallen in love with some nice, workaholic professor who rarely left the safety of his office? She just had to feel this way about a man who took being shot at as a typical job hazard. There was no good way to look at it, so she decided to change the subject.

"Any news about Jake Wyatt?"

Ross shook his head. "None. There's been no sign of the prowler, and as far as I know, Wyatt hasn't had any meetings or dealings with the government for days now. I don't like it."

"Isn't that good?"

"The idea that he's backed off is too good to be true. I think something's brewing. I want to know what it is."

"Any more parties coming up? I can keep working on him."

"Not until next week, unfortunately. But Otieno's cousin Joseph works as an aide for one of the officials involved in the development plans, and he's been briefing us on what happens in the meetings with Wyatt. He'll keep us posted until then."

"What? You mean I'm not your only spy? How disappointing."

Ross grinned. "Sorry."

"I guess it's just as well. My espionage skills are better than I thought, but not that much better. I don't think I'll be putting them on my résumé. We archaeologists are a pretty conservative bunch."

"That reminds me," he said. "I made a few phone calls this morning about your research permit, and I'm planning to bring up the subject in my meetings today. No guarantees, but this should at least get the wheels turning."

"Thank you, Ross," she said, touched that he would offer his help. She smiled at him, feeling warm inside. That was the kind of thing a man would do for someone he cared about, wasn't it? He wouldn't go to all that trouble for just a friend, even if that friend was also a lover.

"I'm glad to do it," he said. "I thought I ought to get started now. These things can take a long time, and I won't be able to do much to help next month when I'm back in the rain forest."

"Oh," she said. "I see."

It was painful to hear the certainty in his voice when he spoke of leaving Kenya in a few weeks. He wasn't even thinking twice about going.

She made her voice deliberately casual. "You haven't considered sticking around to help expand the park? I thought you said something about that when we were at the embassy."

"To Des Peters? Whatever I said to him was probably just intended to make a point. I've done a little preliminary setup work with the Park Bureau, but it's not really necessary. Things will be in good hands here, and I need to get back to our real project."

"Of course," Lilah said, her voice not betraying the tight feeling in her throat. And in her heart.

When they pulled into a street-side parking spot in Nairobi, they were immediately surrounded by a crowd of skinny young boys insisting that they would watch the car for Ross. He nodded, solemnly handed out a few shillings to the oldest ones, and thanked them in Swahili.

"What was that all about?" Lilah asked.

Ross grinned. "It's an ingenious system, actually. No one puts money into the parking meters. Instead, the kids get paid, and they wait until the policeman comes down the street, then run ahead of him and slip a coin into your meter for you. That way, the boys make money, the city gets paid, and you never have to worry about getting a parking ticket."

Nairobi was hot under the morning sun, but the air was spicy and sweet, free of the clouds of diesel exhaust that would accumulate by later in the day.

Lilah managed to take care of her errands with a minimum of trouble, and then wandered through the city market, a winding area of corrugated tin stalls selling everything from African statues to beaded jewelry. By the time she remembered to check her watch, it was almost time to meet Ross.

The Bradford office was on the fifth floor of one of the tall buildings on Kenyatta Avenue, in the busy center of the city.

"Come on in," Ross said as Lilah poked her head through the open door. The floor, and every other available surface, was littered with boxes and piles of paper.

"You may not believe it," he said dryly, "but I've cleared out most of what used to be in here. I don't think my father ever threw anything out."

"I'll bet he knew exactly where to find everything, though," Lilah said, picking her way into the room and moving a stack of folders off a chair.

"You're right, he did."

Ross handed her a pile of letters. "Here's the mail that's come in for your group. I just need to make a quick call to the Park Bureau. The secretary left me an urgent message to phone them."

"I'll wait," Lilah said, thumbing idly through the letters.

There were only two envelopes addressed to her; a large one from the university with some general information about the funding for the excavation, and the other a small white one with no stamp and no return address. Clearly it had been hand delivered. She fingered it curiously. Who would be writing to her from a local address?

The envelope slit open easily, and with amazement, Lilah scanned the brief note inside. It was from Jake Wyatt himself, and in his thick, bold handwriting, he was inviting her to his house for further discussion of the "offer" he had made her.

She gripped the paper, rereading it with growing excitement. Wait until she told Ross about—

"What the hell?" Ross said into the phone, slamming one hand down hard on the desktop. "He did what? How?"

Lilah looked up, surprised, and saw that his face had tightened into lines of anger and disbelief.

"Where did he get the money to do that? He doesn't have that kind of capital! Hell, no, if I knew I wouldn't be asking you. When did you learn about this?"

Ross sucked in his breath through gritted teeth as he listened, reaching up to rake his fingers through his hair. "Right. Fine. Find out everything you can, and call me at home, tonight. I'll talk to you then.

"Damn Jake Wyatt," he said, hanging up. "I knew something was going on."

"What happened?"

"This morning, out of the blue, Wyatt became more than a mere supporter of the factory. He somehow came up with hard currency equal to several million U.S. dollars, and is now the principal investor in the project."

"I didn't know he was so wealthy."

"Neither did I," Ross said grimly. "Neither did anyone. In fact, I would have bet the ranch—and I did—that he was definitely *not* that wealthy."

He stood up abruptly and strode over to the window, staring out, his shoulders square and tense.

"This is going to change everything. The major problem with the factory project was lack of funding to get it off the ground. Now that won't be an issue. Wyatt has done exactly what it takes to get the support he needs. Damn it! I never saw this coming. How the hell did he get all that money?"

Lilah watched him anxiously, not knowing what to say.

"And do you know what else is strange?" Ross continued, turning to face her.

"What?"

"The profit he'll bring in as an investor in the factory shouldn't be nearly enough to justify risking such a huge amount. It isn't a deal I'd make, and Wyatt isn't stupid."

"He must be convinced that this is the only way to have the factory. He must think you'd win otherwise."

"And he'd be right," Ross said. "I know he wants that factory, but why does he want it so badly? It looks like he'll do anything, even set himself up to lose money, to see it built. It makes no sense."

"Could this be a personal thing?" Lilah ventured. She had, after all, seen the looks they had exchanged that night at the embassy.

"A vendetta against me?" Ross shook his head. "I might actually be flattered that he thought I merited several million dollars' worth of hate, but no. Jake works by money alone, which can mean only one thing—he knows something I don't. I need to find out what's really going on here."

He walked back to the desk and picked up the telephone receiver.

"What are you doing?"

"Something I should have done already," he said, dialing.

"Diane? This is Ross. Let me talk to Charlie. What? Yes, I know it's 8:00 p.m. there. Well, you're in the office now, why wouldn't he be?"

Ross frowned into the phone. "What do you mean, 'because he has a life?' Since when? Well, good for him. Look, tomorrow morning I want you or Charlie to do a check on Jake Wyatt for me. Use any source you can. Bribe people if you have to, just get me a list of his in-

ternational business connections. I want any financial information you can dig up—investments, hidden bank accounts, all of that. The sooner the better.''

He hung up. "That may help, but I'm not counting on
it. I'm going to have to see what I can find out locally
about where that money came from.''

"Does it matter? I mean, he has it. Isn't that what
counts?''

"Maybe. But I find the whole thing very strange. I want
information.''

Information? About Jake Wyatt? Lilah glanced down
at the note in her lap. If that was what Ross wanted, then
she was in the perfect position to help him.

And she would.

"So, Miss Evans, I'll get right down to it," Jake Wyatt
said, pouring Lilah a cup of strong amber tea. "I want to
know if you've given any thought to what we talked about
that evening at the embassy.''

Lilah added a splash of milk to her cup, and a cube of
sugar from the small bowl on the table.

It was late afternoon, and they were sitting on wicker
chairs on the front porch of Jake's house, surrounded on
all sides by savanna. She knew that the canyon, and the
Bradford ranch, were only a few miles to the east, but
insignificant things like roads and fences somehow van-
ished into the expanse of green land and blue sky.

"Call me Lilah, please,'' she said, glad that her voice
sounded more relaxed than she felt.

She had volunteered to meet with Jake, to find out what
she could about this startling development in the factory
plans, but she had realized as soon as she arrived that it
wouldn't be as simple as she had thought. The days since
the embassy party had faded her initial impression of Jake,

but now she was getting the same feeling that this man was dangerous.

"Lilah, then," he said, her name rolling smoothly off his tongue. "Well, Lilah?" His azure eyes bit into her.

She smiled at him. "Maybe you could tell me exactly what you have in mind."

"It's very simple. Time...for you to have your excavation. That's what you want, isn't it?"

"More than anything. But how can you promise me that?"

"Believe me, I can. Is Ross still clinging to his idea about the wildlife reserve?"

"Very firmly," Lilah said, trying to keep irony out of her voice. That certainly was an understatement.

"Pity for him, then. The factory is going up on that land and it's going up soon. Even if he tries to back out now, the government will force him to give up the property. You're in the right place right now, my dear. This is the winners' circle."

"Lucky for me," she said blandly. She was experiencing a problem that she hadn't had to deal with the last time she spoke with Jake—the desire to use a swift right hook to take that self-congratulatory smirk off his face. "But what makes you so sure?"

Jake bolted the cooled remains of his tea in one shot, as if it were whiskey. "Why am I sure? Because I just put enough money into the factory project to show the government whose side to be on. Does the equivalent of three and a half million American dollars convince you, too?"

"Well," said Lilah, letting false warmth color her voice. "It just might. Congratulations, it sounds like you've won the game."

"That's what I've been trying to tell you," he said.

"And you've won, too. I'll give you all the time you want at that canyon."

"That's a very generous offer."

Jake smiled benevolently. "I'm a generous man."

"Are you an archaeology fan?"

"Oh, I'm interested in all sorts of things," he said. "You could say that I enjoy doing favors for my friends."

"I'm flattered."

"Of course, I always assume that my friends would do the same for me, given the opportunity."

Aha, Lilah thought. She'd suspected from the start that he wanted something from her. Finding out what that was would be both interesting and useful.

"That sounds fair," she said.

"Good. Because there's a way you can help me. I want..." He paused, frowning. "Just a minute."

There was a low mechanical rumble in the distance which had been there for a while, getting steadily louder, but Lilah hadn't paid any attention until Jake did.

She looked past him to see that a truck was lumbering up the dirt road toward the house. It was medium-size and heavy, the size of the typical freight trucks Lilah had seen traveling along the Mombasa highway. But this one was mud-splattered and dusty, with no identifying marks. The back was canvas-wrapped and secured with ropes, and as Lilah glanced curiously at it, she thought she saw the shapes of several large crates loaded inside.

It was a generally uninteresting truck. What was very interesting, though, was Jake's reaction to its arrival. With lightning quickness, a flash of anger exploded across his profile, and he sat up, stiffly straight, and stared at the truck.

But the expression was gone in a flash, leaving Lilah wondering if she'd imagined it. The porch was dappled with shadows of sun shining through leaves and wicker, and it was hard to be sure of what she'd seen.

He turned back to her, totally composed. "That must be the shipment of building materials I ordered. It's arrived early. I don't like being interrupted when I have a guest."

"Oh, that's fine," Lilah said brightly, watching him, her heart suddenly thudding in her chest. "I can wait while you deal with it."

"Come inside," Jake said. "You can look at my African statue collection while you wait."

His tone left no room for objection. Lilah stood up, allowing him to guide her into the house as the truck approached. She glanced back to see that the road dead-ended at a large garage building about a quarter mile past the house.

"I have some pieces you'll like," Jake was saying to her. He had one hand on her shoulder, and was walking close to her. "Good ones from Zaire and Nigeria. This way."

He walked her into the living room, where a number of carved wooden statues were displayed on shelves.

"This won't take long," he said. "I'll be back in a few minutes."

Lilah listened as the sound of Jake's footsteps moved down the hall. What was going on? Had she really seen that flash of fury on Jake's face?

She moved quietly across the room, and cautiously eased open the hall door. The hallway was empty, but Lilah could hear the faint sound of Jake's voice coming from a room far down the hall.

He was indeed angry, she realized, as she moved closer, testing the wood floor for squeaks. His words were rapid and sharpened into muffled staccato beats.

She leaned toward the door and listened.

"...three days early, goddamn it!" Jake's voice was a snarl. "This is sloppy, and I do not do sloppy business. What the hell do you think we're dealing with?"

There was a pause, and Lilah heard the creak of floorboards as Jake began to pace. "Goddamn right it won't happen again. This isn't what I pay you for. One more time and you're finished. Permanently. Do you understand me?"

There was another pause.

"Good," Jake said, and something about his tone made Lilah realize that she had caught the very end of the phone conversation. She turned quickly, and stepping as softly as she could, fled back toward the living room, closing the door hastily behind her.

She wasn't a moment too soon. Barely two minutes after she stopped in front of the statue shelves, the door opened and Jake walked into the room.

Lilah pressed her lips together hard, trying to calm her breathing, and kept her head ducked away from Jake as if she were absorbed in looking at the metal mask she had blindly grabbed.

"I've taken care of it," he said evenly. "Sorry. I'm putting a new addition on the kitchen, so I had to be sure they left the bags of cement in the right place."

"Oh, really?" Lilah looked up with a smile as her breathing quieted. "You're doing it yourself?"

"Yes, bloody lot of work, but I think it'll be worth it."

She could hear the rumble of the truck coming back along the road by the house, and she could tell by Jake's quick glance toward the window that he did, too.

He moved forward. "How do you like my collection? I bought that mask you're holding in Zaire. That's gold, you know, not brass."

Lilah stroked her finger over the almond-shaped eyes and long, straight nose. "It must be valuable."

"Very. Every one of these pieces is either rare or antique. This collection should be in a vault. I wouldn't waste my time on worthless art."

"Of course," Lilah murmured. The metal was cool in her hands and she ran her thumbs over its cheeks, which were decorated with complex, carefully hammered designs. "What are these patterns for? They look like they must have some ritual meaning."

Jake shrugged. "I didn't ask. Heavy, isn't it? That's a lot of gold. You wouldn't believe how much it cost me."

He shifted on his feet, and raised a hand to wipe the sheen of sweat on his face. "Let's go back out to the porch. It's too bloody hot in here."

Outside, the savanna around Jake's house was as quiet and peaceful as if the mysterious truck had never come to disturb it. The breeze rustled the tall grass beyond the road, and birds twittered from the branches of the trees nearby.

Lilah shot a quick glance toward the distant storage building, but it appeared undisturbed.

"How long do you expect to be working on your kitchen?" she asked casually as she settled into her wicker chair.

Jake, positioning himself opposite her, looked up with narrowed eyes. "As long as it takes."

"Oh. Well, do you plan to—"

"It just occurred to me that I've forgotten something," he said suddenly. "I should congratulate you."

"Me? Why?"

"On your excavation. I hear you've made interesting new discoveries down there."

"Yes..." Lilah said, astonished. How had he heard

about that? It had only been a few days since they started turning up artifacts, and they hadn't discussed it with anyone yet.

Jake was watching her with a smooth, satisfied expression, and she realized that he had neatly turned the tables on her.

"How did you hear about the new finds?"

"I told you that I'm interested in all sorts of things."

"But we haven't made it public yet." Lilah couldn't believe it. Was he paying someone down at camp to report to him? One of the workers they'd hired, maybe? But no, that couldn't be it. They hadn't had any extra help since the previous week. It was only her group at the site now.

He smiled at the look on her face. "I have ways of keeping myself informed."

"I can see that," she said, disturbed.

"This must give you even more reason to want to keep working at the site," he said.

"Yes. It does."

"Then I think we can help each other." Jake's flat eyes made Lilah think of a winter sky, pale blue and spiked with needles of ice. She could read nothing in them.

He leaned forward. "There's something I want you to get for me...."

Chapter 12

The paint on the inside walls of the summerhouse was peeling, Ross noticed, as he stacked boxes of old papers on the floor. For some reason, it bothered him. The tiny building was one of the places he'd always thought of as his own.

Although it was only a few hundred feet from the ranch house, it was separated by a thicket of aloe and sisal plants, and all of its windows overlooked the savanna. He wasn't sure why it had been built in the first place, except that everyone in the area also had one, so it must have been the fashion once.

Theirs had never been used much. It would have served as an extra bedroom if the house had ever overflowed with guests, but Ross couldn't recall that happening. He had played in here when he was young, and his mother had come here to write letters or have tea with friends, but after Ross left for school, and Claire died, it had become a storage area.

Boxes were now piled on the faded cushioned seats, and he was having a hard time facing the chore of sorting through them all. He sighed, remembering how he had once wished for siblings. That wish still held. A brother or sister to help with all of this was just what he needed.

There was a soft knock on the open door, and he looked up to see Lilah standing there.

"You look lost in thought," she said. "May I interrupt?"

"Absolutely." He was glad to see her. Her appearance chased away all of the melancholy, cobwebby feelings creeping around inside him, and brought him back to the present, which was where he'd far rather be.

Especially with Lilah here, framed by the sunny space of the doorway, her blue dress making her look as if she'd just come from a garden party.

He couldn't help noticing the curve of her waist under the soft cotton, and the shadowy outline of her legs as the sun filtered through her skirt. Ross pulled his gaze away, rubbing a hand over his forehead. He hadn't seen her since Nairobi, and he'd swear he was having withdrawal symptoms.

It wasn't just that he missed touching her, or missed the scent and taste of her. He did, but what really troubled him was this sudden uplifted feeling, of peace, of...damn it, completeness, that came from her mere presence. He seemed to be developing a hole inside himself that only Lilah could fill, a hole that nagged and twinged with emptiness when she wasn't with him.

The thought that he might begin to need her—really need her to feel whole—was chilling. He'd learned early in life—at his father's knee, so to speak—the terrible rejection and pain that came with depending on anyone else's love to ensure his own happiness. He'd had no choice as a child, but he was an adult now, and he was damned if he'd ever make himself that vulnerable again. Was he wrong to assume that this time limit of six weeks would protect him?

No. He wasn't so weak that it would be a problem. If he was glad to see her, it was because he'd been worried about her, that was all, and having her back safely from Wyatt's house eased his mind.

"How did it go?" he asked.

Lilah gave him a significant look. "Something weird is going on over there. If you understand it, then explain it to me, because I sure don't."

Ross was immediately alarmed. "Are you all right?"

Her cheeks were flushed, and she looked anxious, as if she had hurried here to tell him something.

"Oh, I'm fine," she said. "And I couldn't get anything useful out of him about the money or his investment in the factory. He's very coolheaded...*if* things are going as planned. But listen to this."

She began to describe the incident with the truck. Ross was intrigued, more by her claim that Jake had been shaken up by the appearance of the truck than by the incident itself. After all, trucks went in and out of a working cattle ranch every day.

"And then, he practically dragged me into the living room, supposedly to look at his statue collection. I couldn't see a thing from there, which I know was intentional. Jake said something about the truck arriving early with building materials for an addition to the kitchen."

Ross frowned. That was strange. Since when did building materials arrive in canvas-wrapped crates?

"How big were the crates?"

"Big," Lilah said definitely. "And wide. Maybe six

feet long, I'm not sure because I only got a glimpse through the back of the truck.''

"How many did you see?''

"At least four.''

"Did Wyatt say anything else about them?''

"Wait,'' she said, her eyes beginning to gleam. "You haven't heard the good part yet. He disappeared into the house, and I followed him.''

"You what?'' Ross had a feeling that he wasn't going to like what he was about to hear.

She grinned. "I followed him. He went down the hall to make a phone call. He sounded angry, so I listened in.''

Ross looked incredulously at her. He'd been right. He didn't like this one bit. He closed his eyes for a brief, pained moment, imagining what could have happened if Jake had caught Lilah sneaking around his house.

"And?'' he said, his voice strained.

She widened her eyes. "He wasn't just angry, he was furious. He said something about the truck being three days early, and called it sloppy. He threatened the person on the other end, and said that it had better never happen again, or that person was finished. Permanently.''

Ross's interest in what she was saying won out over his urge to shake her. "What else?''

"I had to run after that or he would have seen me,'' she said apologetically. "What do you think it was all about?''

That was a good question. It could be anything—stolen equipment, illegal pesticides, antiquities...or even construction materials, unlikely as it sounded. There was no way to know for sure, but if Lilah had seen something that Jake wanted to keep unseen, then this accident of timing could be dangerous.

"What happened when he came back?" Ross asked.

"He kept me inside, talking, until the truck was gone, and then we went back to the porch. I asked him a few questions about the kitchen plans."

"You pressed him on this?"

"I thought it would be interesting to hear what he said. He was extremely vague about the whole thing, I might add."

Ross didn't like the way this was developing. "Is there any reason at all for Jake to think that you were suspicious about that truck?"

She was quiet for a moment. "No," she said finally, as if she were sure. "I really don't think so."

"Good. Just the same, I think you should avoid him for a while, until we have a better idea of what's going on."

"I can't."

"Why not?"

"Because I said I'd come back to his house in a few days."

Ross looked sharply at her, not liking the feeling of being one step behind. She had scheduled another meeting with Wyatt? Lilah was taking to this "intrigue thing," as she called it, like a duck to water.

"I don't recall hearing this part of the story," he said coolly. "Why does Wyatt want to see you again?"

She hesitated, and Ross felt a finger of apprehension trailing up his back. Was there something she hadn't told him? Could Lilah, of all people, be keeping secrets?

"Why does he want to see you again?" he repeated. "What exactly have you two been discussing?"

"Well," she said, and took a deep breath. "There's something I didn't mention about the first conversation I had with Jake. He...er...made me an offer."

A cold knot formed in his stomach. "What kind of offer?"

"He said that when the property was taken over by the developers, he would make sure that I was given as much time at the site as I wanted."

"I see," Ross said tightly. "In exchange for what?"

Lilah looked nervously at him. "I don't know. I think he wants me to owe him. When I was over there today, he asked me to bring him some maps of your ranch." She paused, frowning. "Ross, I was going to tell you all of this."

"Were you? When? It sounds to me like you've been using Wyatt's offer as a backup plan, just in case you don't get your research permit."

"That's not true at all. I was—"

"Keeping all your options open?" he said coldly.

"No! If I were trying to play you against Jake, I wouldn't be telling you about it."

Ross just looked at her. It had been clear from the beginning that Lilah had her own agenda, but he'd let himself be blindsided anyway. How could he have been so naive? After all, why should she ally herself with him? The excavation was her first priority, and if she thought Jake Wyatt was in a position to give that to her...

"Taking Wyatt up on his offer would be a big mistake," he said. "Believe me. I guarantee that it'll be more trouble than any damned archaeological site is worth."

"Ross," Lilah stepped up to him, and put a hand on his arm. "Listen to me. Of course, Jake's offer would be tempting to someone in my position, but if I joined forces with him—"

"The hell you will," he snapped. "If you think I'm going to sit back and let you get involved with that bastard, you're wrong. You don't know Wyatt like I do. He'll hurt you, Lilah. Don't believe his promises. He doesn't care about anything but himself.''

''I know that,'' she said urgently. ''I'm trying to tell you that it's not an issue. I'm on your side, Ross, and that's not going to change, whatever happens to your ranch or my excavation.''

He searched her face and saw nothing but sincerity written there. It was hard to imagine that anyone could lie so convincingly. Was she telling him the truth? He was shaken by how much he wanted to believe her.

''I mean it,'' Lilah said. ''If it'll help convince you, I'll stay away from Jake. I'll just work at the site and let you take over this intrigue thing.''

Her eyes were wide and anxious, and her fingers tightened around his arm. ''Ross,'' she said. ''Trust me. Please.''

He took a deep breath. Looking at her, he had to admit that he did believe her. He didn't know why, because there wasn't one solid, secure reason for it, but the trust came from a place deep inside him, beyond logic or reason. It wasn't like him to take such a risk, but he did, hoping to God that he wasn't being a fool.

He lifted Lilah's hand, twining his fingers into hers. ''Why are you so determined to help me?'' he asked quietly.

She looked away. ''Lots of reasons.''

''What are they?''

''I told you already.''

''You told me that you think the reserve is a good thing, and that you like me. That doesn't stack up very high against your willingness to put yourself on the line for me.''

Lilah was starting to look uncomfortable. ''I just want to help,'' she mumbled. ''It's...it's like you said in the car, Ross, about your job. I don't want to hide away and not be involved, because I think this reserve is important.''

He nodded slowly, not satisfied. It was a strange explanation, but he let it stand for the moment.

''So,'' he said. ''Wyatt wants you to bring him maps. What's he going to do, start sketching his factory plans? He shouldn't be in such a hurry. He hasn't won a damn thing yet.''

But the confidence in Ross's voice was forced. Everything had been in a state of turmoil since Jake's announcement, and just as he had feared, support for the reserve project was wavering. Suddenly no one in Nairobi would give him a straight answer, and he had spent the entire morning on the phone, arguing with various bureaucrats.

He sighed, and reached up to rub the tense muscles at the base of his neck.

''Wait,'' Lilah said, watching him. ''Let me do that. Sit down.''

She stepped behind him, and began to attack the knots in his shoulders with warm and surprisingly strong hands.

''Don't worry,'' she said. ''Jake Wyatt won't win a damn thing. This is far from over.''

Ross leaned back, letting himself relax against her. Lilah's fingers seemed to be burning right into his skin, sending their fiery heat down deep inside him. He was grateful for the fire in her voice, as well. This wasn't her battle, but she had made it hers, and she was standing right beside him to help him fight it. It was more than he would have ever asked of her, and he didn't understand why she was doing it, but the sudden and powerful sense that he was not alone was an incredible relief.

''Lilah,'' he said, turning around so that she stood before him, "Don't take any more risks like you did today. It's not worth it."

"It is worth it," she argued, typically. "If I'd heard something about the money—"

"No," he said firmly, taking her by the waist and giving her a tiny shake. "Even the ranch is not worth having something happen to you. Promise me that you'll be more careful."

She began to look stubborn, and Ross wondered wearily if he was in for an argument.

"I was careful," she insisted.

"Sneaking around in Jake Wyatt's house to spy on him does not fit my definition of careful," he said. "I'm grateful, and impressed, but I don't want you to do it again."

"Yes, but I think we should find out what's in those crates," she said, sidestepping him. "Don't you think they might be important?"

"Important in general? Probably. Important to the issue of the ranch and the developers? Maybe, maybe not. Wyatt has a history of using illegal chemicals on his cattle. You could have seen a shipment of those arriving, or one of a hundred other shady things that he could be involved with. I'll find out what I can. Now, promise me that you'll be careful. No more risks."

"Okay, okay," she said grudgingly. "I promise. Satisfied?"

"Yes." Ross reached out and pulled her down into his lap. She came willingly, breaking into a grin, and linked her arms around his shoulders as he began to kiss her neck. Her skin was sweet and sun-warmed, and red on her nape.

"You have a sunburn," he murmured against her neck, touching the hot skin gently with his mouth. His breath must have tickled her, because he felt her shiver slightly as he spoke.

"I know," she said. "I can feel it. Is it bad?"

"Not very. What's happening at the site?"

"We're still working on the soil level we uncovered. New tools and bones keep turning up, and it's looking really good. I can't wait to get the potassium-argon dating results back."

As much as he intended to have a reasonable conversation with her, Ross was unable to keep from touching her with a series of kisses on her neck and jaw as she spoke. He curved his arm around her waist and pulled her even more snugly against him.

She was addictive, there was no doubt about it. He couldn't keep his damn hands off her, and her presence wove such a spell over him that he didn't even care. Fortunately, she had a little more presence of mind, and began to squirm slightly.

"Hey," she said weakly, with a little grin, then sighed as he pressed his mouth into the shadow between her breasts. "Hey. You can't just ask me questions, then do that...I can't think."

"Sorry." He forced himself to stop kissing, and sat up straight to look at her.

Lilah's cheeks were pink and her eyes were dancing as she returned the gaze, and her soft, happy expression warmed him. It was hard to imagine leaving her in only a few more weeks.

A sudden awareness of where his thoughts were headed hit him like a splash of cold water. He *was* leaving Kenya, and there was absolutely no question about it. What the hell was wrong with him?

"Ross? Are you all right?" Lilah's face furrowed with concern.

"I'm fine," he said immediately, but he knew that he wasn't. He had used the six-week time limit as an excuse to let down his guard, as if it were a talisman to keep him safely unattached. But the plan had spun around and reversed itself cruelly.

"Okay," she said, as the merest flicker of a hurt expression crossed her face. "It's just that you seem strange all of a sudden. Distant. I thought maybe you—"

"I'm fine," he repeated. What if he continued down the path he had cut, and stayed here because of her, opening himself to the vulnerability of loving her, changing his life to that degree...

No, it wasn't possible. He had to fight this feeling before it took him over completely.

Lilah's eyes were the color of savanna grasses in the late summer sun, and the beauty and clarity of them made his throat tighten as he looked at her.

"Are you still worried that I might be considering Jake's offer?" she said.

"No," Ross said. "Not at all. I'm just tired."

"You have a right to be tired," she said sympathetically, and reached up to caress the side of his face. "It's enough to have to deal with clearing out the office, and the house, and getting your father's affairs in order, without having this problem with the developers on top of it."

Ross smiled briefly. "I have a history of sink-or-swim living."

Her touch was hypnotic, and he had to resist the urge to lean his head into her hand. It was time to break this off, and set himself back on the track he had been on before Lilah stepped into his life. It was imperative that he do it now.

"Lilah..." he began raggedly, and the tension in his own voice surprised him. He couldn't remember ever feeling so torn. Every hard-won survival tactic in his body insisted that he tell her it was over, but something else, something deeper and more intuitive, shouted for him to be silent.

"What?" she said, looking at him, and as Ross gazed back at her, he couldn't speak. He couldn't do it, and it appalled him. He wanted her so much that he didn't care about anything but being with her now, and to hell with the future and whatever it held.

He took a deep breath. "I have to make some phone calls. Do you need a ride back to camp?"

"No, I brought one of the cars," she said, then stood up, obviously disturbed. "But you need to tell me what you want me to do about Jake."

"He wants you to meet with him again? At his house?"

"Right, with maps. Should I give them to him?"

"The maps aren't a problem, but I don't want you to go to his house again. It's not safe. Arrange to meet him somewhere public."

"Okay," she said. "Although I really don't think there would be any problem with going there. Nothing is going to happen to me, and it would be easier than—"

"No," Ross said definitely.

She shrugged. "It's your game. I'll send him a note and have him meet me next time I'm in Nairobi. Do you have any spare maps I can hand over? I need the ones I have down at the field site."

"That box is full of them," he said, pointing to a carton on the floor. "I'll go through it later this evening and dig out a few for you."

"No, you have enough to do. I can find them, if you don't mind me taking the box down to camp. I'll have time to rummage around in it before dinner."

Ross nodded. "Fine."

"Great." She picked up the carton, frowning at him over the top of it. "Well. I guess I'll see you later. Sometime. Bye."

She turned to go, and bumped the edge of the box awkwardly against the door frame.

"Wait." He stood up and strode over to her, lifting the box out of her arms. "I'll take this to the car for you. What are you doing tonight?"

She looked speculatively at him as they walked. "Why?"

Ross was tired of arguing with himself. "Because you have a standing invitation at Hotel Bradford. Will you come up when you've finished working?"

"I don't know," she hedged. "I have a lot to do. It'll be late by the time I'm done."

"Come late, then."

He loaded the box into the back of Lilah's car, then turned to her. She looked upset, and he knew that it was his fault. He lifted his hand to brush a tendril of hair out of her eyes.

She smiled slightly. "Are you sure you want me to come up? I know you're tired."

"I'm sure."

She hesitated. "What amenities do you offer? Heated pool?"

"Hot bath."

"Good enough. What else?"

"A very attentive hotel keeper."

"Mmm." She flicked her eyes up to meet his. "Sounds tempting. Okay, I'm convinced. I'll try not to be too late."

"Don't worry about that," he said. "I'll wait for you."

For as long as it takes.

Chapter 13

"What on earth are you doing?" Elliot asked, appearing in the doorway of Lilah's tent, and looking with bemusement at the piles of papers that she had stacked on her cot.

"Looking for maps," she said. "Is dinner ready?"

"That's why I'm here. To fetch you before you lose your place at the feeding trough. It's spaghetti tonight."

"Ah. Peter must be cooking again."

"How did you guess? And am I the only one to notice that he's so thin and pale, he actually looks like a noodle? They do say that you are what you eat."

"He's not so pale anymore."

"With that sunburn? Now he looks like he's been covered with tomato sauce. It all fits."

Lilah grinned. "Does this mean that after a few more nights of Peter's cooking, we'll turn into noodles, too?"

Elliot glanced down at his rounded waistline. "It could

only help me,'' he said. "Are you coming? Or should I save you a plate?"

"I'll be there in a minute." She had turned up one old map of the area, but if there were any more in the box, it wouldn't hurt to have them as well. And she was enjoying poking around in the old papers. There was a certain voyeuristic pleasure in going through a box of someone else's stuff, especially when that person was Ross. He was so confusing that any supplementary information was welcome.

Unfortunately, the contents of the box were mostly uninteresting, even to her. There was a jumble of old receipts, lined notebook pages with figures jotted down by Hugh, clippings of articles about cattle and ranch issues, and various postcards addressed to Claire from friends around the world.

Toward the bottom, though, something caught her eye. It was a dark red, leather-bound book, slim and flat, packed into the sea of loose papers. Lilah picked it up curiously, and opened into the middle of its gold-edged pages.

The page was dated April 20, 1969, and the delicate, loopy handwriting marked itself as that of a woman. Lilah let her eyes skim down the page, her gaze immediately catching a name. Jake.

Jake? There it was again.

...told Hugh I was going shopping in town, but actually spent the day at Jake's ranch...have to invent an excuse for the bracelet he gave me so that I can wear it at home...I think Hugh knows about us but doesn't care. He's busy with the ranch and I'm bored, as usual....

"Oh, my God," Lilah said, and slammed the book shut, her cheeks flaming as she realized exactly what she had found. This was Ross's mother's diary, and from peeking at only one page, she had suddenly learned far more about Claire Bradford than she had ever wanted to know.

She dropped the book, not even wanting to touch it, but it was too late to keep the few sentences she'd seen from etching themselves into her mind. Could Claire Bradford have been involved with Jake Wyatt? Unless there was another ranch-owning Jake around, the diary entry certainly made it sound as if he had been on Claire's list of affairs.

Ross had said that his mother's infidelities were common knowledge, but did he know about this particular affair? Lilah chewed her lip anxiously. What if he didn't know? How horrible for Ross to learn that his own mother had been sleeping with Jake Wyatt.

She shuddered, not wanting to be the one to tell him. She didn't even want to mention that she'd found the book in the first place. Tough as Ross might be, it had to be painful to read the details of your own mother's secret love life. Maybe she should just put the diary back in the box and pretend she'd never seen it.

"Lilah!" Denise's voice came clearly across camp and through the canvas wall of her tent. "Come eat! Or we'll fight over your share of the spaghetti!"

Lilah doubted that, but she was hungry nonetheless. She stood up, glaring down at the book on her bed. Why did Claire have to keep a stupid diary? Maybe Ross wouldn't want to read it, and it would go to its rest in the trash heap where it should have ended up in the first place.

"Lilah!"

"Coming!" she called, shooting the diary one last baleful look, then turned to dash out of the tent.

* * *

There was one light burning in the ranch house when Lilah drove up a little before midnight, and she looked at the faint yellow glow with a wry smile. Ross was probably doing his ever-present paperwork, or on the phone with New York, as the offices there began to open for the day.

The *askari* was walking across the front lawn as Lilah stepped out of her car. He was shadowy and hard to see in the darkness, but the shape of the rifle slung over one shoulder was clear.

She waved to him a little doubtfully, and was relieved when he waved back, apparently having been told to expect her.

Ross was in the library, working at the big rolltop desk, his profile illuminated by the pool of light from the little table lamp.

"Is this the reservation desk?" she said from the doorway. "I'd like to check in."

He must have seen her approach out of the corner of his eye, because he didn't seem startled as she spoke, but looked up and smiled, rubbing his eyes. "Hi."

"Hi. I was afraid that you might have gone to sleep."

"Would you have turned around and gone home if I had?"

"No...I would have stumbled around in the dark, broken a few valuable antiques, and eventually found you and crawled into bed with you. That would have taken your hotel rating down to three stars, though."

"Lucky I had enough work to keep me up."

Lilah came into the room and sat down on one of the leather chairs near his desk, her heart beating anxiously. "Ross," she said, "I need to talk to you about something."

He turned his chair to face her. "What?"

"I found something kind of unexpected in that box of papers I was searching through."

"Did you find the maps for Wyatt?"

"Yes, I have those. But I found something else."

He looked inquiringly at her.

"Um, maybe you saw it already? A book? Red, leather-bound?" she said hopefully. "Does that sound familiar?"

Ross shook his head, waiting for her to continue.

"Oh," she said unhappily. So, he didn't know about the diary. Great. Could that mean that he also didn't know about Claire's affair with Jake? "It...ah...belonged to your mother."

"Most of the things stored in the summerhouse did."

"Yes, well, this book seems to be her diary," she said, then added in a rush, "and I don't know if you want to read it or not, but I really don't think you should, because like you said yourself, the past is over, and there isn't much use in bringing it up again, especially in this case, because it probably isn't worth reading anyway. Right? Right. After all, the past is—"

"Over," Ross finished for her. "I believe you already said that."

"I did? Oh." Lilah watched him for any reaction to this news, but so far she saw none.

Ross was gazing at her thoughtfully. "I get the feeling that you have a reason for not wanting me to read this diary?"

"Well, not really," she said uncomfortably. "I just don't think it would be a good idea, that's all."

"Thank you. And the truth, please?"

Damn. She was going to have to tell him.

"I didn't read it," she said defensively. "I was just wondering what it was, so I opened it, and saw a few sentences. I just don't think that you should—"

"Lilah," Ross said softly, with an odd look in his eyes. "Are you trying to protect me from something?"

She looked at him mulishly, and didn't answer.

"Tell me what you read," he said. "Please."

She sighed. "Not much. But enough to get the feeling that your mother might have been involved with...Jake Wyatt. I could be wrong, of course."

Ross's brief smile was without humor. "No, you're probably right. I've suspected that for a long time. It's hard to ignore the gossip around here."

"Are you upset?"

He shrugged. "Not really. And I'm certainly not surprised, except that I didn't realize Claire's taste in men was quite so bad." He paused. "You really were worried that I'd be upset by this?"

Lilah stared at him, trying to read something in the cool mask of his face. He seemed to be taking it well, and she knew that she should be relieved, but something didn't seem quite right.

"I was very worried," she said. "Ever since I found that book this evening, I've been trying to figure out the best way to tell you about it. I thought you'd be crushed."

"I don't crush easily."

"I guess not," she said slowly. "I guess I forgot that I don't ever have to worry about hard-shelled Ross Bradford."

"Were you trying to protect me?"

"I didn't want you to be hurt by this."

"You don't need to worry," he said. "But I like the fact that you did. I can't remember the last time someone wanted to protect me."

"I'll bet," Lilah said. "You don't let anyone see you hurt, so why should anyone ever see a need to protect you?"

"You did, though. Why?"

"Because I'm not that easy to fool," she said. "I think there's more to you underneath the walls you let people see."

He laughed. "Don't let your archaeological instincts overwhelm you. There's no need to look for anything hidden in me."

"You won't let me anyway."

He frowned. "What's that supposed to mean?"

Lilah felt what might be the first twinges of upcoming heartbreak as she looked at him. "You seem so determined to keep yourself apart, to not let anyone get close to you. I wonder why."

"Common sense," he said. "I don't expect too much from anyone, and no one ever has to give me more than they want to."

"Oh," Lilah said. "I didn't realize it was so simple."

"It is," he said sharply. "I don't depend on anyone but myself. If everyone lived like that, there would be a lot fewer disappointed and bitter people in the world."

"And a lot more lonely and isolated ones."

He exhaled hard. "Lilah, what's the point of this?"

"The point is that I want to know you," she said. "And that gets tough when you refuse to talk about personal things."

"Things like what, exactly?"

"Your father, for a start. Why you didn't come home for fifteen years."

Ross's jaw tightened. "You really want to hear about that? It's a bad story, Lilah. My father believed in tradition and loyalty, and in his mind, I betrayed both of those principles when I refused to become a rancher. Rejecting the ranching life was rejecting the Bradford name, according to Hugh. He thought he had every right to cut me off.''

''Do you agree?''

''Hell, no. Loyalty is supposed to go both ways. But my father didn't...''

''Didn't what?''

Ross snorted. ''It's nothing. Otieno has been trying to convince me that my father was starting to change his views about all that. Softening in his old age, or something.''

''Do you think it might be true?''

''Who knows. I have a hard time imagining it, and it doesn't really matter anyway.''

''Maybe you just won't let it matter to you,'' she said. ''Because you're afraid of being hurt all over again. Maybe you've gotten into the habit of not letting other people matter to you, and that's why you sometimes seem so guarded, and so alone. You don't have to be, Ross. You—''

''Lilah.'' Ross reached out from where he sat to catch her hands and pull her firmly toward him. ''Stop. We're here together. Neither of us are alone now.''

But we are, and I think you know it, too, she wanted to say. But as she stood before him, he pushed aside the edge of her shirt, and began to trail kisses on the sensitive skin just above the waistband of her jeans.

The taut strength of his lean fingers on her hips, and the touch of his mouth on her skin began that spiraling feeling of desire that left her weak and aching for him. He moved his head lower, and the sensation of his lips pressing against her, between her legs, as his breath came hot and maddening through the rough denim, was more than she could stand.

''Oh, Ross,'' she groaned, crumpling down over him,

her knees suddenly weakening. Her face was buried in his hair, and as she bent down, Ross wrapped his arms around her and moved forward, out of his chair, back toward the soft leather couch.

He was rougher this time, holding her with a desperate hunger that made Lilah feel as if he were trying to seize something beyond her physical self, something which he seemed to feel was slipping away as inexorably as the minutes that passed.

It surprised, and even awed her, this passion with which he touched her, the urgency that radiated from him as they struggled out of their clothes, and the desire in his eyes as his kiss claimed her. His mouth was hot and demanding, and although Lilah responded eagerly, even her own reeling desire for Ross didn't seem to match the intensity of his need for her.

She lifted herself toward him, pressing up against him, and felt him pause.

"Wait," he said hoarsely. "This is too fast. You haven't—"

"It's okay," she whispered. "Don't wait."

With a groan, he gave in. Lilah gasped at the feel of him inside her, and at the roughness with which he was taking her; a savage melding of bodies that roused an answering fierceness within her.

One of Ross's legs hooked tightly around hers as his body suddenly stiffened. He threw back his head as his release came swiftly, with an untamed intensity that Lilah could feel exploding through him in waves.

She held him until he stirred, raising himself up on one elbow to look down at her. Lilah smiled up at him intimately, reaching up to slide her fingers over his chest, then saw that his eyes were troubled, and wondered why.

But he immediately drove any questions from her mind

as he reached down, his fingertips moving in a sensual sweep over her belly and the curve of her hip, to find her most sensitive spot.

Lilah closed her eyes and moaned softly as he began to stroke her, his fingers twined into her triangle of soft curls, moving in a slow, deliberate rhythm as she gasped and bit her lips, shifting her hips under his touch.

"I'm not going to leave you behind tonight," Ross said, and Lilah flicked her own desire-dazed eyes open for a brief glimpse of him watching her intently. What was it about his face that caught her attention? She couldn't think. The erotic pleasure was surging inside her, and the only thing she was clearly conscious of were his rough fingertips buried in her softness.

As his hands played her body, the sensations suddenly peaked and burst inside her with a wild, shuddering ecstasy.

She opened her eyes again as the tremors died away, leaving her weak and languid with warm satisfaction, and she snuggled up against him.

"That was wonderful," she said, kissing his shoulder.

"I'm glad," Ross said. He sounded pleased, but also...relieved? Lilah had the sudden feeling that he had been disturbed by his own feverish need for her. It seemed as if he could only relax once he had proved that he could reduce her to the same state of desperate desire, as if wanting her more than she wanted him felt too dangerous.

A small sigh escaped her. By carefully maintaining that balance of sexual need, Ross was still trying to protect himself.

"Lilah?" He looked inquiringly at her.

She gazed up at him, feeling close and far away at the same time. "I feel limp all over," she said.

"Are you tired?" He traced a finger down her cheek,

and the warm concern in his eyes made her heart ache. Ross was a man made of contradictions, and she loved him, which tangled her up into the heart of them.

"A little," she said, relaxing as he ran his fingers through her hair. "Let's not move for a while, though, okay?"

"All right."

They lay there for a few minutes, nestled into the warmth of each others' bodies, and Lilah thought sleepily that at the moment it was easy to forget her worries about their relationship and feel almost completely contented and at peace, curled up in Ross's strong arms.

"Ross," she murmured, "are you going to read that diary?"

He exhaled, and she felt his chest move against her back. "I haven't decided yet," he admitted. "There may be things in there that I should know."

"I doubt it," she said. "It's better to let stuff like that rest. I wish you wouldn't read it."

"Sweet Lilah," he said, pressing a kiss into the back of her neck. "Trying to protect me again."

She yawned. "Well," she said sleepily, "someone has to."

His lips curved into a smile that she could feel against her skin. "I'll think about what you said."

"But you'll do what you want to do anyway," Lilah said. "I know. Well, I'll bring the diary up next time I come. Or you can come down and get it any time but Saturday night. We're doing a group evening on the town in Nairobi."

"Sounds like fun."

"It's really just an excuse to get a break from camp cooking. Want to come?"

"I'd love to, but I'm having dinner with Otieno's family."

His hand was lazily stroking her hip as they talked, and Lilah began to feel a shivery sensation spreading through her body again, slowly and pleasantly awakening her sleepy limbs with the familiar warm current of desire.

She rolled over to press her front against his, gazing up at him with an expression that made interest flicker in his eyes.

"I thought you were tired," he said softly, gazing at her with a slightly amused, slightly wicked expression.

"Oh, not so tired that I couldn't be persuaded to stay up for a good reason," she said mischievously.

Ross grinned, and his strong arms tightened around her, letting her feel the stirring of his own body. "I think we could come up with one. We might even learn to do this without having an argument first."

Lilah felt her warm contentment waver. "Can we?" she said. "Arguments happen when two people want different things."

"But we don't. I want the same thing you do."

She looked sharply at him. "You do?"

"I thought you knew that already. I'm doing my damnedest to make it work, Lilah, and it's all because of you. You made me realize how important it is."

"I did?"

He nodded. "You're committed, and you don't give up. I respect that."

A flash of hope rocketed through her. "I'm committed because I care, Ross," she said, gripping his hand tightly. "This is a once-in-a-lifetime chance, and I want to make it work."

He nodded. "I agree. It won't be easy, but we can do

it. If we're lucky, we might even get it approved before your six weeks are up.''

She frowned, suddenly wary. ''What?''

''I've been pushing my government contacts to speed up the paperwork. I know you'll feel more secure once you have the permit in your hand.''

Lilah gave a choked laugh. ''Research permit,'' she said. ''Right.''

''That is what you want, isn't it?''

''Of course,'' she said. ''That's exactly it.''

''He was talking about the *research permit?*'' Denise said incredulously. It was the next morning, and Lilah was in the lab tent, watching her friend sketch a drawing of one of the stone tools. ''That man is obviously in denial. What did you say?''

''I said, 'Ross, you thick-headed, hard-hearted man, I wasn't talking about the research permit. I was talking about you. I'm in love with you and I want to know that in a few weeks you won't just wave goodbye and thank me for the memories.'''

Denise dropped her pencil. ''You did? Oh, you did not. What did you really say?''

Lilah gave a small, rueful grin. ''I really said something like 'Of course the research permit is what I want.'''

''Wimp.''

''I know. I was just so embarrassed. I can't believe that even for one minute, I thought he was talking about our relationship. How stupid am I?''

''Not stupid. Just a fool for love.''

''Thanks.''

''I think,'' Denise said, adjusting the light over her work, ''that you should tell him how you feel and see what happens.''

"Right, and watch him disappear in a cloud of dust. He has a wall around his heart, and it's pretty clear that I've been scraping up against it lately."

"Hmm. The tall, dark, aloof type. Will he let himself be made vulnerable by love? Or will he remain untouched, tragically guarding his wounded soul forever?"

"You're making this sound like a made-for-TV movie," Lilah said crossly. "I have a serious problem here."

"You sure do," Denise agreed. "But let me remind you. Time is running out. Go ahead, shake him up a little."

"Easy for you to say. I'm not sure how much shaking he can take." Lilah paused, frowning. "How strange. That just reminded me of something Elliot said, right after he met Ross."

"What?"

"He told me that in his opinion, Ross seemed unnaturally self-controlled. He said it made him nervous."

"So?"

"Well, Elliot was right. Ross tries to keep up these walls, and this tight control over his emotions, but it isn't natural for him, and it isn't working. There's this fierceness in him that keeps showing through. He seems like he's right on the edge...of something."

"What?"

"I don't know. But I think I'd like to find out."

Denise looked dryly at her. "Maybe that's why Elliot is nervous."

Chapter 14

The noon sun burned down over the savanna, washing the sea of green grass with dazzling light. It had been nearly two weeks since the last storm of the rainy season, and the land was beginning to dry and harden. Soon it would be summer, and the verdant grass would fade to a dusty gold, rustling softly against the red earth.

But he would be gone by then, Ross reminded himself, shifting the Land Rover into a lower gear to navigate the pitted road. By the time the water holes dried up and the sky turned to brilliant summer azure, he would be back at work on the Zaire project.

He sighed. Back on the firing line, back in the company of men. Fierce, dedicated men, who gave up the comforts of home and family for the heat and disease and political turmoil of the rain forest. Sacrifice on the altar of conservation. Was it really worth it?

He was disturbed to find that he didn't have a ready answer. The passion was still there, the belief in his work and the desire to make a difference, but there was a void at the core of it all, growing bigger all the time.

He glanced over at Lilah, in the passenger seat, her hair whipping in the breeze that streamed through the open window.

Her eyes sparkled with excitement. "So, where are we going?"

"It's a surprise," he said. "We'll be there soon."

"This beats my usual lunch break. Anything is better than an hour in the shade with a bunch of grouchy archaeologists who are as sick of peanut butter sandwiches as I am."

He grinned. "Tension at camp?"

"The usual. Nothing life-threatening." She shrugged, and settled back into her seat. "Ted and I have been disagreeing about everything, but that's old news."

"Is that why he glared at me when I came to get you? I had the feeling it was personal."

She laughed. "Oh, probably. He doesn't approve of you, you know. Calls you a conservation commando. It was meant as an insult, but it's the most creative thing I've heard him say in months."

"Ted seems to have a lot to say about me."

"I think he'd like me to…reconsider my involvement with you," Lilah said delicately. "He doesn't find you suitable."

"And how do you find me, Lilah?"

"Complicated," she said immediately, and a wistful expression crossed her face before she smiled. "But suitable."

Ross raised his eyebrows. He wasn't sure what answer he'd expected, but that hadn't been it. He should have known better than to ask leading questions.

"Ross," Lilah began.

"Yes?"

"I don't mean to imply that I don't trust you, but do you really know where you're going? For the past ten minutes you've been driving like you're lost or looking for something. What's happening?"

"I know where I'm going," he said. "I just don't know where it is."

She frowned. "Okay…"

"It moves," he explained, squinting toward the thicket of bushes and trees around the west watering hole. He could see the sparkle of blue water through the thorny tangle, and then suddenly, something else. "Aha."

Lilah stared at him. "Aha, what?"

"Hold on," he said, swinging the car off the dirt road and onto the thick savanna grass. Springs squeaked as the car jolted and bumped over the open plain.

"What are you doing?" she cried, grabbing the dashboard with both hands.

"You'll see in a minute. Right now, you're on hole patrol."

"Excuse me?"

"Watch the ground right in front of the car for aardvark holes, then tell me, so I can avoid them."

"*Aardvark* holes? Okay," she said doubtfully, trying to lean forward as she bounced in her seat. "There!"

"Where?" Ross asked, just as a front tire hit the depression and bounced with a crash and a neck-wrenching jolt.

He braked slightly. "It would help if you told me to swerve left or right."

"Well, I—hey! Left!"

Ross neatly avoided the next hazard, then slowed the car behind a small rise in the land. He shifted into first gear, and let the car creep slowly and quietly toward the top of the ridge.

"Ow," Lilah said, rubbing her neck. "How big is an aardvark anyway?"

"Big enough."

Ross killed the engine, and the animal sounds of the savanna floated in through the open windows of the car. The grove of trees was just below them, with the pond-size watering hole shimmering silver-blue in the center. Birds were nesting in the trees, chirping excitedly, and making periodic swoops through the air and down to the water.

"What are we—" Lilah began, and stopped as Ross touched her mouth with his fingers.

"Shh," he cautioned, trying to ignore the feel of her smooth, curved lips, and the stirring of desire that rose in him. There would be time for that later. Right now, he had something to show her. "On the far side," he murmured. "In the bushes. Do you see them?"

There was a flash of tawny color in the thick green tangle, and Ross heard Lilah's breath catch as the first lioness rose in a languid feline stretch. The cat gave a great yawn, turned and settled down again, nearly camouflaged by the screen of low-hanging bushes around her.

Lilah's eyes were wide with sudden comprehension as she turned to him. "Oh, Ross..."

"I just had a report from one of the herders that he'd spotted a male and three females in this area. I thought you might like to see them."

"How beautiful," she whispered.

The closest lioness raised her head and gazed around with only the mildest interest. The whole pride wasn't visible from their vantage point, but Ross was willing to bet that all the cats were down there, lounging in the shade of the trees.

"They came from the park," he said. "This is the first time I've seen lions so far into the ranch."

She smiled. "We'll make sure they get to stay."

Their eyes met for a moment, and Ross felt Lilah's warmth and optimism cover him like a healing balm. He was acting like a proud five-year-old, for God's sake, showing off the lions as if they were his very own, but the awe and pleasure on her face kept him from feeling foolish. And they were his lions, in a way. They were part of his dream, and having Lilah here to share it strengthened his flagging confidence.

"You don't mind that I brought you here?" he asked.

"Mind? No, this is wonderful. I wonder about myself, coming to a place like Kenya and spending all my time with my nose in the dirt. Some people might think I'm strange."

"I thought you liked the dirt."

"No, dirt is dirt, wherever you are. It's what pops out of it that I like. But lions..." She sighed. "They're right up there with stone tools. Wow."

"High praise."

She nodded, and moved over to nestle against his shoulder as they looked down at the sleeping lion. Ross slid his arm around her, holding her slim body against him, and bent his head to bury his face in her hair. She smelled familiar, sweet and comforting, and strands of her silky hair tickled his nose.

"Ross?"

"Hmm?"

"Why don't you ever ask me questions about my family or my background?"

He straightened, surprised. "Do you want me to ask?"

"Yes. It would tell me that you want to know me."

"I already know you."

"Do you?" Her voice was sad. "I wonder."

Ross frowned. Why the hell would he ask her personal questions? That was the last thing he wanted her to do, and he'd assumed that she would prefer the same courtesy.

"I grew up in the Chicago suburbs," she said suddenly, as if she'd just made a decision. "My parents still live there. My dad is a high-school teacher, and Mom is a librarian. I'm the first Ph.D. in my family."

She continued, and Ross didn't try to stop her. As she spoke, he grew unwillingly fascinated with the portrait of Lilah taking shape. He saw the quiet, tree-lined streets of her first home, saw her family, saw the childhood he'd always wanted for himself. Not idyllic, not perfect, but loving and safe and real through all the ups and downs of a normal life.

He felt a tightness in his throat as his mind moved back through his own past, before the resentful, troubled isolation of his adolescence, to the time before he'd left for boarding school, when he'd been living here at the ranch.

The memories felt stiff and bright, fresher than they should be for such old images, and Ross was shocked to realize why.

Over the past twenty years, through boarding school, and then through what he thought of as his exile, he'd kept those memories at a distance, unable to stand the pain of missing home.

Missing Otieno, Mama Ruth, the rolling savanna, the endless sky...even his parents, in an odd way. He'd rejected his home after his father had rejected him, but there was more here, so much more, and it belonged to him in a way so primal that it could never truly be renounced or forgotten.

Lilah had stopped speaking, and was watching him. "Are you okay?" she asked softly.

"I'm fine," he said, and looked away, staring out over the plains, struggling to get control of himself. The sudden intimacy surrounding them was both compelling and frightening, and Ross could feel himself tensing with the effort of resisting it.

He cleared his throat. "Tell me more."

"Are you sure you want me to?"

"Yes," he said quickly, wanting a distraction from the disturbing emotions welling up inside him. He wanted words, any words, to fill the air and give him something to focus on.

But Lilah managed to throw him off balance once again.

"Do you want to hear about my engagement?" she asked.

"Engagement?" Ross was feeling too ragged to control the shock of surprise and dismay that shot through him. "When? To who?"

"To another professor. His name was Jeff Ryan. We started dating two years ago, and he eventually proposed. I said yes, and I actually would have married him." She shook her head wryly.

Ross took a deep breath. "What happened?"

"He dumped me for a twenty-year-old in his senior seminar. He said that I cared too much about my work, and didn't pay enough attention to him.

"You know what?" she continued, when Ross didn't speak. "He was right. I was a workaholic. But I think that was my way of hiding from the fact that the relationship was a mistake. It's funny, but I only just figured that out. For the longest time, I thought I had loved him..."

She shrugged. "But I didn't. Not really. I finally know that for sure."

"How do you know?"

Lilah met his eyes. "Trust me," she said with quiet emphasis. "I know."

Chapter 15

It took Lilah a minute to notice that something about the camp looked odd. The archaeologists were returning from an early dinner in Nairobi, and even in the fuzzy, remaining evening light, she could tell that something was wrong.

The tent flaps, that was it. They were hanging open, unzipped from top to bottom, and Lilah was certain that she, at least, had zipped hers closed before they left a few hours ago.

She parked the car and got out, hurrying forward before anyone else realized what was going on. The open door of her tent gaped darkly at her. Frowning, she stepped inside.

"What...?"

Lilah froze in the doorway, staring around the small space. The floor of her tent was ankle deep in clothes, papers and the rest of her personal belongings, as well as the contents of the box from the Bradfords' summerhouse.

Her mattress had been picked up and dumped off her cot, and her duffel bags and suitcase were open and upside down on the floor, empty. It looked as if a cyclone had hit the tent.

She opened her mouth to say something—anything—and found that she couldn't speak. Almost automatically, she did a visual check of her things to see what was missing, fully expecting to discover that she had been robbed.

But, incredibly, the few valuables she had—her jewelry, a shortwave radio and a calculator—were all present. It was hard to tell in the mess, but nothing seemed to be missing.

An outraged exclamation from next door told Lilah that her tent wasn't the only one in this state.

She looked outside to see Ted burst out of his own tent.

He looked around wildly, and saw her standing there. "My tent…! What? How? Is your…?"

"Yes, mine, too. Are you missing anything?"

"How am I supposed to know? It's a disaster! My papers are all over the floor. The draft of my article for *American Antiquity* is scattered everywhere! What the hell happened?"

"I haven't got a clue."

"Well, I do!" Ted shouted. "We've been robbed! Tell that to Ross Bradford! Elliot! We've been robbed!"

He disappeared back into his tent and Lilah could hear the sounds of vigorous rummaging coming from inside.

"My watch! My watch is gone!" Ted's voice came, slightly muffled, through the canvas wall. "That watch was a gift! Ross Bradford is going to have to compensate me for this. He never told us that the ranch was unsafe. He should have warned us that this could happen. This is his fault!"

Elliot came up to Lilah, his face grim. "This is unbelievable. What are you missing?"

"Nothing, as far as I can tell," she said, wincing as Ted continued his diatribe. "You?"

"Maybe a little cash. I think I left some sitting on my table. Nothing worth the trouble of wrecking the place, though, that's for sure. What's Ted yelling about?"

"His watch is gone. He's upset."

There was sudden silence from inside Ted's tent.

"Ted?" called Elliot. "Was the watch valuable?"

There was no response from inside the tent.

"That's a real shame," Elliot said sympathetically. "I'm sorry about that. I have an extra watch I can lend you for now, at least."

"That won't be necessary," Ted said finally, stiffly. "Mine seems to be here after all. It's no wonder I didn't notice it, though, in this mess."

It suddenly occurred to Lilah that no one had checked the lab tent. An apprehensive chill began to curl up through her. If it was in a similar state, if artifacts, data and the valuable microscopes and computer were dumped to the ground in the same reckless way…

Just the idea made her stomach clench into a giant knot of anxiety.

Lilah ran across camp to the lab tent, and tore aside the loosely hanging flap. What she saw there made her want to drop to the ground and cry.

Boxes of artifacts had been overturned on the floor, and were now hopelessly mixed and jumbled into a giant mess of stone chips and bone fragments. Documents, blank forms and Denise's drawings all drifted around the tent, rustling in the slight breeze.

The microscopes were unharmed, and so was the little laptop computer, but anything that could have been opened or emptied had been, and Lilah knew that it would be days of work before everything could be put back into order.

"Oh, my God," someone said behind her, and Lilah turned to see Peter Lee staring past her into the tent. He had been working late every night, studying prehistoric blade-making techniques by fitting together hundreds of stone flakes and their original core rocks. It was slow, frustrating work harder than the most difficult jigsaw puzzle, and now all of his hard-won progress had been swept down to scatter on the floor.

Peter looked as if he was about to be sick, and faced with the chaos that was once their orderly lab tent, Lilah was choked by a hot rush of fury. She forced herself to take a few deep breaths, then gripped Peter's shoulder and walked him away from the tent.

"I can't believe it," he said, over and over. "I can't— why would someone do this?"

Lilah shook her head helplessly. The grad student wasn't the only one who wanted an answer to that question.

"And they didn't even *take* anything," Peter said angrily, as if a robbery at least would have explained the senseless wreckage. "Not a thing! The microscopes, the computer…it's all here! What was this for? Who hates us this much?"

Hate? It did seem like a hate crime, Lilah had to admit. Why else would the camp have been attacked so ruthlessly? But Lilah was equally mystified as to who they could have offended. There were the ranch workers who came down daily to help with the excavation, but they were good men who seemed pleased with the steady work and wages, and Lilah couldn't imagine any of them having a reason to be vindictive.

"What a night," Elliot said, coming up to them, taking in the grad student's gray face. "Pete, are you missing anything?"

"Data," the young man said darkly. "A thesis. Funding for another season of fieldwork. A reason to stay here. Other than that, no."

"Now, now," Elliot cautioned. "One step at a time. We'll work this out. Fieldwork is always full of... surprises, right?" He gave a weak smile.

"This is a little more surprising than I expected," Lilah said. "It's downright weird, Elliot. Why would someone trash the camp but not take anything?"

"Sabotage," Peter muttered. "Pointless vandalism."

"Maybe," Lilah said. "But it doesn't make sense. All the destruction was incidental. Aside from what was dropped or knocked over, nothing was damaged. Vandals would have broken things, smashed things. Whoever did this just emptied everything out, like they were looking for something."

"But what?" Peter asked.

"Valuable artifacts," Elliot speculated. "All sorts of rumors can get started about excavations. People think of King Tut when they think of archaeology. If someone came here looking for treasure, and all they saw were bone pieces and stone tools, they might have been angry enough to wreck the camp."

"So this could happen again?" Peter looked uneasy. "If someone else has the same idea."

"No," Elliot said. "We need to make sure the camp isn't left unguarded again. Those *askaris* that Ross mentioned earlier..." He looked at Lilah. "What do you think?"

"I think we have no choice," she said. "Let's get them down here. Tonight. We'll all feel safer with protection.

Elliot, would you mind driving up to the house and telling Ross what happened? I want to start putting the lab back together.'' Her head ached, and she felt too angry and exhausted to handle the added emotional weight of seeing Ross.

It was going to be a long night. As Elliot drove off toward the ranch house, Lilah returned to the lab tent, steeling herself to face the sickening mess there. Too many of the stone tools littering the floor had chipped or broken against each other as they fell. Others had lost their labels and become anonymous bits of stone without data to link them to their original positions at the site. It was a terrible, senseless waste, and as Lilah crawled around on her hands and knees, picking through the wreckage, she felt numb with rage at the thought of some stranger sweeping their hard work into a heap on the floor.

The students joined her to help, but the light mood from dinner was shattered. Everyone worked silently and methodically, lost in their own thoughts as they sorted through the jumbled sea of artifacts.

Lilah was sitting cross-legged on the floor, with her back to the door, sorting papers, when she heard a rustle of canvas behind her, and then felt a hand on her shoulder.

"Lilah," said Ross's deep voice, and she looked up to see him standing behind her. "Can you take a break?"

"A break? Why not," she said, frustration making her thump the pile of papers back down to the floor. "This certainly isn't going to get finished tonight."

Elliot was waiting for them outside the tent. "He wanted to see the damage for himself," he said, nodding to Ross.

"Well, there it is," Lilah said, waving her hand back toward the lab tent. "Feast your eyes on the destruction of a lot of hard work."

Ross reached up to rub a hand over his forehead. "I'm sorry. I should have been faster about arranging an *askari* for you—"

"Don't say that. You have enough to do. There was no reason to expect something like this."

"No," Ross said. "There wasn't. But a hell of a lot of unexpected things have been happening lately. I should have been better prepared."

"Whatever," Lilah said flatly. "It doesn't matter now."

"You're sure that there's nothing missing?"

"If so, nobody's noticed. All the valuables are here."

"And the excavation area wasn't damaged?"

"Not even touched. The tarps are all in place, undisturbed. But they certainly did a job on the tents, whoever they were."

He exhaled slowly. "This is very strange."

"Yeah, isn't it." Lilah's voice was bitter. "And I thought we had enough to deal with already. I wonder what else is headed our way."

She took a shaky breath, trying to ease the hot, tight feeling in her chest, and was caught by surprise as Ross put an arm around her shoulders. "Come on," he said. "Let's go for a walk."

At his touch, Lilah felt her choked-up emotions loosening suddenly, rising up inside her in a churning swell. She swallowed hard, feeling the pricking of tears behind her eyes, and silently allowed him to lead her out of camp, toward the road.

The sky was clear, and the chirping of the frogs in a pond nearby was a musical backdrop to the warm, starry darkness.

Ross was warm, too, and smelled faintly spicy, and as

they walked along the road, she slowly let herself relax against his side.

"I'm having a rotten night," she said finally, apologetically.

He nodded. "I know."

"What happened at camp...it makes no sense. I've gone over all kinds of possibilities in my mind—"

"Like what?"

"Crazy ideas. Drugs, data theft, government conspiracies, aliens..." She shrugged, with a half smile. "Nothing at all realistic. I just don't understand why anyone would have searched the camp. Or what they could have been looking for. Or even if they found it."

"Searched," Ross repeated. "That's interesting. So you think that whoever tore apart your tents was looking for something specific."

"Yes, don't you? That part seems clear. But who and why...I haven't got a clue."

"Whoever it was knew that your camp would be empty this evening."

"Right, but how? I know I told *you* about the trip the other night, but I certainly wouldn't have mentioned it to anyone else. I haven't even *seen* anyone else. I've been down here, working, and so has the rest of the group. The only way someone could have known that we'd be gone would be if..." She paused, not liking where her thoughts were taking her. "Ross, do you think someone could be watching our camp?"

It wasn't a pleasant idea. The night was dark under the sliver of moon, and the tangled vegetation along the road suddenly seemed deep and forbidding, thick with shadows and mystery.

"It wouldn't be very hard to eavesdrop on us," she added, her apprehension growing. It wasn't the first time this possibility had crossed her mind. She had also wondered about spies the other day at Jake Wyatt's house, when he had surprised her with his up-to-date knowledge of what was going on at the site. In the wake of the other drama of the day, she had forgotten all about it.

"You know," she said to Ross, "I didn't tell you about one strange thing that happened at Jake's. He congratulated me on the excavation."

"What was strange about that?"

"He meant the latest part. The tool cache we found. I still don't understand how he heard about it so quickly."

"Did you ask him how he knew?"

"Yes, but he didn't really answer me. Just said something enigmatic like 'I have my ways of knowing.' I can't remember exactly. Don't you think that's a little weird?"

"Not really. I know he has connections in the Park Bureau. Last week, before we went to Nairobi, I phoned a few people to discuss your research permit, so his sources there must have filled him in."

"Oh," Lilah said. "That does make more sense. I couldn't imagine a reason why Jake would care enough about our excavation to have someone spying on us." She smiled. "I told you that I was coming up with crazy ideas."

"It's not crazy," he said, releasing her to cross his arms against his chest. He stared down at the road as they walked. "Not any crazier than what's actually happening around here."

He shook his head slowly, grimly. "I don't like this," he said under his breath. "I don't like this at all."

"Do you think there's a connection between our camp being ransacked and the prowler at your house?"

"I don't know what to think," he said, stopping in his tracks and raising his hands. There was more frustration in his voice than Lilah had ever heard before. "I can't explain anything. I hate this constant feeling of being two steps behind. Every time I look one way, something hits from the other direction."

His hands had tightened into fists, and he looked down at them, frowning, then unclenched them slowly, returning them to his sides. "I am not used to this," he muttered.

"Feeling out of control?"

It was the wrong thing to say. Ross turned on her, his eyes fierce and his answer reflexively swift. "No! I'm simply surprised that a quick trip to tie up business in Kenya could turn out to be so goddamned complicated!"

There was no time for Lilah to react before he turned away, taking a deep breath.

"I don't know if the prowler is connected to the attack on your camp," he said flatly, not looking at her. "Or even if he's connected to the sale of the ranch, and you'd think I'd at least have figured *that* out by now. I don't know why your tents were searched, what the person was looking for, what the prowler was doing in my house, where Jake got all the money to back the factory project..."

Ross's voice was becoming less controlled as he spoke, and Lilah stared at him, astonished, watching his composure crack. Violent emotion seemed to be leaking from him, coloring the air with a dark mixture of anger and desperation that was terrible to see.

She responded instinctively, reaching out to comfort him. "Ross," she said, gripping his arm, "it'll be all right. Please, don't worry. I'm here, I'll help you. We can do this together. It's going to be okay."

Still holding him, she pressed a kiss into his shoulder, and felt his body stiffen. He looked down at her, his face suddenly distant and guarded, as if he'd just become conscious of how he appeared to her.

"Of course it'll work out," he said coolly. "I'll make sure of that."

Without you. The rebuff was clear. She'd gotten too close, and Ross had just flung up his walls so quickly that she'd practically grazed her nose on them. She let go of his arm and stepped back, suddenly resentful. Why was it so damned hard for this man to let go and simply talk about how he felt? Emotion only came out of him in a burst, against his will and to his regret, and she was losing patience.

"Oh, sorry," she said sharply. "Did I scare you by noticing that you were actually being honest about your feelings for a change?"

"What?" He frowned at her.

"You're so good at shoving people away when they get too close to knowing you. Do I really feel like such a threat?"

"This topic is sounding a little too familiar," he said. "Are we back to this again?"

There was a clear warning in his voice, but Lilah didn't care. "Yes," she said pointedly. "We are back to this. Bradford rule number one, which is never let yourself be vulnerable. Why not? What's so dangerous about showing me that you're worried and confused about everything that's been happening here?"

"Why is this an issue?"

"Because I'm tired of being shut out! Stop keeping me at arm's length. Talk to me."

Ross shook his head stonily. "If you're looking for someone to cry on your shoulder, I'm not your man, Lilah. Don't expect that from me, or you'll be very disappointed."

"Cry or don't cry, I don't care. All I want is for you to trust me enough to be honest with me!"

"What the hell are you talking about? I've never lied to you."

"Wrong. You lie every time you *feel* something and pretend you don't. You can't be honest about who you are, because you can't let yourself trust me. You have this idea that if you let me get close enough, I'll hurt you."

Ross exhaled hard, in a sound that was almost a growl. "Lilah, what is it you want from me?"

"Talk to me! I want you to tell me about the things that matter!"

"Which are what?"

"Everything! Your frustration with what's been happening here. Your fear that Jake Wyatt might get his factory. Things about your past, and your family. How you feel about your father's death, and this affair between your mother and Jake."

"I told you that the affair doesn't bother me," he said, raising his voice. He took another deep breath.

"Really? Or was that just another one of your stoic pretenses? I have no way of knowing. It really doesn't upset you to think about Jake and your mother, together, his hands on her—"

"Enough!" Ross burst out. "It was one of a hundred affairs! What the hell would have happened to me if I'd gotten upset about every single one?"

They stood staring at each other, their breathing rough in the suddenly silent darkness.

"So you didn't let yourself," Lilah said softly. "You closed off. And you did that when your father was always too busy with the ranch, and then you did it later when your mother died, and again when your father rejected you. You've spent your whole life defending your heart, but you don't have to do it anymore.''

Naked pain was written on Ross's face, and seeing it twisted Lilah's heart. Was she wrong to confront him like this? No, she had to make him listen, had to make him understand that these walls of his harmed him far more than they helped.

"Ross," she said. "Trust me. Don't spend your life with a shell around the core of you just to keep from getting hurt—"

"For God's sake," he exclaimed. "This is all I hear anymore. Between you and Otieno this topic is wearing thin. I would like to know what qualifies both of you to tell me how to live my life."

"Because," Lilah said, "you're convinced that you have to be alone, but I know it isn't true."

"No?"

"No! For a start, you have me."

"Do I?" he said wearily. "And why are you so concerned about me?"

"Because I love you!"

There was a moment of shocked silence as the echo of her impulsive confession hung in the air. It was too late to retract the words. Desperately, Lilah searched Ross's face for some hint of a reaction. He stood as if frozen, his expression betraying nothing.

She took a deep breath. "Ross," she repeated, her voice wavering only a little. "I love you."

Slowly, he seemed to hear her, the impact of her words breaking over him like a wave. "Oh, God, Lilah..." he said raggedly, and the raw emotion in his voice sent wild, vibrant hope bubbling up inside her. He loved her, he had to. Surely he was about to say so.

But he didn't continue, and the stillness became unbearable.

"I...I've been wanting to tell you—" Lilah stammered, trying to fill the void.

"Don't," he said. He took an uneven breath and said, "I'm going to be leaving here in three weeks."

It was as if he were reciting a pledge to himself, as if they both needed to hear it and be reminded.

Lilah took a stunned step backward, and Ross caught her arm. She twisted unsuccessfully in his grip. "Let go of me," she said in a choked voice.

"No. We need to talk about this."

"Talk? Why?" Her eyes stung with suppressed tears of humiliation and pain, and she blinked fiercely, willing them away. "You just said all that you needed to. This *affair* ends in a few weeks! Thanks for the reminder. I made the mistake of thinking of you in the long term."

"You don't understand."

"Oh, believe me, I understand perfectly. So you can spare me the speech about how you like me a lot but just don't want a relationship right now. I heard it before, and I should have listened. Is this what you really mean when you close off? Are you warning me not to expect too much, since I'm only a quick affair to you?"

Ross's fingers bit into her arm. "Stop," he ordered. "It's not like that at all."

Her face burned as she faced him. "I think it is, and you just can't stand to hear it said so plainly, because it embarrasses you. I'm good for a diversion while you're here. A little fun, a little sex, but God forbid I might actually start to care about you, because then you feel guilty that you don't care back. It's good to know where I stand, at least."

"Lilah, damn it, I...do care."

"Please. Don't try to make me feel better. I'll be fine. I've got plenty of work to do. I certainly won't waste any time being upset. After all, it's better that we cleared this up, right? It's good that we're being honest with each other."

"No," Ross said. "It's not good. It's more complicated than that."

"It's okay," she said tightly. "Really."

After all, he'd never lied to her about where he stood, and never promised her a thing. She'd known from the start that this was a short-term affair, due to end when they went their separate ways. She'd been ignoring her worries, pretending that fate would wave a magic wand and change everything to suit her. It hadn't happened, and now she needed to deal with it like an adult.

Her heart felt numb, frozen suddenly, and she knew that she would have to try to thaw it again little by little, or else the flood of misery might just overwhelm her.

"Don't worry about this," she said. "I'll still help you with Jake."

"To hell with Jake!" he exploded. "Do you think that makes any difference to me now?"

"Yes," said Lilah. Her little smile felt glued on, and her eyes were hot. "Of course it does. Look, Ross, you don't have to love me. This isn't an all-or-nothing situation. We're friends, and I'll help you. I just don't think we should...sleep together anymore. That complicates things on my end."

She drew a shuddery breath. Damn it, she'd been expecting this. Why was it still a thousand times more awful than she'd ever imagined? "I should go."

Ross reached up to rub a hand over his forehead as if he were trying to scrub away an ache. "No," he said roughly. "This isn't over. I want you to understand what's really happening here."

"I do. And of course it isn't over. I told you, we're friends. Telling you that I...care about you wouldn't mean much if I were ready to dump you the minute you didn't do everything my way, right?"

"That's not what I meant," he muttered.

Lilah could feel the pain inside her swell, threatening to explode in a hot torrent of tears, and she didn't think that she could stand to let this conversation drag out any longer.

"I have to go," she said desperately. "There's so much to do.... We can talk about this some other time, okay?"

She turned and began to walk, moving as fast as she could without running, back down the road toward camp. Ross quickly caught up with her.

"I want to talk about this now," he said, catching her arm again.

"I don't," she said, and kept walking.

He held on. "Lilah, wait."

She began to pull away, then they both stopped, surprised as Ted appeared on the road below them.

"There you are," he said, hurrying up to them. "Lilah, Elliot said that you have a disk copy of the stone tool data? I need it to check the numbers on the pieces we're putting back in order."

"I'll get it for you," Lilah said immediately, but Ross kept hold of her arm.

Ted, for the first time noticing the tension hovering thickly around them, looked suspiciously at Ross. "Is everything all right here?"

"Everything is fine," Ross growled. "Lilah will be there soon."

Ted scowled. "I need that disk now. We're *busy*. I have to check the artifacts, and then I have to record the—"

"Soon," Ross repeated dangerously. "Go back to camp and wait."

Ted fidgeted, flicking his eyes to Lilah. "Will you hurry?" he appealed. "I need—"

"I'm coming now," she said, turning to Ross. He met her eyes, and she forced herself to hold his gaze. "Let me go, Ross."

Slowly, he released her, and she stepped away.

"Bye," she said with difficulty, not trusting her voice to add anything else.

He didn't answer, only watched, his face dark and still, as she and Ted turned back toward camp.

Getting out of Ross's immediate presence helped a little. Lilah felt numb all over, and the shell-shocked, frozen sensation scared her. The pain lurked, dark and turbulent, inside her, but it seemed to hover on the edges of her consciousness, as if something kept it from surging up to overwhelm her.

The rest of the evening moved by in a blur, but she must have functioned reasonably well, because aside from a few odd and concerned looks, no one bothered her. She went back to work in the lab tent, and managed to finish sorting the pile of papers into their original folders by midnight, when everyone else started to yawn and wander toward bed.

Lilah wasn't tired. The idea of going to her small cot and lying there alone in the dark, prey to all of the thoughts and feelings which would inevitably come in a rush, made her think that maybe she would rather get started on sorting the bone pieces back into some kind of order.

She was sitting alone in the tiny pool of lamplight when Elliot poked his head in through the tent flap.

"Still up?" he said. "Go to bed, Lilah. Don't take too much of this cleaning onto your own shoulders. We'll all work on it tomorrow."

"I don't mind," she said in a low voice. "I'm not tired."

He frowned and stepped into the tent. "Are you feeling all right? You seem distracted tonight. Denise went to bed early with a stomachache. I hope we didn't eat anything bad at dinner."

"No, I feel healthy enough."

"Something else bothering you then?" He fixed her with a keen eye under shaggy brows. "You don't seem like yourself."

Lilah opened her mouth, then closed it again. "I'm okay," she said quietly. "See you tomorrow, Elliot."

When he had gone, Lilah half listened as the sounds of camp died away. She heard the rustle of the wind moving through the acacia trees and the soft footsteps of the new *askari* as he walked his slow beat around the edge of camp.

The intermittent animal sounds in the night seemed eerie and distant, and Lilah suddenly felt utterly alone as she sat there in the lab tent, shadows hovering at the edges of her circle of cold light.

She took a deep, experimental breath, feeling it shudder through her lungs.

I will be fine. She took another breath. *I will be fine.*

She didn't feel fine. The frozen misery inside her began to thaw and swell, churning and rising until she felt that it was breaking over her head, drowning her in icy-hot waves.

Ross knew that she loved him, but he didn't love her.

The only thing left to do was to get over him, and she was terrified that she wouldn't be able to. She had seen this coming from the very beginning, and had ignored it, but it was finally time to stop fooling herself.

Very quietly, she put her head down on the table and cried.

Chapter 16

The constant horn blasts of Nairobi's afternoon traffic came bouncing up to Ross's open office window, and were blown right inside with the airstream from the ancient fan whirring away there. The stacks of papers on the desk flapped and rustled in the mechanical breeze, adding their noise to that of the traffic, the fan and the banging of the construction crew who were renovating the offices two floors below.

Ross might not have noticed any of this on a better day, but he had started the morning with a fierce headache and a foul mood, both of which had steadily worsened as the day wore on.

Today was not actually as bad as yesterday, or the day before that, when he had been unable to stare at his work for more than five minutes before he found himself lost in a mental replay of what had happened with Lilah.

Her face haunted him, along with the memory of the

rush of joy he'd felt when she'd shocked him by admitting that she loved him.

But that happiness faltered and fell before the awareness of what this all meant, of what he had done. She had wanted to hear him echo that love back to her, and she deserved to hear it, but he just couldn't bring himself to say the words.

Loving Lilah would mean a negation of the security he had spent his life developing; it meant losing the strength of knowing that he needed only himself. Loving her would twist his soul and heart and life into hers. That was far too much power to trust anyone else with.

She accused him of keeping her at a distance, but the truth was, he had already allowed her to get far too close. Now the future without her looked gray and lifeless, and he knew, angrily, that he was feeling the consequences of his own recklessness.

There was a knock on the office door, and Ross looked up irritably. Maya, his father's longtime secretary, was only in a few days a week now that the ranch was no longer doing business, but unfortunately, this was not one of her workdays. Ross didn't feel like dealing with visitors today, and wished that she was there to send them away.

The knock came again, and he growled, "Come in!" just as the door began to open.

Dr. Elliot Morris cautiously poked in his head. Seeing Ross, the man broke into a smile. "Well, then, I am in the right place. I had the number, but the door wasn't marked."

"I took down the sign last week," Ross said shortly, wondering why Elliot was here to bother him.

Elliot nodded absently, looking around. "Ah. Of course. Moving out, I see."

"Right. Can I do something for you, Dr. Morris?"

"Oh, no, not really," Elliot said genially. "I'm just here to pick up the mail. This is where I get it, right? Lilah said—"

"This is the place," Ross confirmed, and pointed to a metal box by the door. "In there. I haven't sorted it yet."

"No matter. I can do that." Elliot began to shuffle through the pile of letters in the box, tossing a few to the side. "There should be several days' worth in here. No one has picked it up since Lilah did, last week."

Ross wished that Elliot would just go away and leave him alone. Why did the man have to insert Lilah's name into every damn sentence he spoke?

But Elliot was feeling chatty. "Did you hear about the results of the potassium-argon dating of the site? Lilah's guess about the age was right on track. It's about four hundred thousand years old, give or take a chunk of time on either side, of course. Pretty neat, don't you think?"

"Quite."

"You really ought to come by and see the excavation. You'd be amazed at the amount we've taken out of the hillside."

"I'm sure," Ross said, and sighed. Elliot was not going to go away, so perhaps he should attempt to be polite.

Halfheartedly, he asked, "Is your camp back together now?"

"More or less. We've been working hard, especially Lilah." Elliot shook his head, marveling. "I knew she was determined to make this excavation a success, but I've never seen anyone so dedicated. These past few days she's been up at the crack of dawn, and she barely takes two breaks for meals between then and midnight." He frowned. "I wonder if perhaps she's working a little too hard, though."

"What do you mean?"

"Well," Elliot said, "I'm sure it's nothing, but she just doesn't look good lately. She's tense, and has dark circles under her eyes. I don't think she's getting enough sleep, and she's very quiet most of the time. I hope she's not getting sick. Does that sound like any tropical disease you know of?"

"Hard to say," Ross muttered. How interesting, that Elliot had worked this news so casually into the conversation. He looked sharply at the other man, but Elliot's face was as bland as a baby's.

"I'm probably overreacting," Elliot said. "I always worry about Lilah. She's been putting her energy into this excavation for a long time. My wife Mary Beth and I keep trying to lure her out of the library by setting up dinner dates at our house. We invite nice young men over, but so far, nothing has worked out."

"I'm sure that's not for lack of interest," Ross said with a chill in his voice, instantly disliking the whole category of "nice young men" interested in Lilah.

"Men's interest?" Elliot snorted. "No. Lilah's the one with the lack of interest. She doesn't get attached easily, you know."

"Oh?"

"It's self-protection," Elliot said authoritatively. "She's so fiercely loyal that when she falls in love, she does it with her whole heart. So think how bad it would be if she devoted herself to the wrong person. That piece of pond scum she called a fiancé is a perfect example. We all hated him, but she would have followed him to the ends of the earth. Until he broke her heart, that is. I suppose you know all about that."

Ross nodded shortly.

"She's a lot wiser now," Elliot said. "I think that only

one thing could get Lilah to fall in love again...." He trailed off provocatively.

Ross couldn't help himself. "What?"

"A grand passion," the other man said solemnly. "Someone who she loves so much that she'll risk opening herself up again. Someone who she knows she'll love forever."

Ross's guts felt as though they were knotting and twisting inside him. Could that be true? When Lilah had said that she loved him, could she have meant this all-encompassing love that Elliot was describing? It didn't seem possible. It was hard to even imagine a love so strong.

And how could he, of all people, ever be that "grand passion" for Lilah? How could he ever accept or deserve devotion like that? That kind of love demanded marriage, children, shared dreams, a storybook future that could crumble in a hundred soul-shattering ways.

"I'm sure she'll find the right person someday," Ross said tightly, although the idea of anyone else being the object of Lilah's love made him feel physically sick.

"Oh, I think so, too," Elliot said cheerfully. "I'll certainly keep doing my best to help. It's the least I can do for a friend."

Ross didn't answer.

"I should be getting back to camp," Elliot said, scooping up the pile of mail he had sorted out. "Really, do come down and see the site one of these days."

He dropped the mail into his bag, then suddenly raised his bushy eyebrows. "I almost forgot. Lilah asked me to give this to you. She said you wanted it."

He pulled out a flat red book and handed it to Ross.

Claire's diary. Ross took the book with some distaste.

The binding was cool and smooth under his fingers, like the skin of a snake.

"Thank you," he said, and set the book on a chair. He didn't feel like handling it now, and still hadn't decided whether or not to read it.

"You bet. Thank you for the mail. See you later."

Something was nagging at Ross, but it was something he couldn't quite put a finger on.

"Elliot," he said abruptly, startling himself as the words came out. "You're married."

Elliot looked surprised. "Yes. Thirty-five years this September."

"Married, as in to love until death do you part, in sickness and health...all of that."

"Well, yes." Elliot looked puzzled. "That's generally the way it goes."

"But it doesn't go that way," Ross said. "People can't keep commitments like that. It's more like love until you get in my way. Love until I have something better to do."

"Well, I don't know about that," Elliot said doubtfully. "I suppose it all depends on how hard you both try. Commitment isn't easy. Marriage is no blissful happily-ever-after."

"Exactly," Ross said bitterly, remembering his parents, possible contenders for the "World's Worst Marriage" title.

"But," Elliot said, holding up one hand, "that doesn't mean it can't be done, and done in a way to make you proud of the years behind you and happy about the years ahead. Mary Beth and I both believe in our relationship."

"Aren't you worried that she might stop feeling that way?"

Elliot considered. "I suppose there's always that danger."

"But you seem to think the risk is worth it."

"Of course. There's always a risk, but should I let that keep me from working for something I believe in?"

"Damn," Ross muttered, surprised by a wave of déjà vu.

This sounded just like his discussion with Lilah that day as they drove to Nairobi, but then they had been talking about his conservation work in Central Africa, and *he* had been the one arguing for risk-taking and bravery in the face of being hurt.

"After all," Elliot said gently, "what could be more precious and worthwhile than the relationships we build with people we love?"

Ross could feel Elliot's eyes on him, and when he looked up, he thought he saw quiet sympathy in the other man's gaze.

"Nothing," Elliot said firmly, answering his own question. "Nothing else matters so much. How we love is who we are. Some people take an entire lifetime to figure that out, and by then it's too late."

He checked his watch, and gave Ross a brief wave. "I'll see you when you come down to visit us," he said, and closed the office door behind himself.

Ross stared, dumbstruck, at the space Elliot had just occupied, memories of another conversation forming in his mind.

Otieno, speaking of Hugh, had said, "…at the end of a life, it is not land or business which truly matters, but *umoja* that can make one man understand who he is."

Umoja. Unity. Hugh had chosen to give himself to the ranch rather than to his family. Was he one of the people Elliot described, who had learned the value of emotional ties too late?

Otieno would say so.

And what about himself? It was a strange, unstable feeling to turn the focus around to his own life, and Ross suddenly didn't like what he saw. He had, like his father, built a life centered on his work. He was, as his father had been, alone. Did that mean that he, too, would realize one day that he had made terrible mistakes as he shaped his life?

He pushed back the chair and stood up, running his palms over the smooth wood of the desktop. He could see the glimmer of his reflection on the polished mahogany surface. The desk, once cluttered with the miscellany of his father's life, was clean for the first time in years.

Ross felt the symbolism keenly. His own soul felt chaotic, crammed with fragments of memories and emotions. Somewhere in the clutter was the pale gleam of his own underlying self, and it felt imperative that he uncover it soon.

"Denise?"

"Mmm?"

Lilah pushed aside the canvas flap and peered into the dim interior of her friend's tent. "How are you feeling?"

"Don't ask."

"I guess that means you don't want any lunch?"

"Lunch?" Denise rolled over on her cot and groaned. "I remember lunch. We don't get along well. The last time I ran into lunch it ran out of me."

"Ugh."

"Yeah, no kidding. The bug has me bad."

"Can I get you anything?"

"No, I'll be fine. Eventually. This is my punishment for being the only one in my Mexico tour group who didn't get Montezuma's revenge. I gloated, and now I'm paying for it. How's it going down at the site?"

It was lunch break, and Lilah had come up to check on Denise, who had been sick since the night they all had gone to Nairobi.

"It's going well," she said. "You heard the results of the potassium-argon dating?"

"Lilah, that's old news. I heard about it days ago."

"Oh. Sorry."

Denise raised her head to peer at Lilah. "You know," she said, "you seem really out of it lately. Am I just sick and crazy or is there something wrong?"

"No, nothing's wrong."

Denise was too sick to notice that Lilah's wan voice belied her words. "Good. So, how's Ross?"

"I haven't seen him," Lilah said. "I really should go. You need to sleep."

"Sleep," her friend grumbled. "That's all I've been doing. I feel like hell. A few more days of this and I'll have Frankenstein and Godzilla fighting over who gets to marry me."

Lilah smiled. "I'd better get back to work—"

"Don't," Denise said suddenly. "Take the afternoon off."

"Why?"

"So you can go see Ross. Work isn't the only important thing in life. Carpe diem, Lilah, remember? Seize the day. Don't get cold feet now, girl. We don't have that much time left."

Carpe diem, indeed. Denise's inspirational mottoes only worked in the short term, Lilah had to admit. She had been sitting in the Land Rover for fifteen minutes, keys in the ignition, trying to find the courage to drive up to the ranch house.

Was it stupidity or masochism that made her ache to

go find Ross? Her mind had been tormenting her with replays of their last encounter, his awful, telling silence in the wake of her confession of love. But the worst part, more agonizing even than those memories of pain and humiliation, was the simple fact that she missed him desperately. In spite of his not loving her, in spite of his rejection, having him suddenly vanish from her life was like losing a chunk of her soul.

Maybe she could just go up to say hello, to show him with a confident smile that she was doing fine, thank you. Let him think that she had already moved on; that her passionate declaration of love had been more a result of that night's emotional overload than of any deep, lasting feelings. Maybe, if she could at least recover her pride, she could bury the heart-pain deep inside herself until it slowly healed over. It was the best thing to do.

But her resolve had deserted her again by the time she arrived at the ranch house. She knocked on the front door, her heart in her throat and her carefully confident smile cracking at the edges. Maybe Ross wouldn't even be home, and she could turn around and pretend that she had never—

"Lilah?"

His voice came from behind her, and just the sound of it made her quiver. She turned slowly, stretching her tight smile.

He had come around the side of the house, car keys dangling from his hand. If he was surprised to see her, he didn't show it.

"Were you looking for me? I was out back."

"Hi," she said in a rush. "I brought your box. You know, the one with all the papers that I took down to camp? I thought you might want it back, so I just stopped by. It's in the car. I'll get it."

"Wait." Ross moved forward, blocking her path to the car, and Lilah gulped. Yes, this had been a bad idea. Seeing him made her want to scream, to cry, to throw herself at him and demand that he love her. Her own desperation frightened her.

"You came to bring me the box," he said. "I see."

She nodded. "And...and I wanted to say hello. See how you were. It's been a little while, and I just wondered..."

"I'm fine," he said quietly, looking at her with unreadable eyes. "How are you?"

He didn't look fine, Lilah thought. He looked exhausted, as if only ragged willpower and momentum were keeping him on his feet.

His gaze burned hot on her face as he waited for an answer.

"Me?" she said. "Oh, great. Fine. We've been working hard down at the site. You...should come by sometime."

"Yes, I've been hearing that I should," he said, with a strange half smile.

She swallowed hard. "I...noticed that you've been staying away, and I hope it's not...because of me."

"It is," he said. "I thought it would be better that way."

Lilah stiffened. "What's that supposed to mean? I know I came on a little strong the other night, but you certainly don't have to worry about it happening again."

Ross frowned, and Lilah bit her lip. This wasn't going well at all. "I'm sorry," she said. "I didn't come up here to pick a fight. Mostly I wanted to remind you that we have unfinished business together. Jake Wyatt is still waiting for those maps."

He measured her with a look. "I didn't forget. But I

didn't expect you to want to help me anymore, considering what happened between us.''

"Then you haven't been listening to me. Ross, I tried to tell you that I don't put conditions on friendship. Of course I still want to help you. I care about you. Whatever else happened is beside the point.''

"I see.''

"Do you?'' Lilah could feel frustration welling up in her. "I don't think so. You have this don't-touch-me detachment that won't let you believe me. I get hung without a trial, because you won't even give me a chance to prove that I won't disappoint you or hurt you.''

Ross didn't answer, so Lilah jammed her hands in her pockets and stared at the ground, misery sitting like a swollen lump in her chest.

Why had she come here? What had she expected anyway? The man didn't love her, and here she was again, practically begging for something she couldn't have.

"Let's get that box,'' she said, moving forward to step around him. But Ross moved, too, intercepting her, and she found herself chest-to-chest with him.

He stared down into her eyes as if trying to see into her soul, and Lilah met his gaze, her insides curling and dying with longing for him. She knew every inch of his face by now, and the familiarity of it tore her heart.

"Ross...'' she whispered. "Why can't you just let yourself trust me?''

Pain flashed rawly across his face, and his hands rose haltingly, then dropped before he touched her. He closed his eyes, drawing an uneven breath.

"Why?'' she demanded. "What more can I do?''

He opened his eyes, and she was shocked by how old they suddenly seemed, full of a loneliness that she wouldn't wish on anyone.

"This is what I don't understand," he said slowly. "All along, I never promised you anything. I took everything you offered me, and gave you damn little in return. I hurt you. But here you are, telling me that you care about me, that you want to *help* me. I don't deserve this. I didn't ask for this. Lilah, what the hell are you doing here?"

It took her a minute to find her voice. "How can you even ask me that?" she said finally.

"After everything that's happened, you came back to find me, instead of writing me off. Why haven't you given up? Why do you still want to help me? Don't you see that I'm offering you nothing?"

"Oh, I see that very clearly," she said in a choked voice, and suddenly, the cotton-wool feeling in her throat gave way and tears flooded her eyes. She sobbed as she faced him, and felt something else break loose within her. It was too much to stand there, loving this man, wanting him, facing down his demons again and again.

Lilah launched herself at him, seized two fistfuls of his shirt, and shook him, feeling buttons and cloth give way under the force of her anger and frustration.

"Damn you, Ross Bradford!" she shouted into his stunned face. "You're too much of a coward to see what's right in front of you! What did you think I meant when I told you that I love you?"

Chapter 17

The Land Rover jolted over the rough road as Lilah hurtled back toward camp, cursing Ross, cursing herself, trying to replace anguish with rage.

How could she have been such a fool? Ross Bradford wasn't capable of falling in love, and indulging stupid romantic fantasies about him was the worst thing she could do to herself. *No more,* she vowed. No more hoping, no more longing, no more thinking. There was only one way to get through this, one way to keep herself sane and functioning, and that was action.

After work tomorrow, she was going to take those maps to Jake Wyatt. That would give Ross something to mull over. He could spurn her love if he wanted to, but even in the face of rejection, Lilah Evans still kept her promises. So there, Ross, she thought fiercely. That should throw you and your stubborn, cynical world view into a tailspin. Maybe someday you'll wake up and understand what it means to be in love, but by then I'll be long gone and you'll be alone, wondering what you missed.

Unfortunately, Jake wasn't at home when Lilah arrived the next day. There was no answer when she knocked, and even from the porch, she could sense the stillness of an empty house.

She squinted into the distance, listening for the sound of an engine, but the silence of the savanna was broken only by the faint cries of birds. Heat waves rippled the air over the empty road, and not far away, Jake's mysterious storage building shimmered like a mirage.

Storage building...

What a convenient accident of timing, Lilah thought with rising excitement. Here she was, all alone, with no one but the birds to notice if she just happened to take a peek in there to get a closer look at those crates of "building materials" Jake had had delivered. Ross might think that they weren't worth investigating, but he hadn't been the one to see the look on Jake's face that day. There was something strange going on, Lilah was sure of it, and this was her chance to prove it.

On closer inspection, the storage building turned out to be an ugly, utilitarian structure of gray cinder block. Two padlocked garage doors were the only entrances, unless one counted the row of narrow ventilation windows just below the roof, twelve feet from the ground.

Lilah pulled the Land Rover around to the far side, and killed the engine. Scrambling quickly over the warm hood, she climbed onto the car's roof and rose unsteadily to her feet, her fingers scraping against the rough concrete wall.

The windows were encrusted with dirt and cobwebs, and rusted into their metal frames. Lilah squinted through one, reaching up to try to rub away some of the grime, then gasped as the entire plate of glass pushed away from the crumbling metal to fall inside with a crash.

She froze, panicking, as if the sound of breaking glass would bring Jake running.

But aside from the steady, gentle hiss of the breeze, everything was quiet and still under the afternoon sun. Lilah took a deep breath, and poked her head through the open space where the window had been.

The building was dim and musty, and streaks of afternoon sunlight cut through the haze of dust in the air, illuminating the shapes of stored equipment piled along the concrete walls. Directly below her was a workbench, cluttered with tools and scraps of wood. Three rusty bicycles leaned up against the bench, and a wooden rocking chair with a shredded seat gathered cobwebs in the corner.

What she didn't see was even one large wooden crate.

Frowning, Lilah leaned farther in, trying to see to the back of the long building. But everything there was shadowy and indistinct. She needed a closer look.

The window was tight, and she gripped the slight overhang of the roof as she eased herself through, grateful for her jeans as the rusty metal frame scraped against her legs. It wasn't much of a drop to the workbench below, and suddenly she was inside, kicked-up dust tickling her nose.

As her eyes adjusted to the dim light, she saw that the back of the building was filled with construction supplies: boards, bricks and bags of cement stacked against the far wall. The clutter was considerable, and if she hadn't been looking for them, she never would have noticed the hulking canvas-draped forms hidden in the shadows behind a bin of scrap lumber.

The crates! Adrenaline raced through her, and she

rubbed her damp palms on her jeans. Now, to find out what was inside.

She pulled off the canvas, and discovered a sheet of paper attached to the top crate. It was a carbon copy of a shipping document, decorated with official-looking stamps and signatures. The smudged script was almost illegible, but she was able to decipher a few words: *school furnishings* and *St. Luke's Mission, Meru District.*

School furnishings? A Catholic mission? Lilah's skin began to prickle. This was getting stranger by the minute, and she would have bet money that it wasn't textbooks and chalk that Jake Wyatt had locked up in his storage building.

There was only one way to find out. She retrieved a screwdriver from the workbench, and eyed the rough wood. There was no subtle way to open the crate. It would have to be all or nothing.

She wedged the screwdriver blade under the first slat. The wood snapped off with a crack that made her jump, and she tossed it aside. If only it weren't so dark in here! She could see something pale inside the crate.

Lilah pried off another slat, looked again, and gasped.

The blunt tip of a milky-white tusk jutted out at her, its luminous length widening as it curved back into the shadows of the long box. The crate was full of tusks, gleaming faintly at her in the dim light.

Ivory. Jake was smuggling ivory. Of course.

"My God," she whispered. Judging from the size and number of the tusks, the four crates had to hold more than a thousand pounds of the stuff. She calculated quickly, remembering Ross's remark that black-market ivory sold for several hundred dollars a pound, then sucked in an awed breath. There was almost a million dollars' worth of ivory here. No wonder Jake had been tense.

The seriousness of her discovery came crashing over Lilah like a wave, and her sense of adventure suddenly fled, leaving her cold, scared and fighting a rising feeling of panic. This was not a game, and it never had been, in spite of her jokes to Ross about espionage and spies. The flat blue ruthlessness in Jake's eyes, the chill that she had sensed from the beginning...all were warnings that the man was far more dangerous than she or Ross had ever guessed.

She forced herself to calm down and breathe evenly. A report of what she had found would not be enough. She'd carried her cheap handheld camera in with her, and she only hoped that the tiny flash would be bright enough to get a few clear pictures. She stuffed the forged shipping document into her jeans pocket and paused, hands shaking, just long enough to click away the roll of film. Fear was burning through her, rushing her as she turned to go. There was no time to waste. That broken-out window was a clear sign that someone had been in here, and she didn't even want to imagine what Jake might do if he caught her here now.

The phone on Ross's desk shrilled, insistent in the quiet office. It was late afternoon, and the construction crews downstairs had quit for the day, giving him welcome relief from the incessant banging and sawing noises that had been echoing up through the floor.

The phone rang again, and he put down his pen to reach for it.

"Yes?"

Silence.

"Hello," he said impatiently, and there was a quick, sharp click on the other end.

Ross frowned and replaced the receiver. He focused

back on his work, trying to recapture his train of thought, but the brief interruption made him aware of the ache in his back from sitting in the creaky chair all day.

He pushed back from the desk, stood up, and stretched, walking over to the window.

Yesterday's encounter with Lilah had left him reeling, and spending last night alone at the ranch house had made things worse. He hadn't been able to sleep, so he had wandered through the dark rooms, lost among real and imagined shadows.

Lilah's face lingered in his mind, taunting him with how much he missed her. God, how he missed her. Last night, he'd felt an old, familiar ache spreading through him, hollowing him out from the center. He recognized it, helplessly, feeling as if a forgotten enemy from a long time past had suddenly tapped him on the shoulder and waved.

The air around him was cold and empty. He was alone, and he was lonely. Desperately, screamingly lonely, and last night he had wanted to pound his fists on the pillow with frustration. He'd thought he was beyond that, but now he wondered if the feeling had been there all along, quietly gathering strength.

He took a deep breath, and turned his face to the sunlight.

There was a flash of red on the chair by the window, and he focused on it. Claire's diary. He had, perhaps intentionally, forgotten about it. He picked up the book, fingering the leather binding thoughtfully.

The phone rang again, and he dropped the book back onto the chair. ''Yes?''

Again, silence.

''Oh, for God's sake,'' Ross said into the receiver. Was the line malfunctioning? They had frequent problems with the telephone system, but he would swear that he was connected to someone. He could almost, barely, hear the caller breathing over the normal background hiss of the line.

"This is Ross Bradford," he said irritably. "Can I do something for you? If not, then stop tying up my damned phone."

He didn't expect an answer, so it was a shock when he got one.

Ross had moved the receiver away from his ear, about to hang up again, when a low, muffled voice floated out of it.

"I can do something for you."

He snatched the phone back, his fingers tightening around it. "What did you say?"

"I can help you."

The voice was soft, but male, with a Kenyan accent, and the words were almost lost in the static on the line.

"What makes you think I need help?"

"I can tell you something about Jake Wyatt."

"Fine," Ross said. "Tell me."

"Not like this. I must meet you."

"Meet me? Why? Who are you?"

There was only silence and static on the line, but Ross could tell that his strange caller was still there.

"What do you want?" he asked, more gently. This was probably a dead end, but just in case...

"I want to help you. I have something important to show you."

"All right. Come to my office tomorrow morning, and we'll—"

"No!" The voice was suddenly urgent. "I must meet you right now. It is very important."

Ross frowned. "Where are you?"

"I will come there. Wait for me."

With a click, the caller hung up.

Ross put the receiver down hard. "What the hell is going on?" he muttered. He was supposed to sit here, waiting for this mysterious caller to appear with his mysterious information?

He picked up the phone again and dialed. Otieno was also in town today, closing out the last of the ranch's accounts with local suppliers.

"This is a day for strange things," Otieno said, after hearing Ross's account of the odd phone call. "I'll come there. It's not safe."

"No, I can handle it. What did you mean, 'this is a day for strange things?' Have you heard from your cousin Joseph?"

Wyatt had been scheduled for another government meeting that afternoon, and Ross was anxious to get a report on what had happened.

"Yes, I spoke with him. He was asked to leave the meeting."

"What?"

"Jake Wyatt refused to discuss the project with Joseph in the room."

Ross sat forward in his chair, stunned. "Just Joseph? No other aide?"

"Jake Wyatt pointed to him and said, 'You. Out.' The other aides stayed for the meeting."

"That's crazy!" Ross said. "He knows that Joseph's been talking to us?"

"It seems so."

"How? How could he have known that? Joseph is only a distant cousin of yours, and we haven't discussed this with anyone. This is bad, Otieno. Wyatt may be smart and influential, but he's not psychic, for God's sake."

This wasn't the first time Wyatt had pulled an uncanny move. Ross could remember Lilah's amazement that he had known about the latest development in her excavation. What had Jake told her? "I have my ways of knowing" or something like that.

Something was tugging at the back of Ross's mind, and he was determined to pin it down.

"I'll talk to you tonight," he said to Otieno, and hung up.

There were too many bizarre coincidences piling up. The ransacking of the archaeologists' camp, that was another one. Someone had known that the camp would be empty that night.

Lilah had been positive that he was the only one who had known about their group's trip to Nairobi. Ross even remembered the night she had mentioned it. It was when she'd come up to the house, late, and found him in the library. She had been sitting on the chair, and he had been at his desk.

His desk? Wait. He had been on the phone, at the desk, when he called the Park Bureau to set up a meeting to discuss Lilah's research permit. Jake had known about the new discovery immediately afterward.

And Jake had known about Otieno's cousin, not *before* last week's meeting, which Joseph had attended without a problem, but later, *after* Ross and Otieno had discussed him in that room.

The prowler, the faint tracks beside his desk—Ross had assumed that the man had run away before he did his intended job, but in truth, he had done it.

"Damn it!" Ross said violently, slamming his hands down on the scattered papers. How could he have missed this? There was a bug in his desk, a tiny wireless microphone transmitting to a recorder hidden nearby on the ranch. The prowler had probably been back and forth many times, switching tapes.

What else did Jake Wyatt know? Ross frantically tried to remember any other conversations he had had in that room, and managed to pull up only an ominous sense that Wyatt had heard far, far too much.

Lilah. A cold rush of fear grabbed him, sharp as a knife in his heart. Jake would know now that she had been lying to him. Enough had been said and done in that room to make the deception very clear. If she went to his house, not knowing that he knew everything…

There wasn't time to think about what could happen. He had to find her and warn her before it was too late.

Lilah leaned against the table in the lab tent and made herself take a slow, deep breath.

She was back in camp, and she was safe, so she had to calm down and figure out what to do. An itchy, crawling feeling, as if hostile eyes were burning into her, had turned her flight from Jake's ranch into a mad escape just on the edge of panic.

She had driven straight to Ross's house, only to find it empty, with the only phone for miles locked inside. Ross was still in Nairobi, and even the *askari* was nowhere to be seen, so Lilah had come down to camp to find a safe place to hide the film and the document.

The others were still down at the site, so camp was deserted except for the birds chirping in the trees, and Lilah fidgeted as the camera's noisy little motor finished rewinding the film.

Even if Jake discovered the opened crates and got rid of the ivory, her pictures and the shipping document should be enough to bring him down for good. A roll of film and a piece of paper had suddenly become worth the cost of the Bradford ranch. If she sealed them in a plastic bag, she could hide them outside in the tall grass—

"Hello, Lilah."

The voice behind her was as cold and sharp as a razor blade.

Lilah gasped, and turned to see Jake Wyatt framed by the doorway of the lab tent.

"Jake," she said unsteadily, and attempted a smile. "I didn't hear you coming. You surprised me."

"Really." He stepped into the tent, and the ice-cold blue of his eyes glowed out at her. "That shouldn't have happened. You told me you were always careful."

She couldn't read a thing on his face, and it scared her. "You must want those maps," she said. "They're in the car. I'll—"

"No. I want your camera. Give it to me."

Lilah stared at him, losing hope that this visit could be a coincidence. *He knew.* She couldn't give up those pictures! They were her only proof of his guilt.

Jake snapped his fingers. "Now."

She had to stall. Her friends would be coming up from the site soon. "M-my camera?" she said weakly, still holding it. "Why?"

A dark flash of anger twisted Jake's face, and he stepped closer to her, holding out his hand. "Do you think that I'm stupid?" he said in a low voice. "This game is over. Give me the bloody camera or I'll take it from you."

Lilah froze as the gray metal of a gun suddenly gleamed in his hand. Jake motioned to the camera, and she silently handed it to him.

"Thank you." He snapped open the back and pulled out the roll of film. "Did you find anything interesting in my storage building, Lilah? You left in a hurry."

She shook her head, and he laughed.

"There's a liar hiding behind your pretty face. You found my white gold."

With a jerk of his hand, Jake began to expose the film. "So," he said, as it fell to the floor in loops. "You thought that you'd snap a few photos and ruin me? Wrong. You're a beginner. I've been in business longer than you've been alive."

The end of the roll dropped onto the canvas floor, and Jake kicked it away. "I don't like beginners wasting my time, and I don't like pretty liars!" He threw the empty camera down, smashing it against the ground, and beckoned. "Let's go."

"Where?" Terror glazed her voice. Was he planning to kill her? She had to keep him here until someone came. It couldn't be long now.

"We're going to Ross's house."

"W-we can't. Ross is there." *Please, someone, hurry.*

"No, he isn't. He's at the office and he won't be back any time soon. One of my men just called and dropped him a little bait, so it'll be an hour before he realizes that he's been stood up. Until then, he'll be waiting in his office while I get what I want from his house."

"There'll be an *askari*."

"Not anymore. He's been removed from duty. Now walk, or I'll carry you."

Jake reached out and grabbed the front of her shirt, jerking her forward. She stumbled, and he stepped beside her, his fingers digging into her arm. "Move."

When they arrived at the ranch house, one of the windows had been broken in, and the front door was unlocked.

"Now," Jake said. "Find me the book."

Lilah looked blankly at him. "What book?"

"The diary," he snapped. "I know you gave it to Ross, because it's not at your camp. Where is it? I don't want to waste my time tearing this house apart."

"I don't know," she said automatically, trying to understand what she was hearing. Jake was the one behind the devastation at their camp, and all because he'd wanted Claire Bradford's diary? She was secretly pleased she'd had it in her backpack that evening.

"Lies!" Jake's voice cracked sharply in the quiet house. "You gave it to Ross, so it's here, and we're going to find it.

"Start looking through those shelves," he said, shoving her roughly toward them. "And remember, I'm right next to you, so you won't be going anywhere. The sooner you find me that book, the better for you."

Lilah stumbled forward toward the cluttered shelves, and made a show of searching through them while she desperately tried to think. The gun hovered in her peripheral vision, glinting menacingly in the low light.

"I don't know what Ross did with the book," she said. "What if I can't find it?"

"I wouldn't think about that if I were you," Jake said coldly. "Plan to find it. It's here somewhere."

"Why do you want it so badly?"

"That diary is a loose end. I didn't even know the bloody woman kept one, until you turned it up. She knew all about my ivory business, and I'm not taking any chances on whether she wrote about it, too."

"It's not here," Lilah said, facing him.

"Fine." Jake stepped forward and prodded her with the hard barrel of the gun. "We'll search Ross's room. Move."

Chapter 18

The archaeologists were sitting around the fire when Ross jerked his car to a stop at the edge of camp and jumped out. His first feeling was of relief at the normal dinner scene in front of him, but a moment later he realized that Lilah wasn't there.

"Hi, Ross," said Elliot. "Want some spaghetti?"

"Where's Lilah?"

Elliot blinked, surprised, and Ted began to glare. Ross ignored them both. "Is she here?"

"No, she's been gone since four."

"Where?" Ross's hands clenched into fists at his sides.

Elliot frowned. "She said she had some business to take care of...at someone's house? Mr...White?"

"Wyatt," Denise interrupted. "She went to Jake Wyatt's, but—"

Cold fear clenched Ross's stomach, and before Denise finished her sentence, he was running for the car. He pulled open the door of the Land Rover, and was about to jump in when he heard the slap of feet behind him.

Denise had dashed after him, and she grabbed the edge of the window, breathing hard, and looking faintly green. "Ross, wait! Where are you going?"

"To find Lilah." Ross started the car.

"Do you need help? I'll come."

"No. Stay here in case she comes back."

The Land Rover's strong diesel engine roared as he pulled fast out of camp, with a vague impression of Denise standing at the bottom of the road, staring wide-eyed after him.

Every instinct in Ross's body screamed for him to drive straight to Wyatt's house and demand to know where Lilah was, but he knew that it would be dangerous and useless to go unprepared. He needed to get to the phone in his house and call the police, and he needed his rifle, because he sure as hell wasn't going to sit around waiting for the police to arrive.

There was a strange truck parked outside the ranch house. As soon as he'd seen it, Ross had left his car by the side of the road and approached the house on foot.

He moved quietly up the lawn, only to find the new *askari* sprawled facedown in the grass, all of his weapons missing except for his *rungu,* the short wooden club tied to his belt.

"Damn it," Ross muttered, kneeling down. The man had an ugly bruise on the side of his head, but he was alive, his pulse and breathing steady.

He took the club from the fallen *askari,* and stepped through the open front door, a prowler in his own house. The living room was deserted, but he could hear a voice at the far end of the hall.

Wyatt. There was no mistaking that snarl. What the hell was he doing here? And where was Lilah? Ross moved carefully down the hall. The door to his room was open, and through the space, he could see Wyatt's back.

"...where he'd have put it," Wyatt was saying, anger hardening his words. "Go through those boxes. No, damn it, do it fast. Dump them out."

Ross ducked into the adjoining bathroom, and leaned out carefully, watching as Wyatt flashed a handgun. "Hurry up!"

"I am hurrying," said a new voice. Ross inhaled sharply, a shock of relief coursing through him. Lilah! What had started out as a detour had been the very path he wanted. Thank God she was all right...for now.

"What if it's not here?" Lilah said. "What are you going to do?" There was an edge to her voice. She sounded tired, scared and mad as hell.

"Shut up, and don't ask me stupid questions."

"Everyone knows that I went to see you today. They'll know it was you who—"

"They won't know anything. You came to my ranch, and left. Any trouble you ran into after that has nothing to do with me. I'm completely clear."

"The ivory—"

"Will be on its way in a matter of hours. If anyone comes to ask me questions, that shipment will be long gone. You've got nothing, Lilah."

Ivory! Ross recoiled, shocked, as the events of the past few weeks suddenly snapped into place. Of course. The money for the factory. The mysterious crates. Jake's access to and use of high-tech eavesdropping devices. It was out of place for an average rancher, but it fit the portrait of a well-connected ivory dealer.

"If I find the diary, will you let me go?" Lilah asked.

"You said yourself that I have nothing. It's true, there's no evidence now. I can't do anything to you."

Wyatt wouldn't care, Ross thought grimly. He would shoot Lilah without a second thought. *So help me God, if he hurts her, I'll kill him myself.*

He weighed the club in his hand. It was heavy and solid, but no use against a gun. His only other weapon was surprise, and everything would depend on his ability to get quietly into position behind Wyatt before the man knew he was there. It was the only chance he had, and Lilah's life depended on it.

He held his breath, and stepped forward.

"You've been looking in there long enough," Wyatt snapped. "You're stalling. Get up."

"I'm not done," Lilah said, and gasped as Jake stepped forward quickly and grabbed her, his fingers knotting roughly in her hair.

"You'd better hope that I'm feeling kind when you find me that book," Wyatt said through his teeth, "because otherwise…"

Slowly. Ross choked back violent fury as Wyatt threw Lilah toward the desk. Quietly, he moved through the doorway.

At that moment, Lilah looked up through the hair that had fallen loosely around her face and saw him step silently behind Jake. She choked back a gasp, and ducked her head again.

"What?" Jake said, standing alert. "What was that?"

Ross froze. He was too far into the room to back out unnoticed. And if he went forward, Jake would turn and fire before—

"It's here!" Lilah cried. "The diary! I found it!" She began to shuffle papers wildly.

"Give it to me." Jake stepped forward. "Where is it?"

"I just saw it," Lilah said frantically. "Right here. Wait, it's right here."

Jake leaned down over her. "There's no diary there! What the hell do you think you're doing?"

He cuffed her hard across the face. "I'm warning you, you bitch, don't try to—what?"

The wooden floorboards creaked as Ross stepped quickly behind him.

Jake straightened fast, realizing what was happening, but he was seconds too late. He began to turn, and Ross brought the club crashing down on his arm.

"Bloody hell!" Jake screamed, his arm going limp. The gun cracked loudly, discharging into the wall, and dropped out of his fingers. Out of the corner of his eye, Ross saw Lilah scrambling to grab it as he drew back his arm and hit Jake with enough force to send them both sprawling onto the floor.

Ross landed hard on top of Jake, who used his good arm to backfist Ross's head with a blow that burst around him in a spray of light. He heard Lilah shriek as if from a distance, but the haze faded as he gritted his teeth and grabbed Jake, who was still half pinned under him.

"I should have killed you years ago, you bloody bastard," Jake gasped, twisting, and reaching up for Ross's neck. His thick hand closed on it, and Ross felt Jake's heavy fingers digging into his skin, squeezing hard against his windpipe.

Lilah was yelling something, but Ross was only conscious of Jake's rage-twisted face below him as he drew back his arm.

"Too late," Ross said through his teeth. "You lose."

The punch exploded through his fist with all the pent-up force in his body, and Jake grunted and collapsed back onto the floor, where he lay motionless.

"Ross, get away!" Lilah shouted. "I've got him covered!"

He looked up to see her standing over them, holding the gun, her hands shaking as she pointed it. She stared down at Jake's unconscious body, then turned to Ross.

"On second thought," she said, "he doesn't look like he's going anywhere."

Ross smiled. His face was beginning to throb and swell where Jake had hit him, and he still felt hazy from the blow, but seeing her standing there was all that mattered.

He reached out, gently, and took the gun from her, clicking on the safety. "Are you all right?"

She exhaled unsteadily. "I think so. Thanks to you." Her hazel eyes met his, and he could see wariness and vulnerability struggling on her face.

"Good." Ross stared at her, suddenly at a loss for words. She had been haunting his thoughts, and suddenly being faced with the warm, vibrant reality of her made his voice seize up. There were a hundred things he wanted to say, and they all rose at once inside him, jamming his throat.

She stepped toward him and reached up to touch his face delicately, her fingers tracing the outline of what he knew was going to be a dramatic bruise. "Are *you* all right?"

"I'm fine," he said quickly, instinctively.

"As always." Her eyes were wistful.

Ross swallowed hard. "Actually," he said. "I...my face hurts."

Lilah tilted her head, looking curiously at him. "I'll bet," she said. "I'll find you some ice just as soon as we call the police."

She began to step back, but he caught her waist. "Wait."

"What?"

"I'm not fine at all."

"What's wrong?" she asked softly.

"Everything. I haven't been fine for days. God, Lilah, I've been so damned—"

Lilah's fingers suddenly tightened on his arm and she turned her head sharply, glancing around with wide, worried eyes. A second later, Ross heard it too—the sound of a car pulling up outside the house. He tensed, and moved quickly toward the window, just as a female voice echoed down the hall.

"Ross? Ross? Are you here? Oh, my God, Otieno, the door is wide open, and look at this window. I knew something weird was going on. Ross, where are you?"

Lilah relaxed visibly, and shot him a half-apologetic, half-relieved look. "It's Denise," she said. "Come on."

Denise was charging down the hallway, followed closely by Otieno, and there was nearly a collision in the doorway as Lilah stepped out of the room toward them.

"Lilah!" Denise cried joyfully, seizing her. "You're okay! Ross was so worried that I got scared, so I went out to look for you just in case you were out hiking. Otieno picked me up on the road, and when I told him everything, he drove us straight up here. What's happening? Why is Ross looking at me like that?"

Ross blinked, realizing that he was glaring at Denise, and silently turned his gaze toward the inert form on the floor.

Denise frowned. "Did I interrupt some—yikes, who's that?"

"That's Jake Wyatt," Lilah said. "He smuggles ivory. Somebody needs to call the police."

"I will," Ross said gruffly. The moment was definitely ruined, but it hadn't been the best choice of moments for what he wanted to say. There would be time for that soon. Very soon. He picked up the phone and began to dial.

"To a long excavation!" Elliot said, raising his glass. The group around the campfire cheered, and toasted.

"And shorter work hours," Denise added.

"I'll drink to that," Lilah said, attempting to clink her plastic cup against Denise's, and getting more of a dull thud.

It didn't matter. She had spent most of the day in meetings with officials from the Park Bureau and the Department of Wildlife, being formally thanked for her role in the arrest of Jake Wyatt.

"To luck," she said, grinning at Elliot. As the Minister of Wildlife had been shaking her hand that morning, she had taken a deep breath and tactfully mentioned her small problem with the excavation. Within an hour, she had a signed and stamped research permit giving her team un-limited access to the Bradford site. Yes, things were work-ing out beautifully.

Except regarding Ross. Lilah was trying not to think about him, but she couldn't help it. The way he had looked at her after he'd saved her from Jake still made her heart jump to remember it. And he had seemed dif-ferent, urgent, as if he had something important to say.

But from the moment Otieno and Denise had appeared, things had been frantic and crazy, and she hadn't had a chance to do more than glance his way after the police arrived. There had been too much to explain, too many questions to answer, and after they found the ivory, she had been taken into town to do the whole thing over again officially.

Ross had seized her arm at one point, startling her in

the middle of a circle of policemen, and she looked at him hopefully, her heart in her throat.

"We need to talk," he said. "Soon."

She smiled uncertainly. That could mean anything. "Okay."

"I'll find you."

And then the police had whisked her off to Jake Wyatt's ranch, Ross had disappeared into the chaos of it all, and she hadn't seen him since.

She sighed, and Elliot glanced at her, lifting the champagne bottle. "Want a refill?"

"No, thanks."

Ross probably just wanted to say that he'd be leaving soon, now that the ranch situation was resolved. Now that there was nothing to keep him here. Lilah bit her lip.

"Seen Ross today?" Elliot asked.

Lilah shook her head, and he frowned. "Hmm. Well, he probably has a lot to do. And you were gone most of the day. I'm sure he'll come by."

"Sure."

Denise moved next to them, and crouched down to grab a bag of pretzels sitting nearby. She put a hand on Lilah's shoulder, leaned in close, and said, "So, have you seen Ross?"

"No," Lilah said.

"Oh," her friend said uncomfortably. "Gee. I thought you…well, anyway, I'm sure he's just—"

"Busy." Lilah said. "Right."

"Oh dear. Well. Look, if he's going to be a jerk, then to heck with him. You don't need the kind of guy who just waltzes in and out of…" She paused. "I'm not helping, am I."

Lilah squeezed her hand. "It's okay. I'm happy about

the excavation, and that's what we came here for in the first place, right?''

"Right." Denise didn't look pleased.

"I think I'm going to go for a walk," Lilah said, standing up.

Denise stood up too. "Do you want company?"

"No, I'll be fine. I'm just going to go wander around in the canyon and look at rocks. The usual thing."

"Well, be careful. Look what happened the last time I thought you'd just gone for a walk."

Lilah passed the excavation site and wandered along the canyon floor, instinctively sweeping her eyes across the jumbled mass of stones.

She had to make herself take her own words to heart. The site was what she had come here for, and now she had it. That was what mattered, right? She sighed. Wrong. She sure felt lousy for someone whose plan had worked out so well.

The thought of putting on a happy face as Ross headed back to work and out of her life forever raised a swollen lump of agony that pushed up against her chest until she thought she would suffocate. She couldn't do it. If he came down here to say goodbye, she was going to turn and run. Let him be shocked and angry. It was too much to ask of her.

A stone caught her eye. Lilah instinctively crouched down to get it, but it was only a water-smoothed pebble slightly lighter than the chert she wanted. She cradled it in her palm for a moment, then pitched it aimlessly to the side.

"What did you find?" called a familiar voice behind her.

Lilah blinked, but to her credit, she didn't fall over this

time. Her heart began to beat faster, and she stood up slowly, turning.

Ross was hurrying along the canyon toward her. He was wearing a business suit, the tie only barely loosened around his neck, and he carried a coffee mug, very carefully, in one hand.

She smiled hesitantly. "Haven't we done this before? Now I'm supposed to say something rude, aren't I?"

"Go ahead."

"I can't think of anything," she confessed. "Sorry. How's your face?"

Ross grinned. "Sore. But you should see the other guy. He's in jail."

"And likely to stay there for a long time?"

"No doubt. Kenya isn't kind to ivory dealers. And the officials who were siding with Wyatt are now pretty damn angry with him. It turns out that he intended to use this factory as a cover to help him expand his ivory business."

"So that's why he wanted it so badly."

"Right. It would have been perfect. Trucks going in and out all the time, constant activity right next door. A complete camouflage for his own shipments. He wasn't stupid."

"Just unlucky."

"And up against the formidable Dr. Lilah Evans."

Lilah blushed. "Not so formidable in the end. I should have learned my lesson the first time I trespassed. Never again, I swear. Thank you for saving me."

"No," Ross said, with a look that made her knees feel weak. "Thank *you* for saving *me*."

"Then the ranch is definitely safe? No more industrial threats?"

"I wasn't talking about the ranch, but yes, it's safe. The development plans went down with Jake Wyatt, and

I signed the final papers today. We're now officially standing on the new addition to the Nairobi National Park."

"Oh, Ross, that's great. I'm so glad," Lilah said and paused, scuffing her toe in the dirt. "I...guess you'll be leaving then, if this ranch business is all finished."

"Not necessarily."

Lilah looked warily at him. "What do you mean? I thought you were anxious to get back to work."

"I was. But something has come up. The government has declared Wyatt an international criminal and seized his land. I managed to get the wheels turning on an interesting new idea. It looks like they'll also be adding that land to the park area."

Lilah stared at him. "What? You're serious?"

"Completely. Not bad for a day's work, don't you think?"

"Well...yes! That's incredible news. Congratulations. You must be really happy."

"There's more. Since this will double the current size of the reserve, the Park Bureau decided to bring in extra help."

"Meaning..."

"I pulled a few strings and made sure that ECO got the job. I'll be heading the project, if I decide to stay here."

Lilah was having a hard time assimilating all of this. Ross wasn't leaving? She was staying, and he was staying...if he decided to. What was that supposed to mean?

"Oh," she said. "Well. That would be nice. If you stay, maybe I'll see you around. I'm staying too, you know." Her own voice sounded brittle to her ears.

"Lilah," Ross said. "It's up to you. Do you want me to stay? If you do, then my decision has been made."

He stepped forward and caught her by the shoulders, looking down into her eyes. There was a new expression on his face, a heat that made her catch her breath, but she was still afraid to hope that it could possibly mean what she wanted it to.

"I...I don't understand," she said.

Ross let go of her suddenly, and bent down to pick up the coffee mug. He handed it to her, and she looked at it, surprised. "Ross, this mug is full of sand."

It was one of the plain enameled mugs from camp, but it was packed to its brim with loose, sandy canyon soil. Lilah stared at him, now thoroughly confused.

Ross was watching her expectantly. "Dig in it."

"*Dig* in the mug? Why?"

"Because you told me once that archaeologists always like what pops out of the dirt. Now humor me, please."

"Okay." Lilah stuck her fingers into the mug and began to feel around in the loose sand. "I don't—oh, Ross?"

Her fingers had come across something small and hard, with a shape that made her heart begin to pound. She fished it out, and brushed it off quickly, feeling her mouth go dry as the facets of the diamond caught the late-day sunlight and reflected it as rainbow-hued fire. The stone was set simply in a band of white gold, and Lilah held it tightly, speechless.

"I had it made today," Ross said. "And I had to offer the jeweler everything but my soul to get it done so fast. That's why I took so long to get here."

"I thought you wanted to say goodbye," Lilah whispered, barely getting the words out around the lump in her throat.

"No. Never. Tell me that you want me to stay, Lilah. You have to, because we have a lot to talk about."

"We do?"

"We do," Ross said, and took a deep breath. "You've known all along how important this is, and now I finally understand. I've spent my life keeping people at a distance so that no one would ever hurt me, trying to believe that I didn't lose anything because of it. But when I saw that I could lose you, I knew that any risk was worth taking to keep that from happening."

"I would never hurt you. You have to trust me."

"I do. Completely. God, Lilah, I love you so much, and I need you with me, to share my life. I don't want to be alone anymore."

She was in his arms before she even realized that she had moved. He held her tightly against him, so hard that she could barely breathe, and she pressed herself so close to his chest that she thought she would melt into him.

"You were never alone, really," she mumbled into his shirt.

"But I was," Ross said, bending his head to bury his lips in her hair. "Believing it made it true, until you came along and helped me see that that's not how I want to live my life."

Lilah sniffed and blinked back happy tears. "You should have consulted a good archaeologist years ago."

"This is worth the wait. I hope you still love me."

"Love you? Oh, Ross, so much. You know that."

"Then marry me. I'll keep asking until you agree." He gazed down at her anxiously, his fingers tense against her skin as he waited for her answer.

She could feel a smile, free and delighted, curving up over her face as if it would grow forever. "You really want to marry me? For life? To raise babies and get old together?"

"You're damned right I do. We'll teach those babies

about stone tools and wildlife reserves, and show them that the most worthwhile thing in life is to take risks for what you love. Say yes, Lilah. I want to hear you say it.''

''Yes!'' she said, laughing the word. ''Yes, yes, yes!''

She looked up into his eyes and saw love there, melting what she had once called gray ice. It flared up from the core of him, unguarded and unchecked, and beamed out to wrap her in a light warmer than the sun.

*   *   *   *   *

International bestselling author

JOAN JOHNSTON

**continues her wildly popular Hawk's Way
miniseries with an all-new, longer-length novel**

THE SUBSTITUTE GROOM

HAWK'S WAY

August 1998

Jennifer Wright's hopes and dreams had rested on her summer wedding—until a single moment changed everything. Including the *groom*. Suddenly Jennifer agreed to marry her fiancé's best friend, a darkly handsome Texan she needed—and desperately wanted—almost against her will. But U.S. Air Force Major Colt Whitelaw had sacrificed too much to settle for a marriage of convenience, and that made hiding her passion all the more difficult. And hiding her biggest secret downright impossible...

**"Joan Johnston does contemporary Westerns
to perfection."** —*Publishers Weekly*

Available in August 1998
wherever Silhouette books are sold.

Take 2 bestselling love stories FREE

Plus get a FREE surprise gift!

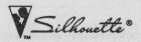

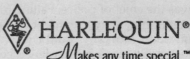

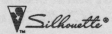

SILHOUETTE·INTIMATE·MOMENTS®
commemorates its

15th Anniversary

15 years of rugged, irresistible heroes!

15 years of warm, wonderful heroines!

15 years of exciting, emotion-filled romance!

In May, June and July 1998 join the celebration as Intimate Moments brings you new stories from some of your favorite authors—authors like:

Marie Ferrarella
Maggie Shayne
Sharon Sala
Beverly Barton
Rachel Lee
Merline Lovelace
and many more!

Don't miss this special event! Look for our distinctive anniversary covers during all three celebration months. Only from Silhouette Intimate Moments, committed to bringing you the best in romance fiction, today, tomorrow—always.

Available at your favorite retail outlet.

INTIMATE MOMENTS®
™ *Silhouette*®